Love & Loss

Stories of the Heart

Love & Loss

Stories of the Heart

edited by
Georgina Hammick

Published by VIRAGO PRESS Limited 1992
20–23 Mandela Street, Camden Town, London NW1 0HQ

Collection, Introduction and Notes Copyright © Georgina Hammick

The right of Georgina Hammick to be identified as the editor of this
work has been asserted in accordance with the Copyright, Designs and
Patents Act 1988.

A CIP Catalogue record for this book is available from the British Library

ISBN 1 85381 292 7

Typeset by Falcon Typographic Art Ltd, Fife, Scotland

Printed in Great Britain

Contents

Acknowledgements

Permission to reproduce stories by the following authors is gratefully acknowledged: Ruth Prawer Jhabvala: to A.M. Heath & Co. Ltd for 'Miss Sahib' from *A Stronger Climate*, John Murray, 1986, Copyright © Ruth Prawer Jhabvala 1986; Sylvia Townsend Warner: to the Executors of the Sylvia Townsend Warner Estate and Viking Penguin, a division of Penguin Books USA Inc., for 'Winter in the Air' from *Selected Stories of Sylvia Townsend Warner*, 1988, Copyright © 1988 by Susannah Pinney and William Maxwell; Doris Lessing: to Jonathan Clowes Ltd and HarperCollins Publishers Inc., on behalf of the author, for 'Flight' from *The Habit of Loving*, MacGibbon & Kee, 1957, Copyright © Doris Lessing 1957; Dorothy Parker: to Duckworth and Viking Penguin, a division of Penguin Books USA Inc., for 'I Live on Your Visits' from *The Portable Dorothy Parker* by Dorothy Parker, Introduction by Brendan Gill, Copyright © 1955 by Dorothy Parker, renewed; Elizabeth Taylor: to the estate of the late Elizabeth Taylor and A.M. Heath for 'The Ambush' from *The Blush and Other Stories*, Peter Davies, 1958, Copyright © Elizabeth Taylor 1958; Kay Boyle: to Abner Stein for 'Black Boy' from *50 Stories*, Penguin, 1981, Copyright © Kay Boyle 1981; Rahila Gupta: to the author for 'Untouchable', Copyright © Rahila Gupta 1991; Alice Munro: to Penguin Books Ltd and the Virgina Barber Literary Agency for 'Simon's Luck', from *The Beggar Maid*, Copyright © Alice Munro 1977, 1978, 1979, Collection first published in Canada in 1978 by The Macmillan Company of Canada Limited under the title *Who Do You Think You Are?*, and first published in Great Britain by Allen Lane, 1980; Elizabeth Bowen: to Curtis Brown, the Literary Executors of the Estate of Elizabeth Bowen and Alfred A. Knopf Inc. for 'Sunday Afternoon' from *The Collected Stories of Elizabeth Bowen*, Jonathan Cape, 1980, Copyright © 1980 Curtis Brown, the Literary Executors of the Estate of Elizabeth Bowen; Pauline Melville: to Curtis Brown for 'Tuxedo' from *Shape Shifter*, Women's Press, 1990, Copyright © Pauline Melville 1990; Grace Paley: to the author, the Elaine Markson Agency and André Deutsch Ltd for 'Samuel' from *Enormous Changes at the Last Minute*, Farrar, Straus & Giroux, 1974 and André Deutsch Ltd 1975, Copyright © Grace Paley 1974; Ailsa Cox: to the author for 'Just Like Robert de Niro', published for the first time in this collection, Copyright © Ailsa Cox 1992; Anna Kavan: to Peter Owen Ltd for 'A Summer Evening' from *My Soul in China*, Peter Owen Ltd, 1975, Copyright © Anna Kavan 1975; Janette Turner Hospital: to the author, Anthony Sheil Literary Associates and the Aaron M. Priest Literary Agency for 'The end-of-the-line end-of-the-world-disc', from *Millennium*, ed. Helen Daniel, Ringwood, Australia, 1991, Copyright © Janette Turner Hospital 1991.

Every effort has been made to trace copyright holders in all copyright material in this book. The editor regrets if there has been any ovesight and suggests the publisher is contacted in any such event.

Introduction

> It is a short word, but it contains all: it means the body, the soul, the life, the entire being. We feel it as we feel the warmth of the blood, we breathe it as we breathe the air, we carry it in ourselves as we carry our thoughts. Nothing more exists for us. It is not a word; it is an inexpressible state indicated by four letters . . .

Maupassant, in this passage from *Our Hearts*, is pretty confident that he can define love, but in the end he decides that language is inadequate. It is certainly true that, as a noun, 'love' remains resolutely abstract. As a verb, it has forfeited some of its potency since Maupassant's time, being forced, increasingly, to do the work that 'like' once did. We can love chocolate bars and *Neighbours*, gardening and football; whereas loss, so often associated in our minds with love, seems to have none of love's elusiveness and ambiguity. The word itself, particularly when spoken, has a dying fall: its very sound is desolate.

The stories in this collection, diverse in form, style and content, all deal, at some level, with aspects of this 'inexpressible state indicated by four letters', and of its loss. I did not want to confine myself to romantic love only, nor to stories in which love and loss is the overt subject matter (although in several of the stories it is). Love, I was reminded while I was reading for this book, can be as powerful an absence as it is a presence: never to have known love, never to have given or received it, never to have experienced its joys or suffered its pains – this is probably the worst loss of all.

> 'Dear Catherine, I am so glad you came before it was dark.' [says Mrs Ingram, in Elizabeth Taylor's story 'The Ambush'] Her seemingly meaningless phrases were often found, later, to have some meaning after all.

Elizabeth Taylor's phrases, and her sentences, are never meaningless, although they frequently contain more than a first reading will easily reveal. Her characteristic strengths of subtlety and penetrating insight are evident in 'The Ambush', a story in which the disclosures only serve to hint at deeper and more complex secrets. Catherine, grieving for her unofficial fiancé, Noël, recently killed in a car crash, is now set, through her bereavement, to lose Noël's beautiful mother (who would have been her mother-in-law), about whom we are told: 'A wake of devotion always followed her and Catherine joined her own homage to the rest.' Mrs Ingram is a decisive person, one who makes plans. These may include marrying Catherine off to her elder son, Esmé, home from abroad for his brother's funeral, and still in the house when Catherine comes to stay. Esmé, whose looks and gestures and voice are disconcertingly like Noël's, who, like Noël, has a fancy and sexually ambiguous name (the one requiring an acute accent, the other a diaeresis), is homosexual – something Mrs Ingram, who is far from stupid, must know even though she chooses to disregard it; something the reader, who is never told, guesses. The guess is confirmed when Esmé's Cockney friend Freddie (like Catherine, he is a painter) arrives at the house.

Mrs Ingram is one of the destructive self-deceivers who, in various guises, turn up again and again in Elizabeth Taylor's fiction. Seemingly sympathetic and generous, actually selfish and manipulative, this enchantress will be capable, we suspect, of doing Catherine enduring harm unless Catherine can find the strength to break away.

'The Ambush' exemplifies, as well as any story in this anthology, the qualities I most often find myself admiring, no matter how unconventional/experimental/fantastical the story may otherwise be: a convincing character or characters in a convincing setting; just the right amount of relevant, telling detail; an intensity in the writing that will not allow the reader off the hook; a precision and economy, where apt, that enables a single sentence to do – and more piercingly – the work of a paragraph; some element of the mysterious or the visionary and an open, rather than a closed, or shutting-down, ending. I confess to a predilection for stories in which place plays, if not an integral, then at least some part, and for writers who, notwithstanding other allegiances/departures, have made certain countries, regions, landscapes, their own. (Within these pages are several examples of these: Grace Paley's New York City, Alice Munro's Ontario, Doris Lessing's Africa, Ruth Prawer Jhabvala's India, Katherine Mansfield's New Zealand, Shena Mackay's Surrey, Elizabeth Bowen's Anglo-Ireland, and so on.) Elizabeth Taylor, too, is as much a writer of place as of character, her place being England in general and the Thames Valley (the setting for 'The Ambush') in particular. There are some marvellously observed descriptions of riverside landscape here, of lock-keepers' houses and gardens – '... like a primitive painting, captivating, bright and *unconvincing*' (my emphasis for Taylor's typical find of the unsettling adjective) – of trees, of light, of the Thames itself. The peculiarities of a house and countryside she has hitherto visited only in the company of Noël intensify Catherine's pain – more than that, they are part of her loss.

> She did not stay long ... It was not the same. She liked young people always, and so she liked the young people she was teaching here; but she could not love them the way she loved her Indian pupils ... by comparison the English children struck her as being cool and distant. And not only the children but everyone she met ... they seemed a colder people somehow, politer perhaps and more considerate than the Indians among whom she had spent so many years, but without (so she put it to herself) *real love.*

In this passage from Ruth Prawer Jhabvala's haunting story of a retired English teacher's life in India in the years following Independence, Miss Tuhy, the 'Miss Sahib' of the title, has made a brief and unsuccessful return to England. The story's central concern is the relationship that develops between the generous-hearted Miss Tuhy, who 'liked and was interested in everyone ... it seemed a privilege to her to be near them and to be aware of what seemed to her their fascinating, their passionate lives', and her landlady's passionate granddaughter Sharmila, who, when we first meet her, is a wayward and attractive child of twelve. Sharmila – on the face of it the embodiment of all the Indian virtues of warmth, colour, charm, drama, so lacking in the English – reveals herself, little by little, as one of life's takers, a monstrous egoist, incapable of *real love.* Jhabvala's exposition of this irony, unsentimental and often wryly humorous ('Unfortunately Sharmila and the children were

ix

all very sick in the bus ... and so could not enjoy the scenery' – an example of innocent-sounding sentences that contrive to convey all manner of selfish and histrionic behaviour), remains true to the Englishwoman's trusting nature that allows her, almost to the end and against all the evidence, to believe the best of her fellow humans.

Love and loss are apparent in 'Miss Sahib', both in the plot itself and as a kind of below-the-surface permeation that has to do with missed chances, wrong choices, lost Empires and ways of life. (I found it interesting to compare Jhabvala's English teacher with the nameless Indian protagonist of Rahila Gupta's 'Untouchable', Miss Tuhy's counterpart in the particular loneliness of the exile, and also in the ambivalence both women feel towards their native and adopted countries and cultures.) In 'Sunday Afternoon', Elizabeth Bowen's chilling glimpse of a certain type of Anglo-Irish attitude towards the Second World War, we are made aware of love because of its absence, while loss reveals itself in the total inability of the people on the lawn to engage with any reality outside their own small sphere. As is customary in Elizabeth Bowen's work, weather and setting play a crucial part as creators and indicators of atmosphere:

> The late May Sunday blazed, but was not warm ... The coldness had been admitted by none of the seven or eight people who, in degrees of elderly beauty, sat here full in the sun, at this sheltered edge of the lawn: they continued to master the coldness, or to deny it, as though with each it were some secret *malaise*. An air of fastidious, stylized melancholy, an air of being secluded behind glass, characterized for Henry these old friends in whose shadow he had grown up ...

These 'old friends' of Henry, members of the Anglo-Irish gentry, appear, in their isolation, almost as dream figures, or as helpless victims of some enchantment that has frozen them for ever on the lawn. The tragedy and suffering of global war cannot touch their lives – any more, one feels, than the violent history of the Ireland they live in has been able to affect them. When later, over tea, they eventually bring themselves to question their visitor about his life in London in the blitz, it is the loss of the valuable contents of Henry's flat, recently bombed, rather than any general or specific loss of life, that succeeds in arousing their concern: "'*Henry*," said Mrs Vesey, "all your beautiful things?'"

Elizabeth Bowen, a master of the short story herself, acknowledged the debt she, and all Katherine Mansfield's successors, owe to Mansfield for the ground she broke for them. In the introduction she wrote to *Thirty-four Short Stories* by K. M. (Collins, 1956), Bowen insists that Mansfield, a self-confessed risk-taker, was never an experimenter for experiment's sake, that she was an innovator rather than a rebel, a writer who did not break with the English traditions of prose narrative she had been born into – 'simply, she passed beyond them'. In the story I've chosen of Mansfield's, 'Life of Ma Parker', where an absence of the definite article in the title accentuates the poignancy, and the irony, contained in 'Life', the innovation is not only in the author's skilful use of time – the way she allows, in a story only half a dozen pages long, Ma Parker's recent and distant past to illuminate her harrowing present – but also in how, without nudging, she forces the reader to compare Ma Parker's 'hard life' with the precious concerns of the 'literary gentleman' she cleans for. The desolate ending, which leaves Ma Parker with nowhere to go to have a 'proper cry' for her dead grandson (and for all the losses of her unhappy life), contrasts painfully with the terrible screams of grief that conclude another, very different – and, for present-day readers who are also mothers, perhaps more horrifying – story about the death of a child: Grace Paley's 'Samuel'.

'Samuel' is brief – not quite as brief as another favourite Paley story of mine, 'Wants' (one that would have fitted the theme of this anthology equally well), but certainly barely more than a thousand words long. So the question is: How does she do it? How is she able to achieve so much cogency and resonance in a story which is over almost as soon as it is begun? How does she manage, out of a few terse sentences, to evoke so vividly the life histories and personalities of the watchers in the subway train? Grace Paley's compression, no less than her genius for storytelling, seems to be little short of miraculous.

Anyone who has ever been stood up on a date, anyone who has ever loved someone who belongs to someone else (and felt guilty about it), will be able to identify with the protagonists of Alice Munro's 'Simon's Luck' and Shena Mackay's 'Evening Surgery', two stories which, unlike in other ways, share an acuity of observation and a common emotional ground of anticipation, disappointment, hope, despair, vulnerability, humiliation – and, above all, pain. It has been said of Munro that her stories have the depth of novels. The depth must be in part to do with structure, most notably in her masterly moving of her stories through different time zones and tenses whereby the past is enabled to shed significant, yet unobtrusive, light on the present (and vice versa); but it also comes from her unrivalled psychological insights and from her truth. By 'truth' I mean her truth to the story she is telling and to its characters, who are never mere ciphers but real human beings with all the ambiguities and contradictions that human beings have. Who could not identify with Rose in 'Simon's Luck' when, expecting her lover's knock, she finds herself confronted instead by the woman at the store:

> Rose knew she ought to offer her something. A glass of wine? She might become mellow and talkative, wanting to stay and finish the bottle. Here was a person Rose had talked to, plenty of times, a friend of sorts, somebody she would have claimed to like, and she could hardly be bothered to acknowledge her. It would have been the same at that moment with anyone who was not Simon.

Munro is not a self-indulgent or self-conscious writer. You can't catch her showing off her language skills just for the sake of them, as lesser writers sometimes do; she never goes in for the mellifluous or the rhetorically effective where there is no place for these to be. This scrupulousness means that, while she is the possessor of a powerful and individual voice, she has – in a period which shows a worrying tendency on the part of both writers and critics to rate style above content – no 'style' as such. Her prose, organic to its subject matter, can be beautiful, eloquent, musical, rich, spare; it can equally, when these are required, be awkward, gauche, boisterous – and a bumpy ride.

The telephone, as so often in unhappy love affairs, becomes an instrument of torture for the protagonists of the Munro and the Mackay stories. Rose, whose self-knowledge is no real protection, foresees herself telephoning Simon and puts herself through the various forms and hells these calls might take. In 'Evening Surgery' there are two telephones. The one in the doctor's surgery is a means by which the appalling senior receptionist, Mavis Blizzard, can humiliate or embarrass the patients; while for the lovesick Catherine at home, the telephone, when not actively capricious and treacherous, is a phantom whose ringing 'was conjured up by her own longing or was some electrical malevolence'. The telephone is not the only enemy in a story where household objects, even a plant, can accuse and be perceived by their victim as part of a conspiracy to punish and reproach. The translation of the ordinary into the extraordinary, of the inanimate into the – often malevolent and menacing – animate, the imbuing of everyday objects with human or animal characteristics ('The sellotape sneered and snarled') or with supernatural powers, all achieved through her enviably original and apposite use of metaphor and simile, are as much hallmarks of Shena Mackay's writing as her lyricism ('. . . the gas fire blooming like a bed of lupins . . .') and what one critic has described as her 'lethal accuracy of observation'. Any tendency the reader might have to think of the Home Counties as middle class, predictable and 'safe' is blown apart by Mackay's version of Surrey which, notwithstanding a brilliant evocation of the county's flora, fauna and architecture, reinvents (or exposes?) it as exotic, random and, at times, murderously dangerous.

I haven't mentioned the humour in the Munro and Mackay stories, another ingredient that links them and places them in the tragi-comedic tradition of Dickens and Chekhov, two masters in the art of juxtaposing the humorous and the tragic to the benefit of both and as an accurate reflection of how life is. In 'Simon's Luck' humour is wry and self-mocking, as befits its protagonist, Rose; in 'Evening Surgery', farce (in the doctor's waiting-room) and gallows humour (in the adulterers' home lives) take turns to point up guilt and shame and pain. An anthology of love and loss that did not include the possibility of laughter would be gloomy reading indeed. Admittedly, there are not too many laughs to be had in George Egerton's proto-feminist piece 'Virgin Soil' (unless, nowadays, they are provoked by the title), nor in Kay Boyle's taut and indelibly shocking 'Black Boy'. There are absolutely none to be got from 'A Summer Evening', the uncompromisingly elegiac lament Anna Kavan wrote shortly before she died. Elsewhere, however, humour is abundantly and variously present, its range extending from Edith

Wharton's hilarious black comedy of old age, 'After Holbein', through Sylvia Townsend Warner's 'Winter in the Air', a witty comedy of manners that manages to depict a quintessentially English way of facing (that is to say, not facing) the break-up of a marriage, while at the same time it shows the real pain and loneliness the break-up will inevitably involve, to the night-in-the-life of Pauline Melville's eponymous hero, Tuxedo. 'Tuxedo' is a *tour de force* of line-by-line, extraordinarily sharp humour, the laughs coming so thick and fast that you can scarcely keep pace with them, the jinxed Tuxedo himself so wonderfully realized that he has stayed with this reader since a first reading of his story. Pauline Melville's has to be one of the most original and exciting voices to emerge in recent years.

Humour is what we expect from Dorothy Parker, and she is in top form in 'I Live on Your Visits', a wincingly recognizable portrait of a jealous and self-pitying mother taunting a teenage son. If it's impossible to sympathize with this monster who lies, who spices her sarcasms with French, Italian and Latin phrases, and whose 'humble' opinion is anything but, we can at least understand her all too well. By the use of significant detail – that indecently crowded fridge – Parker reveals the underlying pathos in a life gone sour through selfishness.

The pleasures of the editor/anthologist – reading; discovering new (or new to me) voices; being reminded of the excellence of old hands – are, I hope, obvious from this Introduction; but there are pains, too, and I'd like to say a little about these. The worst of the pains is this: you cannot have every story, and every writer, you want. For reasons of space, budget, balance – or because a story you rate highly and that would ideally fit the theme has been anthologized too often or too recently; or because a writer you especially admire has never chosen to write on the theme at all – there are bound to be omissions. I knew this, of course, before I embarked, but only in my *head*; it was not until I was confronted with specific disappointments that I really felt it. There isn't room to catalogue loves of mine that, in the editing of this anthology, became losses (and it probably wouldn't be in my interest, anyway, to apprise readers of too many gems that aren't here); however, I would like to touch upon just two instances of ones that 'got away'.

When I was invited to choose stories for this collection, my first reaction was: Hooray – I'll be able to have Han Suyin's *Winter Love*, and I'll be able to include all the 'Elizabeths'. (There are lots of 'Elizabeths', but the ones I particularly had in mind were Bowen, Taylor and Bishop – with Hardwick as a probable fourth). For the Bishop, the natural choice seemed to be her Nova Scotian story 'In the Village', and I'd more or less settled on this when the great idea came: Why not instead preface the collection with Bishop's poem 'One Art' (the one that begins: 'The art of losing isn't hard to master')? Wouldn't the poem act as a perfect indicator, or encapsulation, of what follows? The answer is that it would have done, had Elizabeth Bishop not clearly stated her dislike of 'women only' anthologies, an aversion I knew about but, because I so badly wanted her in, had chosen to 'forget'. However, guilt and doubt caught up with me, and I sought the opinion of Bishop's English publisher, Carmen Callil. Carmen Callil was deeply shocked by my question and said something along the lines of: 'Of course you can't have the poem! Think about it! If Elizabeth Bishop were alive you might be able to persuade her to change her mind – extremely doubtful I should imagine – but she isn't, so you can't.'

Han Suyin's *Winter Love* got away by reason of its length: it's a novella and, if included, would have taken up half this book. (Wishful thinking again, if of a less reprehensible kind, allowed me to believe I could have it. An excerpt might have proved some sort of answer, but I'd made a decision early on not to include excerpts.) I regret the absence of *Winter Love* on three counts: (1) because it's very good indeed, one of the most evocative pictures of wartime London and most sentient chronicles of love and loss I know; (2) because it's out of print (publishers, please note); (3) because not having it means there's no story of romantic/erotic love between women in this anthology. (I read several in the course of my researches, but they didn't match up to *Winter Love* either as literature or in emotional depth.)

Enough about omissions and regrets – and in any case, achieving two Elizabeths out of four is hardly a bad tally. I want to end this Introduction on a positive note by drawing attention to the last story in the anthology. 'The-end-of-the-line end-of-the-world disco', against the prediction of its title and despite the seeming inevitability of disaster inherent in its narrative, is life-affirming in its invention and exuberance, a story that takes extraordinary and marvellous imaginative flight:

> Gladys waves. But what she is seeing is the swooping green of the mango tree in Brisbane. The leaf canopy parts for her and she keeps flying. She is on that wild delicious arc of the swing, soaring up, up, and out from the broken rope.

Georgina Hammick,
Wiltshire, 1992

Ruth Prawer Jhabvala

Miss Sahib

The entrance to the house in which Miss Tuhy lived was up a flight of stairs between a vegetable shop and a cigarette and cold-drink one. The stairs were always dirty, and so was the space around the doorway, with rotted bits of vegetable and empty cigarette packets trampled into the mud. Long practice had taught Miss Tuhy to step around this refuse, smilingly and without rancour, and as she did so she always nodded friendly greetings to the vegetable-seller and the cold-drink man, both of whom usually failed to notice her. Everyone in the neighbourhood had got used to her, for she had lived there, in that same house, for many years.

It was not the sort of place in which one would have expected to find an Englishwoman like Miss Tuhy, but the fact was, she was too poor to live anywhere else. She had nothing but her savings, and these, in spite of her very frugal way of life, could not last for ever; and of course there was always the vexed question of how long she would live. Once, in an uncharacteristically realistic moment, she had calculated that she could afford to go on for another five years, which would bring her up to sixty-five. That seemed fair enough to her, and she did not think she had the right to ask for more. However, most of the time these questions did not arise, for she tended to be too engrossed in the present to' allow fears of the future to disturb her peace of mind.

She was, by profession and by passionate inclination, a teacher, but she had not taught for many years. She had first come to India thirty years ago to take up a teaching post at a school for girls from the first families, and she had taught there and at various other places for as long as she had been allowed. She did it with enthusiasm, for she loved the country and her students. When Independence came and all the other English teachers went home, it never for a moment occurred to her to join them, and she went on teaching as if nothing had changed. And indeed, as far as she was concerned, nothing did change for a number of years, and it was only at the end of that time that it was discovered she was not sufficiently well qualified to go on teaching in an Indian high school. She bowed her head to this decision, for she knew she wasn't; not compared with all those clever Indian girls who held MA degrees in politics, philosophy, psychology, and economics. As a matter of fact, even though they turned out to be her usurpers, she was proud of these girls; for wasn't it she and those like her who had educated them and made them what they now were – sharp, emancipated, centuries ahead of their mothers and grandmothers? So it was not difficult for her to cede to them with a good grace, to enjoy her farewell party, cry a bit at the speeches, and receive with pride and a glow in her heart the silver model of the Taj Mahal which was presented to her as a token of appreciation. After that, she sailed for England – not because she in the least wanted to, but because it was what everyone seemed to expect of her.

She did not stay long. True, no one here said she was not well qualified enough to teach and she had no difficulty in getting a job; but she was not happy. It was not the same. She liked young people always, and so she liked the young people she was teaching here; but she could not love them the way she had loved her Indian pupils. She missed their playfulness, their affection, their sweetness – by comparison the English children struck her as being cool and distant. And not only the children but everyone she met, or only saw in streets and shops: they seemed a colder people somehow, politer perhaps and more considerate than the Indians among whom she had spent so many years, but without (so she put it to herself) *real love*. Even physically the English looked cold to her, with their damp white skins and pale blue eyes, and she longed again to be surrounded by those glowing coloured skins; and those eyes! the dark, large, liquid Indian eyes! and hair that sprang with such abundance from their heads. And besides the people, it was everything else as well. Everything was too dim, too cold. There was no sun, the grass was not green, the flowers not bright enough, and the rain that continually drizzled from a wash-rag sky was a poor substitute for the silver rivers that had come rushing in torrents out of immense, dark-blue, monsoon clouds.

2

So she and her savings returned, improvidently, to India. Everyone still remembered her and was glad to see her again but, once the first warm greetings were over, they were all too busy to have much time to spare for her. She didn't mind, she was just happy to be back; and in any case she had to live rather a long way from her friends because, now that she had no job, she had to be where rents were cheaper. She found the room in the house between the vegetable-seller and the cold-drink shop and lived there contentedly all the week round, only venturing forth on Sundays to visit her former colleagues and pupils. As time went on, these Sunday visits became fewer and further between, for everyone always seemed to be rather busy; anyway, there was less to say now, and also she found it was not always easy to spare the bus-fare to and fro. But it didn't matter, she was even happier staying at home because all her life was there now, and the interest and affection she had formerly bestowed on her colleagues and pupils, she now had as strongly for the other people living in the house, and even for the vegetable-seller and the cold-drink man though her contact with them never went further than smiles and nods.

The house was old, dirty, and inward-looking. In the centre was a courtyard which could be overlooked like a stage from the galleries running all the way round the upper storeys. The house belonged to an old woman who lived on the ground floor with her enormous family of children and grandchildren; the upper floors had been subdivided and let out to various tenants. The stairs and galleries were always crowded, not only with the tenants themselves but with their servants. Everyone in the house except Miss Tuhy kept a servant, a hill-boy, who cleaned and washed and cooked and was frequently beaten and frequently dismissed. There seemed to be an unending supply of these boys; they could be had very cheaply, and slept curled up on the stairs or on a threshold, and ate what was left in the pot.

Miss Tuhy was a shy person who loved other people but found it difficult to make contact with them. On the second floor lived an Anglo-Indian nurse with her grown-up son, and she often sought Miss Tuhy out, to talk in English with her, to ask questions about England, to discuss her problems and those of her son (a rather insipid young man who worked in an airlines office). She felt that she and Miss Tuhy should present a united front against the other neighbours, who were all Hindus and whom she regarded with contempt. But Miss Tuhy did not feel that way. She liked and was interested in everyone, and it seemed a privilege to her to be near them and to be aware of what seemed to her their fascinating, their passionate lives.

Down in the courtyard the old landlady ruled her family with a rod of iron. She kept a tight hold of everything and doled out little sums of pocket-money to her forty-year-old sons. She could often be heard abusing them and their wives, and sometimes she beat them. There was only one person to whom she showed any indulgence – who, in fact, could get away with anything – and that was Sharmila, one of her granddaughters. When Miss Tuhy first came to live in the house, Sharmila was a high-spirited, slapdash girl of twelve, with big black eyes and a rapidly developing figure. Although she had reached the age at which her sisters and cousins were already beginning to observe that reticence which, as grown women, would keep them away from the eyes of strangers, Sharmila still behaved with all the freedom of the smaller children, running round the courtyard and up and down the stairs and in and out of the homes of her grandmother's tenants. She was the first in the house to establish contact with Miss Tuhy, simply by bursting into the room where the English lady lived and looking round and touching things and lifting them up to examine them – 'What's that?' – all Miss Tuhy's treasures: her mother-of-pearl pen-holder, the photograph of her little niece as a bridesmaid, the silver Taj Mahal. Decorating the mantelpiece was a bowl of realistically shaped fruits made of plaster of Paris, and before leaving Sharmila lifted a brightly-coloured banana out of the bowl and held it up and said. 'Can I have it?' After that she came every day, and every day, just before leaving, helped herself to one more fruit until they were all finished and then she took the bowl.

Sharmila was lazy at school all the year round, but she always panicked before her class-promotion exams and came running for help to Miss Tuhy. These were Miss Tuhy's happiest times, for not only was she once again engaged in the happy pursuit of teaching, but she also had Sharmila sitting there with her all day long, bent ardently over her books and biting the tip of her tongue in her eagerness to learn. Miss Tuhy would have dearly loved to

4

teach her the whole year round, and to teach her everything she knew, and with that end in view she had drawn up an ambitious programme for Sharmila to follow; but although sometimes the girl consented to submit to this programme, it was evident that once the terror of exams was past her interest sharply declined, so that sometimes, when Miss Tuhy looked up from a passionate reading of the Romantic poets, she found her pupil fiddling with the strands of hair which always managed to escape from her sober pigtail and her mouth wide open in a yawn she saw no reason to disguise. And indeed Miss Tuhy had finally to admit that Sharmila was right; for what use would all this learning ever be to her when her one purpose in life, her sole duty, was to be married and give satisfaction to the husband who would be chosen for her and to the in-laws in whose house she would be sent to live?

She was just sixteen when she was married. Her grandmother, who usually hated spending money, excelled herself that time and it was a grand and memorable occasion. A big wedding marquee was set up in the courtyard and crammed tight with wedding-guests shimmering in their best clothes; all the tenants were invited too, including Miss Tuhy in her good dress (white dots on a chocolate-brown background) and coral necklace. Like everyone else, she was excitedly awaiting the arrival of the bridegroom and his party. She wondered what sort of a boy they had chosen for her Sharmila. She wanted a tall, bold boy for her, a soldier and a hero; and she had heightened, almost mythological visions of the young couple – decked out in jewels and gorgeous clothes – gaily disporting themselves in a garden full of brightly-coloured flowers. But when at last the band accompanying the bridegroom's party was heard, and everyone shouted 'They have come!' and rushed to the entrance to get the first glimpse, then the figure that descended from the horse amid the jubilation of the trumpets was not, in spite of his garlands and his golden coat, a romantic one. Not only was Sharmila's bridegroom stocky and ill at ease, but he was also no longer very young. Miss Tuhy, who had fought her way to the front with the best of them, turned away in bitter disappointment. There were tears in her eyes. She knew it would not turn out well.

Sharmila came every day to visit her old home. At first she came in order to boast, to show off the saris and shawls and jewellery presented to her on her marriage, and to tell about her strange new life and the house she lived in and all her new family. She was brimming over with excitement and talked non-stop and danced round the courtyard. Some time later she came with different stories, about what her mother-in-law had said to her and what she had answered back, about her sisters-in-law and all the other women, how they tried to get the better of her but how she soon showed them a trick or two: she tucked in her chin and talked in a loud voice and was full of energy and indignation. Sometimes she stayed for several days and did not return till her husband came to coax her back. After a year the first baby arrived, and a year later the second, and after a few more years a third. Sharmila became fat and matronly, and her voice was louder and more raucous. She still came constantly, now with two of the children trailing behind her and a third riding on her hip, and she stayed longer than before, often refusing to go back even when her husband came to plead with her. And in the end she seemed to be there all the time, she and her children, so that, although nothing much was said on the subject, it was generally assumed that she had left her husband and her in-laws' house and had come back to live with her grandmother.

She was a little heavy now to go running up and down the stairs the way she used to: but she still came up to Miss Tuhy's room, and the English lady's heart still beat in the same way when she heard her step on the stair, though it was a different step now, heavier, slower, and accompanied by children's tiny shuffle and patter. 'Miss Sahib!' Sharmila would call from the landing, and Miss Tuhy would fling her door wide open and stand there beaming. Now it was the children who moved from object to object, touching everything and asking to know what it was, while Sharmila, panting a little from her climb up the stairs, flung herself on the narrow bed and allowed Miss Tuhy to tuck a pillow behind her back. When the children had examined all the treasures, they began to play their own games, they crawled all over the floor and made a lot of noise. Their mother lay on the bed and sometimes she laughed and sometimes she sighed and talked about everything that came into her head. They always stayed for several hours, and when they left at last, Miss Tuhy, gorged with bliss, shut the door and carefully cleaned out her little room which the children had so delightfully disordered.

6

When she didn't feel like going upstairs, Sharmila stood in the middle of the courtyard and shouted, 'Miss Sahib!' in her loud voice. Miss Tuhy hurried downstairs, smoothing her dress and adjusting her glasses. She sat with Sharmila in the courtyard and helped her to shell peas. The old grandmother watched them from her bed inside the room: that terrible old woman was bedridden now and quite unable to move, a huge helpless shipwreck wrapped in shawls and blankets. Her speech was blurred and could be understood only by Sharmila, who had become her interpreter and chief functionary. It was Sharmila, not one of the older women of the household, who carried the keys and distributed the stores and knew where the money was kept. While she sat with Miss Tuhy in the courtyard, every now and again the grandmother would make calling noises and then Sharmila would get up and go in to see what she wanted. Inside the room it was dark and smelled of sickness and old age, and Sharmila was glad to come out in the open again.

'Poor old Granny,' she said to Miss Tuhy, who nodded and also looked sad for Granny because she was old and bedridden: as for herself, she did not feel old at all but a young girl, sitting here like this shelling peas and chatting with Sharmila. The children played and sang, the sun shone, along the galleries upstairs the tenants went to and fro hanging out their washing; there was the sound of voices calling and of water running, traffic passed up and down on the road outside, a nearby flour-mill chucked and chucked. 'Poor old Granny,' Sharmila said again. 'When she was young, she was like a queen – tall, beautiful, everyone did what she wanted. If they didn't she stamped her foot, and screamed and waved her arms in the air – like this,' Sharmila demonstrated, flailing her plump arms with bangles up to the elbow and laughing. But then she grew serious and put her face closer to Miss Tuhy's and said in a low, excited voice: 'They say she had a lover, a jeweller from Dariba. He came at nights when everyone was asleep and she opened the door for him.' Miss Tuhy blushed and her heart beat faster; though she tried to check them, a thousand impressions rippled over her mind.

'They say she was a lot like me,' said Sharmila, smiling a little and her eyes hazy with thought. She had beautiful eyes, very large and dark with heavy brows above them; her lips were full and her cheeks plump and healthy. When she was thoughtful or serious, she had a habit of tucking in her chin so that several chins were formed, and this too somehow was attractive, especially as these chins seemed to merge and swell into her very large, tight bust.

But her smile became a frown, and she said, 'Yes, and now look at her, how she is. Three times a day I have to change the sheets under her. This is the way it all ends. Hai,' and she heaved a sigh and a brooding look came on her face. The children, who had been chasing each other round the courtyard, suddenly began to quarrel in loud voices; at that Sharmila sprang up in a rage and caught hold of the biggest child and began to beat him with her fists, but hardly had he uttered the first cry when she stopped and instead lifted him in her arms and held him close, close to her bosom, her eyes shut in rapturous possessiveness as if he were all that she had.

It was one of the other tenants who told Miss Tuhy that Sharmila was having an affair with the son of the Anglo-Indian nurse from upstairs. The tenant told it with a lot of smiles, comments, and gestures, but Miss Tuhy pretended not to understand, she only smiled back at the informer in her gentle way and said 'Good morning', in English and shut the door of her room. She was very much excited. She thought about the young man, whom she had seen often and sometimes talked to: a rather colourless young man, with brown hair and Anglo-Indian features, who always dressed in English clothes and played cricket on Sunday mornings. It seemed impossible to connect him in any way with Sharmila; and how his mother would have hated any such connection! The nurse, fully opening her heart to Miss Tuhy, never tired of expressing her contempt for the other tenants in the house who could not speak English and also did not know how to live decently. She and her son lived very decently, they had chairs and a table in their room and linoleum on the floor and a picture of the Queen of England on the wall. They ate with knife and fork. 'Those others, Miss Tuhy, I wouldn't like you to see,' she said with pinched lips (she was a thin woman with matchstick legs and always wore brown shoes and stockings). 'The dirt. Squalor. You would feel sick, Miss Tuhy. And the worst are those downstairs, the –' and she added a bad word in Hindi (she never said any bad words in English, perhaps she didn't know any). She hated Sharmila and the grandmother and that whole family. But she was often away on

8

night-duty, and then who knew – as the other tenant had hinted – what went on?

Miss Tuhy never slept too well at nights. She often got up and walked round her room and wished it were time to light the fire and make her cup of tea. Those night hours seemed very long, and sometimes, tired of her room, she would go out on the stairs and along the galleries overlooking the courtyard. How silent it was now with everyone asleep! The galleries and the courtyard, so crowded during the day, were empty except where here and there a servant-boy lay sleeping huddled in a corner. There was no traffic on the road outside and the flour-mill was silent. Only the sky seemed alive, with the moon sliding slowly in and out of patches of mist. Miss Tuhy thought about the grandmother and the jeweller for whom she had opened the door when it was like this, silent and empty at nights. She remembered conversations she had heard years ago among her English fellow-teachers. They had always had a lot to say about sensuality in the East. They whispered to each other how some of the older boys were seen in the town entering certain disreputable alleys, while boys who came from princely or landowner families were taught everything there was to know by women on their fathers' estates. And as for the girls – well, they whispered, one had only to look at them, how quickly they ripened: could one ever imagine an English girl so developed at thirteen? It was, they said, the climate; and of course the food they ate, all those curries and spices that heated the blood. Miss Tuhy wondered: if she had been born in India, had grown up under this sun and had eaten the food, would she have been different? Instead of her thin, inadequate, English body, would she have grown up like the grandmother who had opened the door to the jeweller, or like Sharmila with flashing black eyes and a big bust?

Nothing stirred, not a sound from anywhere, as if all those lively people in the house were dead. Miss Tuhy stared and stared down at Sharmila's door and the courtyard washed in moonlight, and wondered was there a secret, was something going on that should not be? She crept along the gallery and up the stairs towards the nurse's door. Here too everything was locked and silent, and if there was a secret, it was being kept. She put her ear to the door and stayed there, listening. She did not feel in the least bad or guilty doing this,

9

for what she wanted was nothing for herself but only to have proof that Sharmila was happy.

She did not seem happy. She was getting very bad-tempered and was forever fighting with her family or with the other tenants. It was a not uncommon sight to have her standing in the middle of the courtyard, arms akimbo, keys at her waist, shouting insults in her loud, somewhat raucous voice. She no longer came to visit Miss Tuhy in her room, and once, when the English lady came to be with her downstairs, she shouted at her that she had enough with one old woman on her hands and did not have time for any more. But that night she came upstairs and brought a little dish of carrot halwa which Miss Tuhy tried to refuse, turning her face away and saying primly that thank you, she was not hungry. 'Are you angry with me, Missie Sahib?' coaxed Sharmila with a smile in her voice, and she dug her forefinger into the halwa and then brought it to Miss Tuhy's lips, saying 'One little lick, just one, for Sharmila', till Miss Tuhy put out her tongue and shyly slid it along Sharmila's finger. She blushed as she did so, and anger and hurt melted out of her heart.

'There!' cried Sharmila, and then she flung herself as usual on the bed. She began to talk, to unburden herself completely. Tears poured down her cheeks as she spoke of her unhappy life and all the troubles brought down upon her by the grandmother who did not give her enough money and treated her like a slave, the other family members who were jealous of her, the servants who stole from her, the shopkeepers who cheated her – 'If it weren't for my children,' she cried, 'why should I go on? I'd make an end of it and get some peace at last.'

'Sh,' said Miss Tuhy, shocked and afraid.

'Why not? What have I got to live for?'

'*You?*' said Miss Tuhy with an incredulous laugh, and looked at that large, full-bloomed figure sprawled there on the narrow bed and rumpling the bedcover from which the embroidery (girls carrying baskets of apples and pansies on their arms) had almost completely faded.

Sharmila said, 'Did I ever tell you about that woman, two doors away from the coal-merchant's house? She was a widow and they treated her like a dog, so one night she took a scarf and hung herself from a hook on the stairs. We all went to have a look at her. Her feet

10

were swinging in the air as if there was a wind blowing. I was only four but I still remember.'

There was an eeric little pause which Miss Tuhy broke as briskly as she could: 'What's the matter with you? A young woman like you with all your life before you – I wonder you're not ashamed.'

'I want to get away from here! I'm so sick of this *house!*'

'Yes, Miss Tuhy,' said the Anglo-Indian nurse a few days later, when the English lady had come to pay her a visit and they both sat drinking tea under the tinted portrait of the Queen, 'I'm just sick and tired of living here, that I can tell you. If I could get out tomorrow, I would. But it's not so easy to find a place, not these days with the rents.' She sighed and poured the two of them strong tea out of an earthenware pot. She drank in as refined a way as Miss Tuhy, without making any noise at all. 'My boy's wanting to go to England, and why not? No future for us here, not with these people.'

Miss Tuhy gave a hitch to her wire-framed glasses and smiled ingratiatingly: 'No young lady for him yet?' she asked, and her voice quavered like an inefficient spy's.

'Oh, he goes with the odd girl or two. Nothing serious. There's time yet. We're not like those others – hurry-curry, muddle-puddle, marry them off at sixteen, and they never even see each other's face! No wonder there's trouble afterwards.' She put her bony brown hand on Miss Tuhy's knee and brought her face close: 'Like that one downstairs, the she-devil. It's so disgusting. I don't even like to tell you.' But her tongue was already wiping round her pale lips in anticipation of the telling.

Miss Tuhy got up abruptly. She dared not listen, and for some unknown reason tears had sprung into her eyes. She went out quickly but the nurse followed her. It was dark on the stairs and Miss Tuhy's tears could not be seen. The nurse clung to her arm: 'With servants,' she whispered into Miss Tuhy's ear. 'She gets them in at night when everyone's asleep. Mary Mother,' said the nurse and crossed herself. Instantly a quotation rose to Miss Tuhy's lips: 'Her sins are forgiven, for she loved much. But to whom little is forgiven, the same loveth little.' The nurse was silent for a moment and then she said, '*She's* not Christian,' with contempt. Miss Tuhy freed her arm and hurried to her own room. She sat in her chair with her hands folded in her lap and her legs trembling. A procession of servants

11

filed through her mind: undersized hill-boys with naked feet and torn shirts, sickly but tough, bent on survival. She heard their voices as they called to each other in their weird hill-accents and laughed with each other, showing pointed teeth. Every few years one of them in the neighbourhood went berserk and murdered his master and ran away with the jewellery and cash, only to be caught the next day on a wild spree at cinemas and country liquor shops. Strange wild boys, wolf-boys: Miss Tuhy had always liked them and felt sorry for them. But now she felt most sorry for Sharmila, and prayed for it not to be true.

It could not be true. Sharmila had such an innocent nature. She was a child. She loved sweet things to eat, and when the bangle-seller came, she was the first to run to meet him. She was also very fond of going to the cinema, and when she came home she told Miss Tuhy the story. She acted out all the important scenes, especially the love-scenes – 'Just as their lips were about to meet, quick as a flash, with her veil flying in the wind, she ran to the next tree and called to him – Arjun! – and he followed her and he put his arms round the tree and this time she did not run away – no, they stood looking at each other, eating each other up with their eyes, and then the music – oh, Missie, Missie, Missie!' she would end and stretch her arms into the air and laugh with longing.

Once, on her little daily shopping trip to the bazaar, Miss Tuhy caught sight of Sharmila in the distance. And seeing her like that, unexpectedly, she saw her as a stranger might, and realized for the first time that the Sharmila she knew no longer existed. Her image of Sharmila was twofold, one superimposed on the other yet also simultaneous, the two images merged in her mind: there was the hoyden schoolgirl, traces of whom still existed in her smile and in certain glances of her eyes, and then there was Sharmila in bloom, the young wife dancing round the courtyard and boasting about her wedding presents. But the woman she now saw in the bazaar was fat and slovenly; the end of her veil, draped carelessly over her breasts, trailed a little in the dust, and the heel of her slipper was trodden over to one side so that she seemed to be dragging her foot when she walked. She was quarrelling with one of the shopkeepers, she was gesticulating and using coarse language; the other shopkeepers leaned out of their stalls to listen, and from the way they grinned and commented to each other, it was obvious that Sharmila was a well-known figure and the scene she was enacting was one she had often played before. Miss Tuhy, in pain, turned and walked away in the opposite direction, even though it meant a longer way home. For the first time she failed to greet the vegetable-seller and the cold-drink man as she passed between their two shops on her way into the house, and when she had to step round the refuse trodden into the mud, she felt a movement of distaste and thought irritably to herself why it was that no one ever took the trouble to clean the place. The stairs of the house too were dirty, and there was a bad smell of sewage. She reached her room with a sigh of relief, but it seemed as if the bad smell came seeping in from under the closed door. Then she heard again Sharmila's anguished voice crying, 'I want to get away! I'm so sick of this *house!*' and she too felt the same anguish to get away from the house and from the streets and crowded bazaars around it.

That night she said to Sharmila, in a bright voice, 'Why don't we all go away somewhere for a lovely holiday?'

Sharmila, who had never had occasion to leave the city she was born in, thought it was a joke and laughed. But Miss Tuhy was very much in earnest. She remembered all the holidays she had gone on years ago when she was still teaching. She had always gone to the Simla hills and stayed in an English boarding-house, and she had taken long walks every day and breathed in the mountain air and collected pine cones. She told Sharmila all about this, and Sharmila too began to get excited and said, 'Let's go', and asked many more questions.

'Sausages and bacon for breakfast every morning,' Miss Tuhy reminisced, and Sharmila, who had never eaten either, clapped her hands with pleasure and gave an affectionate squeeze to her youngest child playing in her lap: 'You'll like that, Munni, na? Shaushage? Hmmm!'

'They'll get wonderful red cheeks up there,' said Miss Tuhy, 'real English apple cheeks,' and she smiled at the sallow city-child dressed in dirty velvet. 'And there'll be pony-rides and wild flowers to pick and lovely cool water from the mountain streams.'

'Let's go!' cried Sharmila with another hug to her child.

'We'll go by train,' said Miss Tuhy. 'And then a bus'll take us up the mountains.'

Sharmila suddenly stopped smiling: 'Yes, and the money? Where's that to come from? You think *she'd* ever give?' and she tossed her head towards the room where her grandmother lay, immobile and groaning but still a power to be reckoned with.

Miss Tuhy waved her aside: 'This'll be *my* treat,' she said.

And why not? The money was there, and what pleasure it would be to spend it on a holiday with Sharmila and the children! She brutally stifled all thoughts of caution, of the future. Money was there to be spent, to take pleasure with, not to eke out a miserable day-by-day existence which, in any case, might end – who knew? – tomorrow or the day after. And then what use would it ever be to her? Her glasses slipped and lay crooked on her nose, her face was flushed: she looked drunk with excitement. 'You'll get such a surprise,' she said. 'When we're sitting in the bus, and it's going up up up, higher and higher, and you'll see the mountains before you, more beautiful than anything you've ever dreamed of.'

Unfortunately Sharmila and the children were all very sick in the bus that carried them up the mountains, and so could not enjoy the scenery. Sharmila, in between retching with abandon, wept loudly that she was dying and cursed the fate that had brought her here instead of leaving her quietly at home where she belonged and was happy. However, once the bus had stopped and they had reached their destination, they began to enjoy themselves. They were amused by the English boarding-house, and at meal-times were lost in wonder not only at the food, the like of which they had never eaten, but also at the tablecloths and the cutlery. Their first walk was undertaken with great enthusiasm, and they collected everything they found on the way – pine cones and flowers and leaves and stones and empty cigarette packets. As Miss Tuhy had promised, they rode on ponies: even Sharmila, gasping and giggling and letting out loud cries of fright, was hoisted on to the back of a pony but had to be helped down again, dissolving in fits of laughter, because she was too heavy. Miss Tuhy revelled in their enjoyment; and for herself she was happy too to be here again among familiar smells of pine and wood-fires and cold air. She loved the pale mists that rose from the mountainside and the rain that rained down so softly. She wished they could stay for ever. But after the third day Sharmila and the children began to get bored and kept asking when they were going home. They no longer cared to go for walks or ride on ponies. When it rained, all four of them sat mournfully by the window, and sighed and moaned and kept asking, what shall we do now? and Sharmila wondered how human beings could bear to live in a place like this; speaking for herself, it was just the same as being dead. Miss Tuhy had to listen not only to their complaints but also to those of the management, for Sharmila and the children were behaving badly – especially in the dining-room where, after the third day, they began demanding pickles and chapattis, and the children spat out the unfamiliar food on the tablecloth while Sharmila abused the hotel servants in bazaar language.

So they went home again earlier than they had intended. They had been away less than ten days, but their excitement on seeing ̶ ̶ ̶ ̶ ̶ ̶ ̶ ̶ ̶ ̶ ̶ ̶ ̶ain was that of long-time voyagers. They had hired ̶ ̶ ̶ ̶ ̶ ̶ station and, as they neared home, they began to point ̶ ̶ ̶familiar landmarks to each other; by the time they had got to their own neighbourhood bazaar, the children were bobbing up and down so much that they were in danger of falling off the carriage, and Sharmila shouted cordial greetings to the shopkeepers with whom she would be fighting again tomorrow. And at home all the relatives and friends crowded into the courtyard to receive them, and there was much kissing and embracing and even a happy tear or two, and the tenants and servants thronged the galleries upstairs to watch the scene and call down their welcome to the travellers. It was a great homecoming.

Only Miss Tuhy was not happy. She did not want to be back. She longed now for the green mountains and the clean, cool air; she also missed the boarding-house with its English landlady and very clean stairs and bathrooms. It was intensely hot in the city and dust-storms were blowing. The sky was covered with an ugly yellow heat haze, and all day hot, restless winds blew dust about. Loudspeaker vans were driven through the streets to advise people to be vaccinated against the current outbreak of smallpox. Miss Tuhy hardly left her room. She felt ill and weak, and contrary to her usual custom, she often lay down on her bed, even during the day. She kept her doors and windows shut, but nevertheless the dust seeped in, and so did the smells and the noise of the house. She no longer went on her daily shopping and preferred not to eat. Sharmila brought food up for her, but Miss Tuhy did not want it, it was too spicy for her and too greasy. 'Just a little taste,' Sharmila begged and brought a morsel to her lips. Miss Tuhy pushed her hand away and cried out, 'Go away! I can't stand the smell!' She meant not only the smell of the food, but also that of Sharmila's heavy, perspiring body.

It was in these days of terrible heat that the grandmother at last managed to die. Miss Tuhy dragged herself up from her bed in order to attend the funeral on the bank of the river. It was during the hottest part of the day, and the sun spread such a pall of white heat that, seen through it, the flames of the pyre looked colourless and quite harmless as they first licked and then rose higher and enveloped the body of the grandmother. The priest chanted and the eldest son poured clarified butter to feed the fire. All the relatives shrieked and wailed and beat their thighs in the traditio   Sh shrieked the loudest – she tore open her breast a. her fists, demanded to be allowed to die, and then she tried to her herself on the pyre and had to be held back by four people. Vultures swayed overhead in the dust-laden sky. The river had dried up and the sand burned underfoot. Everything was white, desolate, empty, for miles and miles and miles around, on earth and, apart from the vultures, in the sky. Sharmila suddenly flung herself on Miss Tuhy and held her in a stifling embrace. She wept that now only she, Miss Tuhy, was left to her, and promised to look after her and tend and care for her as she had done for her dear, dead granny. Miss Tuhy gasped for air and tried to free herself, but Sharmila only clung to her the tighter and her tears fell on and smeared Miss Tuhy's cheeks.

Miss Tuhy's mother had died almost forty years ago, but Miss Tuhy could still vividly recall her funeral. It had drizzled, and rich smells of damp earth had mixed with the more delicate smell of tuberoses and yew. The clergyman's words brought ease and comfort, and weeping was restrained; birds sang cheerfully from out of the wet trees. That's the way to die, thought Miss Tuhy, and bitterness welled up into her hitherto gentle heart. The trouble was, she no longer had the fare home to England, not even on the cheapest route.

Sylvia Townsend Warner

Winter in the Air

T he furniture, assembled once more under the high ceiling of a London room, seemed to be wearing a look of quiet satisfaction, as though, slightly shrugging their polished shoulders, the desk had remarked to the bookcase, the Regency armchair to the Chippendale mirror, 'Well, here we are again.' And then, after a creak or two, silence had fallen on the dustless room.

It was morbidly dustless, morbidly unlittered. Rolling up her apron, Mrs Darbyshire, the charwoman, said, 'I think that is all I can do for you today,' in tones of professional self-righteousness. Indeed, Barbara thought, there was nothing more to ask; everything, from the slight dampness on the floor of the kitchenette to the embonpoint of the cushions on the sofa, was as it should be. She had not seen such neatness for years.

The thought of someone like Mrs Darbyshire had confirmed her decision to live in London again. A London charwoman does her work, takes her money and goes away, sterile as the wind of the desert. She does not spongily, greedily, absorb your concerns, study your nose to see if you have been crying again, count the greying hairs of your head, proffer sympathetic sighs and vacuum pauses and then hurry off to wring herself out, spongily, all over the village, with news of what's going on between those two at Pond House. Not to mention the fact that a London charwoman is immeasurably better at charring.

Except that Mrs Darbyshire went away in trousers, her exit in 1950 was just as the exits of Mrs Shelley had been in the mid-thirties – the same healing order left behind, the same tonic appearance of everything wound up for a fresh start, with a filled kettle sitting on the hotplate ready to be heated. And the flat of now, Barbara thought, in which she was again a single lady, was not very different from the flat of then; it was smaller, and the window glass, replacing glass that had been blown out in an air-raid, was of inferior quality, and the rent was a great deal higher, but the sitting-room and bedroom of the new flat were of the same sober, Victorian proportions, and, considering the housing shortage, she was lucky to get it, above all at such short notice – only two months. Two months and eight days, to be precise, for it was on the seventeenth of August that Willie broke the news, coming slowly across the sunburned lawn to where she stood repainting the front door of Pond House, little thinking how soon she would go out by it and Annelies come in.

'But why?' she had asked. 'Why must she come and live with you? I thought it was all over, months ago.'

'So did I.'

'But Annelies doesn't. Is that it?'

'She is so wretched,' he had said. 'So desperately, incompetently wretched. I can't let her go on suffering like this.'

While they spoke, she continued spreading the blue paint, brushing it into the knots and cajoling it round the door-knocker. Dreamily, under the shock of these tidings, there had persisted a small, steady dissatisfaction because the paint was not the right shade of blue.

The flat of now seemed lighter than the flat of then. This was partly because her pieces of rosewood furniture were now so much paler in tone; twelve years in a country house, with windows open and sun shining in and not enough furniture polish, had bleached the rosewood to a tint of *feuille-morte*. Outside there was a difference, too – more air, more light, welling like fountains from the bombed sites. The room was full of light, as full of light as it was full of silence. In the centre stood the rosewood table, and as she bent over it, it reflected her with the whole length of its uncluttered surface, darkened here and there with old ink-stains like sea-leopard skin.

'I shall leave you the rosewood table,' she had said to Willie. 'It's the only one that is the right height for you, and large enough to hold all your traps.'

'No, don't,' he had said. 'I shall take over the big kitchen table. It's the same height. I've measured it.'

'Very well. But you'll keep the wardrobe?'

'I'd rather not.'

18

'Nonsense! You must have something to keep your clothes in. Or to keep the moths in, for I suppose you'll never remember to shut the doors.'

'That's all right. Annelies has one of these compactum things. It belonged to her husband.'

'I see. How convenient.'

'My God, how I hate these practical conversations! Why must we have them? They always end like this.'

Planning ahead, Barbara had resolved that the furniture should not be arranged in the flat of now as in the flat of then. But London rooms impose a formula. Now, as then, the desk stood in the recess on the left side of the fireplace, and the bookcase in the recess on the right; the sofa had its back to the window; and, on the wall opposite the fireplace, the Chippendale mirror hung above the bureau. Later on, she thought, readjusting the sofa cushions (for Mrs Darbyshire, like Mrs Shelley, had a passion for putting square objects cornerwise) – later on, people too will regroup themselves in this room. Mary Mackenzie's hand will dangle from the arm of the Regency chair as though its rings were too many and too heavy for it, and Julian will project his long legs obliquely from the stool, and Clive Thompson will stand with his back to the room, puffing at the bookcase. They will not have kept their outlines as unyieldingly as the furniture has, but their voices will be the same, and after the first constraint we shall find a great deal to talk about. It will be best, her thoughts went on, planning, foreseeing and planning as they had done during the breathless, interminable weeks before her departure from Pond House – it will be best to get them all here together one evening, when any awkwardness can be tided over by making them a trifle drunk. But that could be later on. It was still only her third day in the flat of now, and one must have a small decency-bit of time in which to lick one's wounds and wring the sea-water of shipwreck out of one's hair. *Such privilege belongs to women* . . . One of the advantages of a solitary life is that it allows one time to verify quotations instead of trailing them about all day, hanging them on gooseberry bushes, leaving them, like rings, above the sink. *Such privilege* . . . Hermione, in *The Winter's Tale*, said it.

Shakespeare was in the bedroom, to countervail against her dislike of it. It was a dislikeable room, mutilated by the remodelling, which had shorn it for a bathroom. The tree beyond the bedroom window, she thought, coming back into the sitting-room with the book in her hand – even the tree, in itself a pleasant thing, must be contemplated as a sparrow-rack, where, from the first light onward, sparrows would congregate and clatter, making sleep impossible.

She found *The Winter's Tale*, and turned to the trial scene. Here it was:

> ... with immodest hatred,
> The child-bed privilege denied, which 'longs
> To women of all fashion. Lastly, hurried
> Here, to this place, i' the open air, before
> I have got strength of limit.

Verifying quotations would indeed be an interesting pursuit if they all turned out to be as wide of the mark as this one. If Willie had shown a spark of even modest hate, she might have known a spark of hope.

She laid Shakespeare on the sofa and presently sat down beside him. To do so was a deliberate act, for she still retained, as a vestige of the last few weeks, an inability to sit down. One says 'a glutton for work', and during her last month at Pond House she had exemplified that odious phrase, rushing gluttonously from one useful deed to another, cleaning, dispatching, repairing, turning out and destroying.

'All this revengeful housecleaning!' Willie had lamented.

'It's only fair to Annelies to get my smell out of the house,' she had replied.

In the first onset of grief, when grief was still pure enough to be magnanimous, the explanation might have been almost true, but not by the time she gave it. By then, she had no more magnanimity than a criminal on the run. There must be nothing left behind by which she could be tracked. A visual recollection of something overlooked and unscotched would strike her, as she lay sleepless – strike her violently, as though the object itself had been catapulted against her face. With her heart hammering and the blood pounding in her ears, she would begin to interrogate herself as to where, in their magpie's nest of a house, she had last set eyes on the red flannel heart embroidered with forget-me-nots, or the mug with 'William' on it that she had bought at Aberdovey. And all the while the most damning piece of evidence had slipped her memory, and only came to light by chance.

Invalided after Dunkirk, Willie had retained from his equipment one of those metal slides that isolate the military button for polishing. Thinking that this would serve the same purpose for the brass knobs on the spice cupboard, she began to search for it in the collector's cabinet, where Willie's father had kept his birds' eggs, where Willie hoarded his oddments. In the third drawer down, she came on the letters, her sight stumbling from Annelies's crisp blue sheets to her own letters, written from the flat of then to the Willie of then. She had looked at them no longer than to think how surprisingly and for the worse her handwriting had altered during the twelve years of happy married illiteracy, when she heard Willie saying, 'I know nothing about it. Do please go away,' to the children at the back door who had come to fetch the things for the jumble sale. Slamming the drawer to, she ran downstairs to recall the children. When she went back to the cabinet, the drawer was locked. Embarrassment tied her tongue.

Three days later, looking like a good dog, Willie laid her letters on the dressing-table.

'I don't approve of what I am doing,' he said. 'But then I don't approve of anything I am doing.' After a pause, he added, 'I think I wish I were dead.'

'Not really,' she answered. 'Not really, my dear.'

They looked at each other in the mirror, then. In the mirror she watched him lay his head on her shoulder – deposit it there, as though it were a sick animal.

But it was from that hour – as though by the restitution of her letters a ghost had been laid or a cork drawn – that Willie began to recover, to ascend from being a mournful cipher in her preparations to becoming their animating spirit. The last joint days at Pond House were spent in a kind of battered exhilaration, with Willie circumventing inquiring droppers-in, beating carpets and sewing on buttons. It was not just speeding the parting guest. He had, somehow or other, to dispose of the mounting excitement with which he awaited Annelies, and to be the life and soul of Barbara's departure was at once a safety valve and a tribute to conjugality.

21

'Write to me, won't you?' he had said, tying on the last luggage label.

'We said we wouldn't write, except on business,' she had replied. 'It would hurt Annelies. You know how sensitive she is, how the least thing makes her suffer agonies.' (She could not deny herself this shaft, and anyhow it did not penetrate.)

'You owe me a letter, Barbara. I gave you back the others. I didn't want to, but I did. I have never been so unhappy as I was that morning.' It was true, as true as that he was now much less unhappy. 'At least write and tell me that you are settled in, that you are all right, that the roof doesn't leak, that there aren't black beetles. It might be called a letter of business, really – though it isn't.'

'I will write,' she had said.

Now she took up Shakespeare, in whose orisons all our sins are comprehended, and patted him. 'Dear Swan!' she said aloud, her voice, in the unexplored depths of the lofty London room, sounding like the voice of a stranger. She could feel her body furtively relaxing while she sat on the sofa, and beginning to enjoy itself. It sighed, and stretched its legs, and burrowed deeper into the cushions, and her nostrils quickened to the smell of furniture polish, as though there were promise in it. She had been happy in her former solitude; presently she would be solitarily happy again. Like the furniture, she would settle down in the old arrangement, and the silence of the room would not intimidate her long; it was no more than a pinpoint of silence in the wide noise of London. The kettle was on the hotplate, filled and ready to be heated. The room sat around her, attentive, ready for her to begin. But first she must write to Willie.

Crossing the room, she seemed to herself to wade through silence, as though she were wading out to sea against a mounting tide. Silence embraced her thighs and almost overthrew her. She sat down at the desk and took a sheet of paper from a pigeonhole. The light from the window fell on the desk over her left shoulder, just as it had done in the flat of then. And, just as she had done in the flat of then, she wrote the date – the date of now – and the words 'My Dear'.

'I am keeping my promise,' she wrote. 'The flat is very comfortable. There are no black beetles, and the person overhead plays Bach by hand, which seems very old-fashioned and soothing. I have found a nice charwoman. She is called Mrs Darbyshire. She wears trousers. I hope –' The pen stopped. What did she hope?

After birthdays and Christmases there came the hour when one was set down to write the letters of thanks. 'Thank you so much for the gorgeous chocolates,' one wrote, or, 'It was very kind of you to give me that nice bottle of scent.' The chocolates had been eaten, the scent had been spilled – but still they had to be thanked for. One's handwriting sagged down the page as if from weariness, the words 'nice' or 'jolly' dogged one from sentence to sentence, and with every recommencement of gratitude the presents and the festivities became more irrevocably over and done with. One stared at the unfinished sentence and wondered what false thing to say next. Yet what she wanted to say to Willie was clear enough in her mind, clear as the printed words on India paper which had levelled themselves at her heart from that speech in *The Winter's Tale*:

> To me can life be no commodity;
> The crown and comfort of my life, your favour
> I do give lost, for I do feel it gone,
> Yet know not how it went . . .

But in real life one cannot write so plainly the plain truth; it would look theatrical. She must think of something she could legitimately hope. A hope about Mrs Darbyshire would do nicely. She wrote, 'I hope she will like me enough to look on me as a permanency.'

Oh, poor Willie! That sentence would not do at all. She tore up the unfinished letter and threw it into the grate, which Mrs Darbyshire had left neatly laid with crumpled paper and sticks and a few well-chosen lumps of coal, in case the lady should wish to light a fire in the evening; for a newly-moved-into place always strikes chilly at first, and though the autumn weather was keeping up wonderfully, almost as mild as spring, one could feel winter in the air.

Doris Lessing

Flight

A bove the old man's head was the dovecote, a tall wire-netted shelf on stilts, full of strutting, preening birds. The sunlight broke on their grey breasts into small rainbows. His ears were lulled by their crooning, his hands stretched up towards his favourite, a homing pigeon, a young plumpbodied bird which stood still when it saw him and cocked a shrewd bright eye.

'Pretty, pretty, pretty,' he said, as he grasped the bird and drew it down, feeling the cold coral claws tighten around his finger. Content, he rested the bird lightly on his chest, and leaned against a tree, gazing out beyond the dovecote into the landscape of a late afternoon. In folds and hollows of sunlight and shade, the dark red soil, which was broken into great clods, stretched wide to a tall horizon. Trees marked the course of the valley; a stream of rich green grass the road.

His eyes travelled homewards along this road until he saw his granddaughter swinging on the gate underneath a frangipani tree. Her hair fell down her back in a wave of sunlight, and her long bare legs repeated the angles of the frangipani stems, bare, shining-brown stems among patterns of pale blossoms.

She was gazing past the pink flowers, past the railway cottage where they lived, along the road to the village.

His mood shifted. He deliberately held out his wrist for the bird to take flight, and caught it again at the moment it spread its wings. He felt the plump shape strive and strain under his fingers; and, in a sudden access of troubled spite, shut the bird into a small box and fastened the bolt. 'Now you stay there,' he muttered; and turned his back on the shelf of birds. He moved warily along the hedge, stalking his granddaughter, who was now looped over the gate, her head loose on her arms, singing. The light happy sound mingled with the crooning of the birds, and his anger mounted.

24

'Hey!' he shouted; saw her jump, look back, and abandon the gate. Her eyes veiled themselves, and she said in a pert neutral voice: 'Hello, Grandad.' Politely she moved towards him, after a lingering backward glance at the road.

'Waiting for Steven, hey?' he said, his fingers curling like claws into his palm.

'Any objection?' she asked lightly, refusing to look at him.

He confronted her, his eyes narrowed, shoulders hunched, tight in a hard knot of pain which included the preening birds, the sunlight, the flowers, herself. He said: 'Think you're old enough to go courting, hey?'

The girl tossed her head at the old-fashioned phrase and sulked, 'Oh, Grandad!'

'Think you want to leave home, hey? Think you can go running around the fields at night?'

Her smile made him see her, as he had every evening of this warm end-of-summer month, swinging hand in hand along the road to the village with that red-handed, red-throated, violent-bodied youth, the son of the postmaster. Misery went to his head and he shouted angrily: 'I'll tell your mother!'

'Tell away!' she said, laughing, and went back to the gate.

He heard her singing, for him to hear:

'I've got you under my skin,
I've got you deep in the heart of . . .'

'Rubbish,' he shouted. 'Rubbish. Impudent little bit of rubbish!'

Growling under his breath he turned towards the dovecote, which was his refuge from the house he shared with his daughter and her husband and their children. But now the house would be empty. Gone all the young girls with their laughter and their squabbling and their teasing. He would be left, uncherished and alone, with that square-fronted, calm-eyed woman, his daughter.

He stooped, muttering, before the dovecote, resenting the absorbed cooing birds.

From the gate the girl shouted: 'Go and tell! Go on, what are you waiting for?'

Obstinately he made his way to the house, with quick, pathetic persistent glances of appeal back at her. But she never looked around. Her defiant but anxious young body stung him into love and repentance. He stopped. 'But I never meant ...' he muttered, waiting for her to turn and run to him. 'I didn't mean ...'

She did not turn. She had forgotten him. Along the road came the young man Steven, with something in his hand. A present for her? The old man stiffened as he watched the gate swing back, and the couple embrace. In the brittle shadows of the frangipani tree his granddaughter, his darling, lay in the arms of the postmaster's son, and her hair flowed back over his shoulder.

'I see you!' shouted the old man spitefully. They did not move. He stumped into the little whitewashed house, hearing the wooden veranda creak angrily under his feet. His daughter was sewing in the front room, threading a needle held to the light.

He stopped again, looking back into the garden. The couple were now sauntering among the bushes, laughing. As he watched he saw the girl escape from the youth with a sudden mischievous movement, and run off through the flowers with him in pursuit. He heard shouts, laughter, a scream, silence.

'But it's not like that at all,' he muttered miserably. 'It's not like that. Why can't you see? Running and giggling, and kissing and kissing. You'll come to something quite different.'

He looked at his daughter with sardonic hatred, hating himself. They were caught and finished, both of them, but the girl was still running free.

'Can't you *see?*' he demanded of his invisible granddaughter, who was at that moment lying in the thick green grass with the postmaster's son.

His daughter looked at him and her eyebrows went up in tired forbearance.

'Put your birds to bed?' she asked, humouring him.

'Lucy,' he said urgently. 'Lucy ...'

'Well, what is it now?'

'She's in the garden with Steven.'

'Now you just sit down and have your tea.'

He stumped his feet alternately, thump, thump, on the hollow wooden floor and shouted: 'She'll marry him. I'm telling you, she'll be marrying him next!'

His daughter rose swiftly, brought him a cup, set him a plate.

'I don't want any tea. I don't want it, I tell you.'

'Now, now,' she crooned. 'What's wrong with it? Why not?'

'She's eighteen. Eighteen!'

'I was married at seventeen and I never regretted it.'

'Liar,' he said. 'Liar. Then you should regret it. Why do you make your girls marry? It's you who do it. What do you do it for? Why?'

'The other three have done fine. They've three fine husbands. Why not Alice?'

'She's the last,' he mourned. 'Can't we keep her a bit longer?'

'Come, now, Dad. She'll be down the road, that's all. She'll be here every day to see you.'

'But it's not the same.' He thought of the other three girls, transformed inside a few months from charming petulant spoiled children into serious young matrons.

'You never did like it when we married,' she said. 'Why not? Every time, it's the same. When I got married you made me feel like it was something wrong. And my girls the same. You get them all crying and miserable the way you go on. Leave Alice alone. She's happy.' She sighed, letting her eyes linger on the sunlit garden. 'She'll marry next month. There's no reason to wait.'

'You've said they can marry?' he said incredulously.

'Yes, Dad, why not?' she said coldly, and took up her sewing.

His eyes stung, and he went out on to the veranda. Wet spread down over his chin and he took out a handkerchief and mopped his whole face. The garden was empty.

From around a corner came the young couple; but their faces were no longer set against him. On the wrist of the postmaster's son balanced a young pigeon, the light gleaming on its breast.

'For me?' said the old man, letting the drops shake off his chin. 'For me?'

'Do you like it?' The girl grabbed his hand and swung on it. 'It's for you, Grandad. Steven brought it for you.' They hung about him, affectionate, concerned, trying to charm away his wet eyes and his misery. They took his arms and directed him to the shelf of birds, one on each side, enclosing him, petting him, saying wordlessly that nothing would be changed, nothing could change, and that they would be with him always. The bird was proof of it, they said, from their lying happy eyes, as they thrust it on him. 'There, Grandad, it's yours. It's for you.'

27

They watched him as he held it on his wrist, stroking its soft, sun-warmed back, watching the wings lift and balance.

'You must shut it up for a bit,' said the girl intimately. 'Until it knows this is its home.'

'Teach your grandmother to suck eggs,' growled the old man.

Released by his half-deliberate anger, they fell back, laughing at him. 'We're glad you like it.' They moved off, now serious and full of purpose, to the gate, where they hung, backs to him, talking quietly. More than anything could their grown-up seriousness shut him out, making him alone; also, it quietened him, took the sting out of their tumbling like puppies on the grass. They had forgotten him again. Well, so they should, the old man reassured himself, feeling his throat clotted with tears, his lips trembling. He held the new bird to his face, for the caress of its silken feathers. Then he shut it in a box and took out his favourite.

'*Now* you can go,' he said aloud. He held it poised, ready for flight, while he looked down the garden towards the boy and the girl. Then, clenched in the pain of loss, he lifted the bird on his wrist and watched it soar. A whirr and a spatter of wings, and a cloud of birds rose into the evening from the dovecote.

At the gate Alice and Steven forgot their talk and watched the birds.

On the veranda, that woman, his daughter, stood gazing, her eyes shaded with a hand that still held her sewing.

It seemed to the old man that the whole afternoon had stilled to watch his gesture of self-command, that even the leaves of the trees had stopped shaking.

Dry-eyed and calm, he let his hands fall to his sides and stood erect, staring up into the sky.

The cloud of shining silver birds flew up and up, with a shrill cleaving of wings, over the dark ploughed land and the darker belts of trees and the bright folds of grass, until they floated high in the sunlight, like a cloud of motes of dust.

They wheeled in a wide circle, tilting their wings so there was flash after flash of light, and one after another they dropped from the sunshine of the upper sky to shadow, one after another, returning to the shadowed earth over trees and grass and field, returning to the valley and the shelter of night.

28

The garden was all a fluster and a flurry of returning birds. Then silence, and the sky was empty.

The old man turned, slowly, taking his time; he lifted his eyes to smile proudly down the garden at his granddaughter. She was staring at him. She did not smile. She was wide-eyed, and pale in the cold shadow, and he saw the tears run shivering off her face.

Dorothy Parker

I Live on Your Visits

The boy came into the hotel room and immediately it seemed even smaller.

'Hey, it's cool in here,' he said. This was not meant as a comment on the temperature. 'Cool', for reasons possibly known in some department of Heaven, was a term then in use among many of those of his age to express approbation.

It was indeed cool in the room, after the hard grey rain in the streets. It was warm, and it was so bright. The many-watted electric bulbs his mother insisted upon were undimmed by the thin frilled shades she had set on the hotel lamps, and there were shiny things everywhere: sheets of mirror along the walls; a square of mirror backing the mirror-plated knob on the door that led to the bedroom; cigarette boxes made of tiny bits of mirror and matchboxes slipped into little mirror jackets placed all about; and, on consoles and desk and table, photographs of himself at two and a half and five and seven and nine framed in broad mirror bands. Whenever his mother settled in a new domicile, and she removed often, those photographs were the first things out of the luggage. The boy hated them. He had had to pass his fifteenth birthday before his body had caught up with his head; there was that head, in those presentments of his former selves, that pale, enormous blob. Once he had asked his mother to put the pictures somewhere else – preferably some small, dark place that could be locked. But he had had the bad fortune to make his request on one of the occasions when she was given to weeping suddenly and long. So the photographs stood out on parade, with their frames twinkling away.

There were twinklings, too, from the silver top of the fat crystal cocktail shaker, but the liquid low within the crystal was pale and dull. There was no shine, either, to the glass his mother held. It was cloudy from the clutch of her hand, and on the inside there were oily dribbles of what it had contained.

His mother shut the door by which she had admitted him, and followed him into the room. She looked at him with her head tilted to the side.

'Well, aren't you going to kiss me?' she said in a charming, wheedling voice, the voice of a little, little girl. 'Aren't you, you beautiful big ox, you?'

'Sure,' he said. He bent down toward her, but she stepped suddenly away. A sharp change came over her. She drew herself tall, with her shoulders back and her head flung high. Her upper lip lifted over her teeth, and her gaze came cold beneath lowered lids. So does one who has refused the white handkerchief regard the firing squad.

'Of course,' she said in a deep, iced voice that gave each word its full due, 'if you do not wish to kiss me, let it be recognized that there is no need for you to do so. I had not meant to overstep. I apologize. *Je vous demande pardon.* I had no desire to force you. I have never forced you. There is none to say I have.'

'Ah, Mom,' he said. He went to her, bent again, and this time kissed her cheek.

There was no change in her, save in the slow, somehow offended lifting of her eyelids. The brows arched as if they drew the lids up with them. 'Thank you,' she said. 'That was gracious of you. I value graciousness. I rank it high. *Mille grazie.*'

'Ah, Mom,' he said.

For the past week, up at his school, he had hoped – and coming down in the train he had hoped so hard that it became prayer – that his mother would not be what he thought of only as 'like that'. His prayer had gone unanswered. He knew by the two voices, by the head first tilted then held high, by the eyelids lowered in disdain then raised in outrage, by the little lisped words and then the elegant enunciation and the lofty diction. He knew.

He stood there and said, 'Ah, Mom.'

'Perhaps,' she said, 'you will award yourself the privilege of meeting a friend of mine. She is a true friend. I am proud that I may say it.'

There was someone else in the room. It was preposterous that he had not seen her, for she was so big. Perhaps his eyes had been

31

dazzled, after the dim-lit hotel corridor; perhaps his attention had been all for his mother. At any rate, there she sat, the true friend, on the sofa covered with embossed cotton fabric of the sickened green that is peculiar to hotel upholsteries. There she sat, at one end of the sofa, and it seemed as if the other end must fly up into the air.

'I can give you but little,' his mother said, 'yet life is still kind enough to let me give you something you will always remember. Through me, you will meet a human being.'

Yes, oh, yes. The voices, the stances, the eyelids – those were the signs. But when his mother divided the race into people and human beings – that was the certainty.

He followed her the little way across the room, trying not to tread on the train of her velvet tea gown that slid along the floor after her and slapped at the heels of her gilt slippers. Fog seemed to rise from his raincoat and his shoes cheeped. He turned out to avoid the coffee table in front of the sofa, came in again too sharply and bumped it.

'Mme Marah,' his mother said, 'may I present my son?'

'Christ, he's a big bastard, isn't he?' the true friend said.

She was a fine one to talk about anybody's being big. Had she risen, she would have stood shoulder against shoulder with him, and she must have outweighed him by sixty pounds. She was dressed in quantities of tweedlike stuff ornamented, surprisingly, with black sequins set on in patterns of little bunches of grapes. On her massive wrists were bands and chains of dull silver, from some of which hung amulets of discolored ivory, like rotted fangs. Over her head and neck was a sort of caul of crisscrossed mauve veiling, splattered with fuzzy black balls. The caul caused her no inconvenience. Puffs of smoke issued sporadically from behind it, and, though the veiling was crisp elsewhere, around the mouth it was of a marshy texture, where drink had passed through it.

His mother became the little girl again. 'Isn't he wonderful?' she said. 'This is my baby. This is Crissy-wiss.'

'What is his name?' the true friend said.

'Why, Christopher, of course,' his mother said.

Christopher, of course. Had he been born earlier, it would have been Peter; earlier again, Michael; he had been not much too late for Jonathan. In the lower forms of his school, there were various Nicholases, several Robins, and here and there a Jeremy

32

coming up. But the members of his own class were in the main Christophers.

'Christopher,' the true friend said. 'Well, that's not too bad. Of course, that downward stroke of the "p" is bound to give him trouble, and I'm never really happy about an "r" and an "i" together. But it's not too bad. Not too. When's your birthday?' she asked the boy.

'The fifteenth of August,' he said.

His mother was no longer the little girl. 'The heat,' she said, 'the cruel August heat. And the stitches. Oh, God, the stitches!'

'So he's a Leo,' the true friend said. 'Awfully big for a Leo. You want to be pretty careful, young man, from October 22nd to November 13th. Keep away from anything electrical.'

'I will,' the boy said. 'Thank you,' he added.

'Let me see your hand,' the true friend said.

The boy gave her his hand.

'Mm,' she said, scanning the palm. 'M-hmm, m-hmm, m-hmm. Oh. Well – *that* can't be helped. Well, you'll have pretty good health, if you just watch that chest of yours. There's a long sickness in your twenties and a bad accident some time around forty-five, but that's about all. There's going to be an unhappy love affair, but you'll get over it. You'll marry and – I can't see if there's two or three children. Probably two and one born dead, or something like that. I don't see much money, any time. Well, you watch your chest.' She gave him back his hand.

'Thank you,' he said.

The little girl came back to his mother. 'Isn't he going to be famous?' she said.

The true friend shrugged. 'It's not in his hand,' she said.

'I always thought he'd write,' his mother said. 'When he was so small you could hardly see him, he used to write little verses. Crissy, what was the one about the bumpety bunny?'

'Oh, Mother!' he said. 'I don't remember!'

'Oh, you do so, too!' she said. 'You're just being modest. It was all about how the bunny went bumpety, bumpety all day long. Of course you remember. Well, you don't seem to write verses any more – least none you show to *me*. And your letters – they're like telegrams. When you write at all, that is. Oh, Marah, why do they have to grow up? And now he's going to be married and have all those children.'

'Two, anyway,' the true friend said. 'I'm not too happy about that third one.'

'I suppose I'll never see him then,' his mother said. 'A lonely old woman, sick and trembling, and no one to take care of me.'

She picked up the true friend's empty glass from the coffee table, filled it and her own from the cocktail shaker, and returned the friend's. She sat down near the sofa.

'Well, sit down, Crissy,' she said. 'And why don't you take off your coat?'

'Why, I don't think I'd better, Mom,' he said. 'You see –'

'He wants to keep his wet coat on,' the true friend said. 'He likes to smell like low tide.'

'Well, you see,' the boy said, 'I can stay just a minute. You see, the train was late and everything, and I told Dad I'd be sure to be there early.'

'Oh?' his mother said. The little girl ran off abruptly. The eyelids came into play.

'It's because the train was late,' he said. 'If it had been on time, I could have stayed awhile. But it had to go and be late, and they're having dinner awfully early tonight.'

'I see,' his mother said. 'I see. I had thought that you would have dinner with me. With your mother. Her only son. But no, that is not to be. I have only an egg, but I would have shared it with you so gladly. So happily. But you are wise, of course. You must think first of your own comfort. Go and fill your stomach with your father. Go eat stalled ox with him.'

'Mother, don't you see?' he said. 'We have to have dinner early because we have to go to bed early. We've got to get up at daybreak because we're driving to the country. You know. I wrote you.'

'Driving?' she said. 'Your father has a new car, I presume.'

'It's the same old heap,' he said. 'Nearly eight years old.'

'Really?' she said. 'Naturally, the buses in which I am obliged to ride are all this year's models.'

'Ah, Mom,' he said.

'Is your father well?' she said.

'He's fine,' he said.

'Why not?' she said. 'What is there could pierce that heart? And how is Mrs Tennant? As I suppose she calls herself.'

'Let's not do this again, will you, Mom?' he said. 'She's Mrs Tennant. You know that. She and Dad have been married for six years.'

'To me,' she said, 'there is only one woman who may rightfully wear a man's name; the one whose son he has sired. But that is only my humble opinion. Who is to listen to it?'

'You get along all right with your stepmother?' the true friend said.

As always, it took him a moment before he could connect the term. It seemed to have nothing to do with Whitey, with her gay little monkey's face and her flying straw-colored hair.

A laugh fell from his mother's lips, hard, like a pellet of ice. 'Such women are sly,' she said. 'They have ways.'

'Well, born on a cusp,' the true friend said. 'You've got to keep considering that.'

His mother turned to the boy. 'I am going to do something that you will agree, in any honesty, that I have never done before,' she said. 'I am going to ask a favor of you. I am going to ask you to take off your coat and sit down, so that for just a few poor minutes it will seem as if you were not going to leave me. Will you let me have that illusion? Do not do it out of affection or gratitude or consideration. Just in simple pity.'

'Yes, sit down, for God's sake,' the true friend said. 'You make people nervous.'

'All right, sure,' the boy said. He took off his raincoat, hung it over his arm, and sat on a small, straight chair.

'He's the biggest damn thing I ever saw,' the true friend said.

'Thank you,' his mother said. 'If you think I ask too much, I plead guilty. *Mea culpa*. Well, now that we are cozy, let us talk, shall we? I see so little of you – I know so little about you. Tell me some things. Tell me what there is about this Mrs Tennant that causes you to rank her so high above me. Is she more beautiful than I am?'

'Mom, please,' he said. 'You know Whitey isn't beautiful. She's just sort of funny-looking. Nice funny.'

'Nice funny,' she said. 'Oh, I'm afraid I could never compete with that. Well, looks aren't everything, I suppose. Tell me, do you consider her a human being?'

'Mother, I don't know,' he said. 'I can't do that kind of talk.'

'Let it pass,' she said. 'Let it be forgotten. Is your father's country place attractive at this time of year?'

'It isn't a place,' he said. 'You know – it's just a big sort of shack. There isn't even any heat. Just fireplaces.'

'Ironic,' she said. 'Bitterly, cruelly ironic. I, who so love an open fire; I, who could sit all day looking into its leaping golds and purples and dreaming happy dreams. And I haven't even a gas log. Well. And who is going to this shack, to share the lovely, glowing fires?'

'Just Dad and Whitey and me,' he said. 'Oh, and the other Whitey, of course.'

His mother looked at the true friend. 'Is it growing dark in here?' she said. 'Or is it just that I think I am going to faint?' She looked again at the boy. 'The *other* Whitey?'

'It's a little dog,' he said. 'Not any particular kind. It's a nice little dog. Whitey saw it out in the street, when it was snowing, and it followed her home, and so they kept it. And whenever Dad – whenever anybody called Whitey, the dog would come, too. So Dad said well, if he thought that was his name, then that was going to *be* his name. So that was why.'

'I am afraid', his mother said, 'that your father is not ageing with dignity. To me, whimsey after forty-five is a matter of nausea.'

'It's an awfully nice little dog,' he said.

'The management does not allow dogs here,' she said. 'I suppose that will be held against me. Marah – this drink. It is as weak as the beating of my heart.'

'Why doesn't he make us some fresh ones?' the true friend said.

'I'm sorry,' the boy said. 'I don't know how to make cocktails.'

'What do they teach you, anyway, in that fancy school of yours?' the true friend said.

His mother tilted her head at the boy. 'Crissy,' she said, 'want to be a big, brave man? Take the bowl and get some nice, cold ice out of the kitchen.'

He took the ice bowl, went into the minuscule kitchen, and took a tray of ice cubes from the tiny refrigerator. When he replaced the tray, he could hardly close the refrigerator door, the shelves were so crowded. There were a cardboard box of eggs, a packet of butter, a cluster of glossy French rolls, three artichokes, two avocados, a plate of tomatoes, a bowl of shelled peas, a grapefruit, a tin of vegetable juices, a glass of red caviar, a cream cheese, an assortment of sliced Italian sausages, and a plump little roasted Cornish Rock hen.

When he returned, his mother was busied with bottles and shaker. He set the bowl of cubes beside them.

'Look, Mom,' he said, 'honestly I've got to –'

His mother looked at him and her lip trembled. 'Just two more minutes,' she whispered. 'Please, oh, please.'

He went and sat again.

She made the drinks, gave one to the true friend, and kept one. She sank into her chair; her head drooped and her body looked as boneless as a skein of yarn.

'Don't you want a drink?' the true friend said.

'No, thanks,' the boy said.

'Might do you good,' the true friend said. 'Might stunt your growth. How long are you going to stay up in this country where you're going?'

'Oh, just over tomorrow night,' he said. 'I have to be back at school Sunday evening.'

His mother stiffened and straightened. Her former coldnesses were as tropical heat to that which took her now.

'Do I understand you to say that you will not be coming in to see me again?' she said. 'Do I understand you aright?'

'I can't, Mom,' he said. 'I won't have a chance. We've got to drive back, and then I have to get the train.'

'I quite comprehend,' she said. 'I had thought, in my tenderness, I would see you again before your return to your school. I had thought, of course, that if you must rush away like a mad thing today, then I would see you again, to make up for it. Disappointments – I thought I had had them all, I thought life could bring forth no new ones. But this – this. That you will not take a little bit of your time from your relatives, who have so much of it, to give to me, your mother. How it must please them that you do not want to see me. How they must laugh together. What a triumph. How they must howl in merriment.'

'Mother, don't say things like that,' he said. 'You shouldn't, even when you're –'

37

'Please!' she said. 'The subject is closed. I will say no more about your father, poor, weak man, and that woman with the dog's name. But you – you. Have you no heart, no bowels, no natural instincts? No. You have not. I must face the fact. Here, in the presence of my friend, I must say what I had thought never, never to say. My son is not a human being!'

The true friend shook her caul and sighed. The boy sat still.

'Your father,' his mother said. 'Does he still see his old friends? *Our* old friends?'

'Why, I don't know, Mom,' he said. 'Yes, they see a lot of people, I guess. There's almost always somebody there. But they're alone a lot of the time. They like it that way.'

'How fortunate,' she said. 'They like being alone. Smug, content, no need – Yes. And the old friends. They do not see me. They are all in twos, they have lives, they know what they're going to be doing six months from now. Why should they see me? Why should they have memories, kindnesses?'

'Probably most of them Pisces,' the true friend said.

'Well, you must go,' the boy's mother said. 'It is late. Late – when is it ever late for me, when my son is with me? But you have told me. I know. I understand, and so I bow my head. Go, Christopher. Go.'

'I'm terribly sorry, Mom,' the boy said. 'But I told you how it is.' He rose and put on his coat.

'Christ, he gets bigger and bigger,' the true friend said.

This time, the eyelids of the boy's mother were lowered at her friend. 'I have always admired tall men,' she said. She turned again to the boy. 'You must go,' she said. 'It is so written. But take happiness with you. Take sweet memories of our little time together. See – I shall show you that I bear no vengefulness. I shall show you that I wish only well to those who have wrought but evil to me. I shall give you a present to take one of them.'

She rose, moved about the room, touched boxes and tables fruitlessly. Then she went to the desk, moved papers and inkstands, and brought forth a small, square box, on top of which was a little plaster poodle, sitting on its hind legs, its front paws curved endearingly, begging.

'This is a souvenir of happier times,' she said. 'But I need no reminders. Take this dear, happy thing to one you love. See! See what it is!'

She touched a spring at the back of the box and the 'Marseillaise' tinkled forth, hesitantly.

'My little music box,' she said. 'That moonlit night, the ship so brilliant, the ocean so still and beckoning.'

'Hey, that's cool, Mom,' he said. 'Thanks ever so much. Whitey'll love it. She loves things like that.'

'Things like that?' she said. 'There are no other things like that, when one gives from one's heart.' She stopped and seemed to ponder. '*Whitey* will love it?' she said. 'Are you telling me that you propose giving it to that so-called Mrs Tennant?' She touched the box; the tinkling ceased.

'I thought you said –' the boy said.

She shook her head at him, slowly. 'Curious,' she said. 'Extraordinary. That my son should have so little perception. This gift, from my poor little store, is not for her. It is for the little dog. The little dog that I may not have.'

'Why, thanks, Mom,' he said. 'Thanks.'

'So go,' she said. 'I would not hold you. Take with you my wishes for your joy, among your loved ones. And when you can, when they will release you for a little while – come to me again. I wait for you. I light a lamp for you. My son, my only child, there are but desert sands for me between your comings. I live on your visits – Chris, I live on your visits.'

Elizabeth Taylor

The Ambush

A few weeks after the funeral, Catherine went back to stay with
the Ingrams. Uncertain, during those weeks, how much grief
was suitable to her – for she and Noël had not been officially
engaged and in the eyes of the world she saw her status as mourner
undecided – she had shown no sign of sorrow, for one tear might
release the rest and one word commit her to too many others. Her
fortitude was prodigious, even alone after the funeral when all that
she had keyed herself up to was over. She avoided the drawer where
his letters were; the air about her, at the art school by day and with
her parents at home, was full of warnings and tensions. She felt
jolted and stunned, as if she had been in his car at the time of the
accident, and she walked about slowly and carefully, suffering from
a stiffness of her limbs and a sensation of vertigo. By the end of the
first month her effort had told on her – the energy spent in fending
off other people and the sympathy they might offer, the holding back
of tears, left her weak and apathetic. The boredom of her grief was
not its easiest part to bear – the irritation of having nothing but her
loss ever enter her mind now, when once she had had so many
thoughts, dulled all her days and her dreams at night. Her parents
were thankful when she took herself off to the Ingrams and they
could come down from their tightrope and relax.

Mrs Ingram met her at the station. Catherine saw her first, standing
on the platform, scanning the carriages as the doors began to open.
She was wearing a mauve gingham frock and her white hair was
blown back from her forehead and from that plane below her high
cheekbone which Noël had had, too, and which made, Catherine
thought, those two faces the most beautiful she had ever known.

'I am here,' she said, setting down her suitcase for a moment while
she was kissed.

'Dear Catherine, I am so glad you came before it was dark.' Her seemingly meaningless phrases were often found, later, to have some meaning after all.

A soldier, for Mrs Ingram's sake, not Catherine's, had lifted the suitcase and was carrying it out to the station-yard. A wake of devotion always followed her and Catherine joined her own homage to the rest.

They got into Mrs Ingram's tinny little shopping car and drove away through the red-brick Thames-side village and down darkening lanes scented with elder-blossom.

'Esmé is still with us,' Mrs Ingram said. 'I wanted you to come before his leave was over.'

Esmé was Noël's elder brother, adored first-born, whom Catherine had heard of for years, resented somewhat on Noël's account and seen fleetingly at the funeral, to which he had come from abroad.

'You will be someone young for him,' Mrs Ingram said.

She drove as if she were a goddess in a chariot, her white hands confident, her head erect. Sometimes she waved to children who pressed back against the hedges, staring.

They turned through iron gates into the tunnel of trees leading up to the house; a haze of gnats danced under the bitten leaves; cow-parsley was grey in the shadows. The drive ended suddenly and they were under the high façade of the house with its rows of Georgian windows diminishing in height at each storey and the panelled door and rounded fanlight. Lights were on on the ground floor and a young man came out of the house and down the steps towards them.

Not quite up to the shock of seeing even a slight resemblance to Noël, Catherine was obliged to look up at what she had steadfastly at the funeral ignored. This brother had the same eyes, shrewd and alert, lines from laughter beneath them – for as a family they seemed to have laughed a great deal. When Mrs Ingram did so, she became even more beautiful – a rare thing in a woman; laughter enlivened her features and never disorganized them. Esmé was heavier than Noël; his features less defined; his colour paler. The beautiful flatness under the cheekbone he lacked. Catherine could imagine him in middle age rather puffy under the eyes and stout and inactive and even, later, gouty as his father had been.

Catherine saw the house in the last of the light – perhaps its most magical time. It was ashen and flat against the dark trees. Beyond the lawns the river slid by and she could hear and smell the tumbling water at the weir. Moths followed them into the lighted hall. Damp had drained colour from great patches of the crimson walls, but the room was in brilliant contrast to outside. The tall clock only tocked, never ticked, Noël had said. On a table was a disarray of flowers and baskets and vases, for Mrs Ingram had left for the station in the middle of building a great pyramid of honeysuckle and peonies. She now, leading Catherine to her room, looked back regretfully at her interrupted work. Could not Esmé have fetched me, then? Catherine wondered, apologetic as always. Or wouldn't he?

From her bedroom's two long windows she would be able to see the river when it was daylight again.

'I hope the weir won't disturb you,' Mrs Ingram said, as if Catherine had never stayed in the house before. 'I never hear it now.'

When Esmé had brought in the suitcase and gone, Mrs Ingram embraced Catherine again. 'So lovely that you are here,' she murmured. 'Come down soon and have a drink after your long journey.'

She looked round the room, pulled at a curtain and rearranged some white geraniums in a pewter mug before she left Catherine alone.

The girl had the most extraordinary feeling of dizziness from so much sudden beauty – the beauty of Mrs Ingram herself whose footsteps were now light and hastening on the oak staircase, and the house and garden and this room scented with pinks and sounding of the river.

On the wall above the writing-table hung a watercolour drawing of Esmé and Noël as children – vaguely done, insipidly pretty and not worthy of their mother's room. They sat on a sofa together and had a picture-book open across their knees. The smocking on their blouses was painstakingly tinted in and Esmé's tawny curls were carefully highlighted though nothing much could be made of Noël's straight black hair. His eyes were round and unseeing and bright as forget-me-nots. Fond drawing by a relative, Catherine thought. She herself had never drawn Noël, either fondly or objectively. The nearest she had got to that, she reflected, was once sketching his foot when he was lying on the lawn after swimming. She had been

42

drawing the gable of the boathouse and branches of a chestnut-tree and, for some reason turning to look at him, began on a corner of the paper to draw his foot with its bony ankle and raised veins. Then he had slapped one foot against the other to chase off a fly. She had rubbed out the sketch, blown at the paper and quickly covered up the smudge with a clump of rushes. She had trembled as if hoping to hide some misdemeanour, but was calm again when he stood up and came to look at her drawing. She had added an imaginary dragonfly above the rushes and then, at his request, a heron. What became of the drawing she could not now recall.

Mrs Ingram was in the hall when Catherine went downstairs. The uncarpeted staircase could be an ordeal, so much of it exposed to the hall, and now Mrs Ingram looking up and smiling as she stripped leaves from the peonies. Voices echoed here, and whatever Esmé said as he came from the library carrying a decanter was lost to Catherine.

She took her glass of whisky and Esmé pulled a chair out from the table for her where she could watch Mrs Ingram's flower-arranging. A pale greyhound lay on a window-seat, and Esmé sat down beside it, fingering its silky ears.

'Other women I know do the flowers in the morning,' he said.

'You need not stay with me.'

She tore some leaves from a stalk with an asperity to match her voice, an asperity Catherine had never heard before, but which she always had felt to be a dreaded possibility in people as decisive as Mrs Ingram.

Esmé sat far back in the shadows stroking the dog's ears, not replying.

This hall was at the heart of the house – open to the garden in fine weather, a place for casual conversations and chance meetings. The last time Catherine was there it had been filled with wreaths, cushions of carnations propped against chair-legs, Mrs Ingram's hoop of roses and camellias lying on the table. It had had a drab symmetry about it, with its suggestion of flowers bought by the dozen and Catherine had seen the glance it received, the weary contempt with which it was put aside as beyond improving.

Now Mrs Ingram carried the big soup tureen of flowers and stood it against the wall, stepped back to view it while Esmé yawned and clapped his hands, then called to his dog and went out into the garden.

Mrs Ingram sank into a chair the moment he had gone as if she had no need now to be busy.

'I shall send you to bed soon,' she told Catherine. 'You look tired after your journey'; and then as Catherine was obediently finishing her whisky she asked, 'How are you getting over Noël?'

At home, no one had dared to say this name and Catherine was unprepared to hear it and could think of no reply.

'Don't defer it, or try to pay off in instalments,' Mrs Ingram said. 'One only pays more in the end.' She sat so still with her elbow among the litter of leaves on the table and her cheek resting on her hand. 'I knew you would take it in this way, poor Catherine, and that is why I asked you to come here.' She gave the smile that was always so much remembered when Catherine had left her and was trying to reassemble the look of her, feature by feature, in her mind. The smile was the only uncertain thing about her, wavering, pleading; deep lines broke up the smoothness of her face and her regality – the Blue Persian look, Noël had called it – vanished.

I love her, Catherine thought. I could never withstand her, no matter what she wanted of me.

When she was in bed, she wondered why such a thought had come to her, when there was no longer anything Mrs Ingram could want of her, no longer anything she could ask her to relinquish. Strangeness and the physical beauty of the place overtook her. She was under this roof again, but the old reason for being there was gone. Listening to the weir, lying in the flower-scented room, between the cool sheets (Mrs Ingram's linen was glassier than anyone else's, she thought), she fell under the spell of the family again, although the one of it she loved was dead. Missing him, it was in this place she wanted to be, no other.

She heard Esmé crossing the gravel again and calling in a low voice to the dog.

In the morning, the garden, drenched with dew, flashed with rainbow colours; the meadows on the other side of the river gently steamed. The sun had already warmed the carpet under the windows. Catherine stood there barefoot looking down on the dazzling scene. She could hear the grating sound of oars in rowlocks before Esmé appeared round the river-bend under the silvery willows. She watched him coming up from the boathouse. His footprints were dark on the dewy grass and the dog's paw-prints ran in circles about them. He was especially tender with his dog, would be with all animals and with children, as some bachelors are, she guessed.

When Catherine had stayed in the house on other occasions, Mrs Ingram had always had breakfast in bed. She had a clever way of not being seen coming downstairs, but of being discovered later very busy about the house, at her desk or coming from the kitchen with a list in her hand, as if she had been about since daybreak, the reins gathered in her hands for hours. This morning, Catherine, coming downstairs, was surprised to hear Mrs Ingram and Esmé talking in the dining-room. 'If you object, I can go to *his* place instead.' That was Esmé. Then his mother said quickly, 'I don't object ...' and paused, as if she were about to add a second clause that would take the meaning from the first. She got as far as saying 'but' and then heard the footsteps in the hall and Catherine came into the room to a tense silence and rearranged expressions.

Mrs Ingram was standing by the window, drinking coffee. Esmé rose from the table and, doing so, scattered some pages of a letter over the carpet. His mother glanced, then glanced away. She really does look as if she has been up since dawn, Catherine thought. Perhaps *she* doesn't sleep, either.

The warmth of Mrs Ingram's smile welcomed her and Catherine regretted the stiffness and timidity of her own that answered it. She felt full of a jerky vagueness, and the beginning of a fear that the house with its associations might undermine her and expose some nerve in an intolerable way. She was constantly alarmed at the possibility of behaving badly and trembled to think of the presumption of not holding back a grief that Mrs Ingram herself seemed able to contain. The strain was not merely of never being herself, but of not knowing who she any longer was.

She took a chair opposite Esmé's and Mrs Ingram came back to the table to pour out coffee, but without sitting down.

'Are you going out sketching this morning?' she asked Catherine; for that was how she had spent her mornings on other visits.

Catherine stared down at her boiled egg as if she were wondering what curious object she had been given, so dismayed was her expression. Esmé, who had put away his letter, looked across at her but wished that he had not. There was a sign of a crack in her sedate composure.

She said: 'Yes, I think I will do that.'

'Then we shall all meet at luncheon.'

Mrs Ingram was brisk, as if now Catherine was disposed of for the morning. This was unlike her, Esmé thought: but his mother was definitely up to something and he wondered for whom ill was boded, Catherine or himself. Some wonderful ill, no doubt, he thought; done for one's good; a great, bracing, visionary ill. Even if I want to paint again, Catherine thought, I don't want to be in the painting *mood* – so exposed and inviting. She had brought her painting materials with her and knew that she must rouse herself to work again and better here, perhaps, than at her own home with its too patent watchfulness, the irritating parental concentration upon her and all her doings and the secret discussions she could imagine just as if she had overheard them. 'Now she is painting again. Such a good sign. We will pretend not to have noticed.'

So after breakfast she went down to the river and along the bank until she reached the lock. Much about the Thames Valley is Victorian – the canopied steamers and the red brick lock-keepers' houses and the little shelters with spiked edges to their wooden roofs like miniature railway platforms. The garden beds of marguerites, calceolarias, were edged with whitewashed stones and slung about with whitened chains; all was neat and two-dimensional, like a primitive painting, captivating, bright and unconvincing.

Beyond the lock was a stretch of river, darkened and smothered by dusty, summer chestnuts; the oily, olive-green water slid by, was brown when the sun went in; a boat tied up in the rushes had no reflection. The other bank, in contrast, was silvery with aspens and willows, with shifting white leaves and light.

She sat on the bank and unpacked her watercolours. The sun was strong now, the light banal, she thought fretfully, narrowing her eyes to blur what she saw too sharply and with too many irrelevances. She felt a deep reluctance to begin painting on this lulled and buzzing mid-morning, and felt too that she had been expelled, excluded from Mrs Ingram's presence where she wanted to be, and sent off to do her painting as a child might be sent to practise scales.

She slapped at the horseflies biting her bare legs. They were always a plague – the towing-path flies – and on other summer days Noël had sat beside her and waved them away with his handkerchief while she painted. Her irritation suddenly heeled over into grief and she dropped her brush, stunned, appalled, as the monstrous pain leapt upon her. Her painting – the faint washes of grey and green which had lifted the paper – dried in the sun, the jar of water was scarcely coloured. She rested her elbows on the drawing-board and covered her eyes with her hands, waiting for this moment to pass. Esmé, going along the towpath to the pub, saw her before she heard his footsteps and would have turned back, but as he hesitated he thought that she had heard him. He was a reticent man but could see no reason for turning his back on sorrow, so against his inclination he went over to her. His dog, following him, sniffed at the paint water and stretched himself out in the shade of some rushes.

Catherine kept her head bent, and began to pack up her painting things as Esmé sat down beside her. She had not been crying. Her face was pale, but her cheekbones were red where her hands had pressed against them. In a few seconds this colour receded and she seemed more in command of herself.

She unpinned the drawing-paper from the board and tore it across.

'Not a good morning?' he asked.

'I am bitten to death by horseflies.'

'Come with me to the pub and have a drink. I will carry all the paraphernalia.'

He had Noël's voice, though he talked too rapidly and stumbled over words. His tongue was not quick enough to keep up with his desire to have the words done with and his part of the conversation over. His manner of speaking was, from nervousness, over-decisive and just when he meant to be tender he sounded stern.

They walked along the towing-path in silence until they reached The Rose and Crown – there, the bar was empty until a woman came through from the kitchen, drying her hands, to serve them. She drew

47

the beer and went back to her cooking. Catherine and Esmé sat on the varnished window-seat and looked out at the river. Conversation was uneasy between them. What they had in common was felt by both to be taboo and he, from lack of interest and living abroad, had no idea of what sort of girl she was. This morning, he began to be moved by her forlornness and blamed his mother for letting her mope: something strenuous and gay should surely have been arranged – though he could not think what.

'Would you like to play darts?' he asked her. She did not in the least want to play darts and did not know how, but his solicitude was so masked, his voice was so abrupt that she timidly agreed. He was patient and encouraging as her darts struck the brick wall, once a tin lampshade, but rarely the board, until, as part of her haphazard throwing – and she had no idea that such a thing could happen – two darts landed together in the bull's-eye. She glowed at his amazement and praise. He called in the landlord's wife to draw them some more beer and to see Catherine's score and said that he had never done such a thing in his life and would never do it.

'But I didn't *know*,' Catherine said happily. 'They might just as easily have gone out of the window.' She could not have imagined that doing something well in a game could be so stimulating.

They left the pub and walked back along the towing-path. Mrs Ingram was sitting on the steps in the sun and she, too, listened to Esmé's account of Catherine's first game of darts and she smiled radiantly, as if this was the nicest, gayest thing that could happen. At luncheon, the three of them were drawn together: by some simple magic, which Catherine could not understand, Mrs Ingram no longer seemed cross or embarrassed with her son, but rather as if she were acquiescing to some delightful plan he had for the future. Only when they were drinking coffee on the terrace and Esmé suggested an afternoon on the river did she detach herself from them again, making too many excuses – a little headache and a letter to write and a vague notion that one of her friends might call. She would not let them delay one moment. They must go alone and if they wanted tea it could be packed for them.

Catherine was disappointed, for it was Mrs Ingram she loved and admired, not Esmé; and Esmé himself looked sulky again. He watched his mother going away from them along the terrace and his eyes were full of contempt, as if he knew some secret she had, which he despised. He stood up and said 'Well, then,' in a hearty voice, trying to seem gaily anticipatory, but not managing it.

Mrs Ingram had a small motor launch which was used for visiting her friends up and down the river, and in this, sitting beside one another in wicker chairs, Esmé and Catherine drove sedately under the summer darkness of the trees. The easy gaiety had gone and Catherine felt helplessly that Mrs Ingram had pushed her off alone with Esmé against his inclination, and she was puzzled to think what motive she could have for doing such a thing. If it was simply to be rid of her, then she need never have invited her; that she might be trying to lay the foundations of something deeper between Esmé and Catherine than this slight acquaintance they had was not in character with her role of possessive mother. Noël had once said: 'It is lucky for you that you love me, not Esmé. Mamma never allows any girls within yards of her darling. They are just to be devoted to one another.' Equally, that Mrs Ingram simply had, as she said, a headache was unthinkable. She was not a woman who would be likely to have headaches or confess to such frailty if she had. She was ordinarily so proudly direct that excuses were alien to her. She would not deign to dissemble or explain. When she did so, Catherine felt uneasily compelled to wonder why.

Some cloud was between mother and son. In other circumstances, Catherine would have thought that it gathered from Mrs Ingram's jealousy. Her coldness might have been caused by Catherine and Esmé wishing to escape together, not from the reverse. For the second time that day Esmé set out to dispel the melancholy his mother had induced in Catherine. She recognized along the river features of the landscape she had discovered with Noël, and Esmé pointed them out to her as if she had never seen them before. Soon, his discourse became more than a commentary upon the river banks and the late Victorian and Edwardian houses, gabled and balconied, the rustic summer-houses, the lawns with urns of geraniums and flag-poles, and weeping copper-beeches, and began to be an excursion back through time; for here, he said, Noël had rammed the boat into the mooring-posts, ('Yes, he told me,' Catherine whispered) and on that island disturbed a wasps' nest in a hollow tree.

49

They were held up outside the lock, and at last the keeper came out and opened the gates. The peace and heat inside the lock were intense. As the water went down, Catherine, grasping a slimy chain, looked long at Esmé, who stood up with the painter over a bollard and was lighting a cigarette. The most veiled of men, she suddenly thought him; his in some ways handsome face expressionless with discretion, the speed of his talk overcoming his reluctance to talk at all, and his easiness, his courtesy – with the lock-keeper at this moment – proclaiming almost that beyond this he was far removed and could not love, be loved, or have any exchange at all that courtesy or kindness did not dictate.

Beyond the lock, she found herself thinking: We shall have to come back through it, in an echo of the triumph with which she used to say this aloud to Noël. Each lock had prolonged their aloneness, as indeed it prolonged her time with Esmé, but it was so much as an echo of an old thought that it came to her that she found herself telling Esmé now how once it had been.

At first, she thought his courtesy had deserted him. 'Oh, look, a kingfisher,' he said.

She looked in the wrong place and it was gone. 'Another thing about the river,' he said. 'We can quite safely bring our unhappiness here. No one can reach it or be contaminated by it, as on dry land. I have felt that I was in quarantine with it these last weeks.'

'But at home . . . ?' Catherine began.

'No, I don't think we can be safe there,' he said rapidly. 'I mean that other people would not be safe from *us*.'

'I wonder if your mother wishes now that she hadn't invited me.'

'My dear little Cathy, what an odd thing to wonder. Or should I not call you "Cathy"?'

'I liked to hear it.' She had blushed with pleasure and surprise. 'I wondered if the sight of me depresses her,' she said humbly. 'I suppose that we have only Noël in common. By the fact of just being myself I can only go on and on reminding her of him.'

'You remind her of yourself and that she loves you. The dead can become too important, just by dying. Any ordeal is yours surely? Coming back to the house and the river and so much obviously that only you and Noël knew about.' He spoke rather aloofly, to imply that being in love was not in his province, though he acknowledged

50

it in hers. 'But I understand', he added, 'that it was probably now or never.'

'I shouldn't have liked it to be never. I love it here, being with your mother and seeing the house again – the *beautiful* house . . .'

'Yes, I think it is the only nice one on the river,' he said. He turned the boat round in mid-stream. 'All of those rose-red villas with their fretwork balconies and the conservatories and so much wisteria . . . yet I miss it when I'm away, and it comes at me with a dismaying, not wholly depressing rush, when I return. Living in one place all of one's youth makes being an expatriate very difficult. I think I shall go and live in London for a bit before I go abroad again. Go by instalments, as it were. It may halve the pains of departure. I must tell Mamma. Until I have done so, know nothing of it, please.'

'Of course not,' Catherine whispered.

Has Esmé said anything to you about leaving here?' Mrs Ingram asked Catherine a day or two later.

'No.'

Wide-eyed surprise, poorly done, thought Mrs Ingram. 'I know he feels concerned about leaving me and may not like to mention it; but he will have to go in the end. He mustn't be tied to my apron-strings for ever.'

'Apron-strings' had too homely a connotation altogether – Esmé and his mother were not just pottering cosily about a kitchen. So fine that they were invisible were the threads with which she drew him to her: it was by the most delicate influence that she had had him break off his long-ago engagement and had later tried to stop him from going abroad, though seeming all the time to speed him on his way. I know that she sometimes does wrong, Catherine thought. But I love her and I should be happy if she cared to dominate me, too. She had wanted to be her daughter-in-law and part of the enchantment. She and Noël would have lived nearby, and come often to the house. 'The children are coming to luncheon,' Mrs Ingram would say. Once, the summer before, Catherine, sitting out on the steps in front of the house, had heard Mrs Ingram in the hall, telephoning a friend. 'Do come over. I shall be alone. The children are going to the cinema.' Bliss had flowed through Catherine. She had shut her eyes, feeling the sun, hearing the sounds of the garden – the birds and insects and the weir. Yes, it was bliss in those days, she thought, and she still sensed the magic of this quieter house, though the river was more melancholy to her and the family diminished and Mrs Ingram's composure no longer completely holding.

Someone called Freddie began to be talked of – a friend of Esmé's, a painter, of whose painting Mrs Ingram disapproved. She compared it unfavourably with Catherine's. It had, she said, that detestable ingredient, virtuosity. 'It allows one to see how clever he has been, and that should never be. I don't want to see the wheels go round or to feel called upon to shout, "Bravo", as if he were some sweating Italian tenor. One should really feel, "How easy it must be! How effortless!" I should think – don't you, Catherine? – that an artist must seem too proud to have tried, too careless to have thought of succeeding.' Esmé said nothing, so Catherine could not judge if he agreed.

Freddie was expected for luncheon, but did not come.

'Perhaps he didn't feel hungry today,' Mrs Ingram said.

So Freddie himself was out of favour along with his paintings, Catherine thought. Mrs Ingram had glanced at Esmé when she had spoken and his face betrayed him by its impassivity.

In the afternoon, Catherine made another attempt to paint, in a tangled part of the garden behind the old stables. In the shade, the nettles and docks were a dark and bitter green and this greenness seemed to tinge the curdy white flowers of elder and cow-parsley. She became gradually absorbed in the shapes and the textures of the leaves – the feathery, the ribbed and spade-like, the giant fern weighted down by a heavy snail. She was pleased with what she was doing and just painting in a bright poppy among the green and silvery green, for contrast, when she saw a snake lying on the path before her at the edge of the shade. It was green, too, of an olive-green to enhance her picture and in a curious way she realized this before she took fright, tiptoeing backwards away from it until she felt safe to turn and run.

She sped up the steps and into the hall, calling for Esmé, then the wonderful sunny slumbrance of the house checked her and she felt disconcerted. A young man came to the drawing-room door, saying, 'I wanted Esmé, too.'

52

Oh, I am glad, for Esmé's sake, that he came at last, thought Catherine, pulling up too suddenly and slipping on a rug.

'Scatter-rugs they call these in America,' said Freddie, coming to steady her. 'A good name. I should like to scatter them all in the river.'

He seemed a very neat young man at a first glance. His suit exactly matched his fawn hair and his blue bow-tie matched his pullover and socks. His voice and his Cockney accent were pert and gay, his small eyes very bright. A second impression revealed his bitten nails and dirty shoes and the fact that his slight build and his clothes made him seem more boyish than he was.

'You sound as if you wanted Esmé in a great hurry,' he said.

'Yes, I saw a snake round by the stables and I think it is an adder.'

'Isn't there a gardener or something?' Freddie asked, looking vaguely out at the terrace.

'I just thought of Esmé first. I left all my painting things there.'

'I shouldn't think a snake would harm them. Did you want me to kill it or something?' he asked reluctantly.

'You see, I am sure they are deadly.'

'Is that supposed to encourage me?'

He went into the back hall and chose a walking-stick from the umbrella-stand. 'Oh, dear, this isn't really up my street. I just hope it's gone away by now. It would have been much better if you had asked a gardener.'

They set out towards the stables and he said: 'My name is Freddie Bassett. I was expected to lunch. Was there much hard feeling?'

'I am a guest. It isn't for me to say.'

'So there was! I ran out of petrol miles from anywhere. So what could I do?'

'You could have telephoned, I suppose.'

'Splendid! I knew I was right to try the story out on you first. You spotted the flaw as Mrs Ingram would have done. How can I get round that one? I telephoned, but the silly girl at the exchange said there was no reply. I don't know what these girls are coming to.'

'No one would believe you.'

'Mrs Ingram will not dare to say so. All right, then, I lost my way.'

'This way,' said Catherine coldly, taking another path.

53

'As a matter of fact, I did.' He seemed surprised to find himself speaking the truth. 'I stopped for a quick one and fell in with a little party. You know how that can be done – complete strangers, but something happens, there is some clemency in the smoke-haze, so that they seem the dearest companions one ever had, one almost weeps with gratitude that they are so sympathetic, so much one's own sort. So helpful in helping one to forget anxiety. I could not tear myself away from them and now I have forgotten them and shall never see them again – only similar ones. When it was closing-time we stayed on, because the landlord was the same sort as well. I felt dreadfully guilty about Esmé, and they were all so sympathetic and so full of condolences and advice about what his mother would say. They came out to see me off and wish me good luck. Then I took the wrong road.'

'Wouldn't it have been better not to have come at all?'

'Surely not? I can stay to dinner instead.'

Catherine felt frightened. I am not his accomplice, she thought. It is nothing to do with me.

'Do you know when Esmé went out?' he asked. 'I want to say that I arrived the minute after.'

'I didn't know that he had gone.'

'He has taken his mother to a meeting. I hope it is a nice long one and that my head will feel better before she comes back.'

They crossed the stables courtyard and Catherine peered through the archway at the path where her painting things were lying beside her folding stool.

'Have I really got to?' Freddie asked. 'Oughtn't I to be wearing puttees or something? I am sure it has kindly gone away.'

But the snake had only moved farther into the sun. Catherine shrank back and for some strange reason put her hands over her ears. 'Oh, Lord!' grumbled Freddie, going forward with the stick held high. Catherine stayed in the courtyard. She heard the stick beating the ground and Freddie swearing, but she would not look. When he came back, he was carrying the stool and the drawing-board and his face was white. 'I take it you don't want to go on with this at the moment,' he said, handing her the unfinished watercolour without glancing at it. 'I just left it there – the snake.'

'You did kill it?'

'Yes, I suddenly went mad with fear. It was a dreadful thing to ask someone from London to do. Are you the girl Noël was engaged to?'

'We weren't engaged.'

'And now, I understand, Mamma wants you to marry Esmé?'

'I think you are rude and absurd,' Catherine said. 'It is none of my business, but I don't know how Esmé can tolerate you.'

She hurried on ahead of him and turned the corner of the house. There was Esmé walking on the lawn, his head down, his hands in his pockets. He paced up and down dejectedly. When he saw Catherine he smiled and then his smile warmed and he came forward eagerly, quite transformed by the sight of Freddie trailing behind, carrying the folding stool.

'It was a poor grass snake,' Mrs Ingram said. 'It would have done no harm to anyone and great good to the garden.'

'I am just a Cockney. How should I know?' said Freddie. 'I did as I was told.'

Catherine could only keep saying how sorry she was.

'I am surprised at you,' Mrs Ingram said teasingly. 'So meticulous in your painting, and to make such a mistake.'

It seemed to be Catherine who had failed. Freddie was triumphantly eating dinner instead of lunch, although Catherine would have staked a great deal against such a possibility. She had listened to his long apology with outraged astonishment ... 'tramping along in the blazing heat with my little petrol can in my hand ... I went all round some village looking for the Post Office. Wonderful honeysuckle all over it and jars of bull's-eyes in the window. I should have thought there would be some regulation against calling them that, when they are nothing of the kind ...'

He is putting off the weak part of his story, about the telephone, Catherine thought with interest.

'... the phone-box was just outside the door and the exchange itself just inside by the bacon-slicing machine. The same pop-eyed old codger who was selling the bull's-eyes went to the switchboard. Twice he got the wrong number. "Skates the Fishmongers here" was one. The third time I truly thought would be lucky, but there was no reply. "There is always someone there. There are hundreds of servants. They are moneyed folk," I said. "Comfortably *placed*, as you might say." "I daresay," he said, sarcastically, as if I were a child, or drunk. "All the same, they're not answering.'"

Esmé bent down and stroked his dog, trying to hide a smile.

'You *might* have answered,' Freddie whined complainingly. 'After I had trudged so far and had such a horrible time and my hands were so *sore* with carrying the petrol can.' He glanced at them, wincing.

'It *is* only pretending, isn't it?' said Mrs Ingram, her voice as sweet as honey. As if she thought that Freddie was over-exciting himself, she changed the conversation.

So Freddie triumphed. He triumphed over his headache and he stayed to dinner and Catherine thought that he would manage to stay the night as well. Esmé was quiet and full of a peace that Catherine could understand. She remembered the contentment of saying those words to herself, 'We are under the same roof.' She had known how beautiful it can be to come to the close of the day and lie down in bed, thinking those words. Then the house itself became haunted, enchanted, spellbound with love.

Her heart began to ache again and her throat almost shut. The flesh is endlessly martyred by grief, humiliated by nausea and vomitings, bothered and alarmed; breath checked and the heart belaboured; the eyes stabbed viciously until they unload their tears and the tongue as bitter as if it had tasted poison. This Freddie does not know, Catherine thought, and she felt pity for Esmé and kinship with him.

Dinner was soon over, for there was hardly any conversation to prolong it. Once Mrs Ingram said to Freddie: 'Catherine paints, too,' and Freddie answered, 'So I saw.'

Beset by midges they drank coffee out on the terrace above the steps. 'An irritating noise,' Freddie said, referring to the weir, and Catherine thought, So it is. The sound is what you are yourself at the moment: if you are in despair, it sounds despairing; tumultuous if you are angry; romantic when you are in love.

Esmé and Freddie never exchanged remarks or glances, and when Mrs Ingram went indoors Catherine felt herself so much in the way that she followed her and was conscious of their nervous silence as she walked away.

Mrs Ingram came from the back hall carrying a bunch of roses. 'I was going to ask you if you would like to come, but don't if you aren't up to it. To Noël's grave, I mean. No, you would rather not, I am sure,' she said quickly. 'It is difficult to guess how other people feel about such a thing. I know it is old-fashioned and unimaginative of me, but I feel comforted when I go there.'

Catherine did not know herself how she felt or would feel, but she went with Mrs Ingram and carried the roses for her. They walked slowly along the scented lane to the church by the river; then through the lych-gate under the limes. She began to be afraid. She remembered the churchyard carpeted with wreaths and the raw earth mounded up ready for its dreadful purpose; the groups of black figures standing, as if stunned, among the graves and the lime-trees only just in leaf which now were ready to flower. She wondered if she would have to face some overpowering monument, for death is alien enough in itself without some of the things which are done afterwards as being appropriate. She hung back on the gravel path as she had done once before and Mrs Ingram, humming peacefully, her pink cardigan hung over her shoulders, stepped quickly across the grass. Following her, raising her eyes only to look at a safely eighteenth-century headstone with a cherub's head and wings and saffron rosettes of lichen all over the crumbling stone, Catherine saw the name 'Ingram' with a sense of shock. But there were groves of Ingrams, among them Noël's father, who was to share the roses. Unlike most of the other riverside families, this had kept its bones in one place for at least two hundred years. The last Ingram had, Catherine was relieved to find, only a simple white wooden cross with his name painted in black. She faced this steadily, feeling that she had been spared an awkwardness. 'Only until the ground has sunk,' Mrs Ingram said, throwing away stale water and going to fetch fresh.

Catherine took a step back, as if she might otherwise sink with the earth. She felt obscenity, not peace, around her.

'I suppose that little liar will be staying the night,' said Mrs Ingram, returning from the water tap. 'I can't pretend that I fancy having him under my roof.'

She knelt down and began to strip leaves off the roses and break off the big blood-red thorns.

When her plans have failed, there are always the flowers to do, Catherine thought. The night I arrived, I suppose that she left them until late as an excuse for sending Esmé to the station – to make us be together from the start. But Esmé wouldn't fall in with the plan – new habit in him, I should think.

Then the words 'my darling Noël' broke across her reflections. For a second, she wondered if she had said them aloud, caught on the in-breath of a sob. But Mrs Ingram finished the flowers calmly and then they walked home along the towing-path. The river was bronze in the sunset and the fluffy meadow-grasses filled with a pinkish light.

Esmé and Freddie were still sitting on the terrace. Freddie was now in Mrs Ingram's wicker chaise-longue, his hands clasped behind his head and his legs stretched out comfortably. Esmé sat, rather awkwardly, with his greyhound across his lap. They both struggled to rise when they saw Mrs Ingram and Catherine crossing the lawn, but Mrs Ingram ignored them and went round the house by a side-way and Catherine followed her.

Catherine went up to bed and stood by the open window, looking out into the dark garden. A misty moonlight furred the grass, like rime, and white ghosts rose off the weir. I have been to the churchyard, she thought, and now I have had enough.

She drew one of the heavy velvet curtains round her like a cloak. I cannot *not* feel when I am here, she thought. Especially when I am so *meant* to feel. Was not Mrs Ingram, she wondered, trying to make her realize the extent of her loss, as if nothing could be accomplished until this was done or any other part of her plan proceeded with.

Mrs Ingram came in to say good night and found Catherine wound up in the curtain.

'So Freddie went – as if he overheard me and meant to prove me wrong.'

She came to the window and they both looked out at the garden, listening to the weir.

On the blanched terrace below Esmé's greyhound appeared, then

Esmé. He went down the steps and was lost in the dark garden. Sometimes he reminded Catherine of his brother. Family likenesses in gestures are stranger than those of feature or build and often more poignant and she had sometimes been moved by such a slight thing as the inclination of his head as he walked, so mysteriously the same as Noël.

'He is going away next week,' Mrs Ingram said.

'And I,' said Catherine quickly. 'I must go too.' She was struggling with tears and her voice was rough and abrupt. She breathed very steadily and presently the tears receded and she said: 'I must get back to work, you know. I must ...'

'What makes it difficult for living here may make it good for painting,' Mrs Ingram said.

'Too beautiful,' Catherine began. She put her hands over her face and tears ran down her wrists and the insides of her arms. Mrs Ingram waited, as if she were measuring the fall of tears and knew when the limit of grief was reached and only then put out her hand and touched Catherine's shoulder.

'You see, I can't stay. You do see?' Her heart had been twice ambushed in this house and now she was desperate to escape. Yet did Mrs Ingram understand? She said nothing. She simply took Catherine in her arms and kissed her – but with a welcoming, a gathering-in gesture as if to one who has come home at last rather than to someone preparing to go away.

Kay Boyle

Black Boy

At that time, it was the forsaken part, it was the other end of the city, and on early spring mornings there was no one about. By soft words, you could woo the horse into the foam, and ride her with the sea knee-deep around her. The waves came in and out there, as indolent as ladies, gathered up their skirts in their hands and, with a murmur, came tiptoeing across the velvet sand.

The wooden promenade was high there, and when the wind was up the water came running under it like wild. On such days, you had to content yourself with riding the horse over the deep white drifts of dry sand on the other side of the walk; the horse's hoofs here made no sound and the sparks of sand stung your face in fury. It had no body to it, like the mile or two of sand packed hard that you could open out on once the tide was down.

My little grandfather, Puss, was alive then, with his delicate gait and ankles, and his belly pouting in his dove-grey clothes. When he saw from the window that the tide was sidling out, he put on his pearl fedora and came stepping down the street. For a minute, he put one foot on the sand, but he was not at ease there. On the boardwalk, over our heads, was some other kind of life in progress. If you looked up, you could see it in motion through the cracks in the timber: rolling-chairs, and women in high heels proceeding, if the weather were fair.

'You know,' my grandfather said, 'I think I might like to have a look at a shop or two along the boardwalk.' Or, 'I suppose you don't feel like leaving the beach for a minute,' or, 'If you would go with me, we might take a chair together, and look at the hats and the dresses and roll along in the sun.'

He was alive then, taking his pick of the broad easy chairs and the black boys.

60

'There's a nice skinny boy,' he'd say. 'He looks as though he might put some action into it. Here you are, Sonny. Push me and the little girl down to the Million Dollar Pier and back.'

The cushions were red with a sheen of dew over them. And Puss settled back on them and took my hand in his. In his mind there was no hesitation about whether he would look at the shops on one side, or out on the vacant side where there was nothing shining but the sea.

'What's your name, Charlie?' Puss would say without turning his head to the black boy pushing the chair behind our shoulders.

'Charlie's my name, sir,' he'd answer with his face dripping down like tar in the sun.

'What's your name, Sonny?' Puss would say another time, and the black boy answered, 'Sonny's my name, sir.'

'What's your name, Big Boy?'

'Big Boy's my name.'

He never wore a smile on his face, the black boy. He was thin as a shadow but darker, and he was pushing and sweating, getting the chair down to the Million Dollar Pier and back again, in and out through the people. If you turned towards the sea for a minute, you could see his face out of the corner of your eye, hanging black as a bat's wing, nodding and nodding like a dark heavy flower.

But in the early morning, he was the only one who came down on to the sand and sat under the beams of the boardwalk, sitting idle there, with a languor fallen on every limb. He had long bones. He sat idle there, with his clothes shrunk up from his wrists and his ankles, with his legs drawn up, looking out at the sea.

'I might be a king if I wanted to be' was what he said to me.

Maybe I was twelve years old, or maybe I was ten when we used to sit eating dog biscuits together. Sometimes, when you broke them in two, a worm fell out and the black boy lifted his sharp finger and flecked it carelessly from off his knee.

'I seen kings,' he said, 'with a kind of cloth over they heads, and kind of jewels-like around here and here. They weren't any blacker than me, if as black,' he said. 'I could be almost anything I made up my mind to be.'

'King Nebuchadnezzar,' I said. 'He wasn't a white man.'

The wind was off the ocean and was filled with alien smells. It was

61

early in the day, and no human sign was given. Overhead were the green beams of the boardwalk and no wheel or step to sound it.

'If I was king,' said the black boy with his biscuit in his fingers, 'I wouldn't put much stock in hanging around here.'

Great crystal jelly-beasts were quivering in a hundred different colours on the wastes of sand around us. The dogs came, jumping them, and when they saw me still sitting still, they wheeled like gulls and sped back to the sea.

'I'd be travelling around,' he said, 'here and there. Now here, now there. I'd change most of my habits.'

His hair grew all over the top of his head in tight dry rosettes. His neck was longer and more shapely than a white man's neck, and his fingers ran in and out of the sand like the blue feet of a bird.

'I wouldn't have much to do with pushing chairs around under them circumstances,' he said. 'I might even give up sleeping out here on the sand.'

Or if you came out when it was starlight, you could see him sitting there in the clear white darkness. I could go and come as I liked, for whenever I went out the door, I had the dogs shouldering behind me. At night, they shook the taste of the house out of their coats and came down across the sand. There he was, with his knees up, sitting idle.

'They used to be all kinds of animals come down here to drink in the dark,' he said. 'They was a kind of a mirage came along and gave that impression. I seen tigers, lions, lambs, deer; I seen ostriches drinking down there side by side with each other. They's the Northern Lights gets crossed some way and switches the wrong picture down.'

It may be that the coast has changed there, for even then it was changing. The lighthouse that had once stood far out on the wild rocks near the outlet was standing then like a lighted torch in the heart of the town. And the deep currents of the sea may have altered so that the clearest water runs in another direction, and houses may have been built down as far as where the brink used to be. But the brink was so perilous then that every word the black boy spoke seemed to fall into a cavern of beauty.

'I seen camels; I seen zebras,' he said. 'I might have caught any one of them if I'd felt inclined.'

And the street was so still and wide then that when Puss stepped out of the house, I could hear him clearing his throat of the sharp salty air. He had no intention of soiling the soles of his boots, but he came down the street to find me.

'If you feel like going with me,' he said, 'we'll take a chair and see the fifty-seven varieties changing on the electric sign.'

And then he saw the black boy sitting quiet. His voice drew up short on his tongue and he touched his white mustache.

'I shouldn't think it a good idea,' he said, and he put his arm through my arm. 'I saw another little oak not three inches high in the Jap's window yesterday. We might roll down the boardwalk and have a look at it. You know,' said Puss, and he put his kid gloves carefully on his fingers, 'that black boy might do you some kind of harm.'

'What kind of harm could he do me?' I said.

'Well,' said Puss with the garlands of lights hanging around him, 'he might steal some money from you. He might knock you down and take your money away.'

'How could he do that?' I said. 'We just sit and talk there.'

Puss looked at me sharply.

'What do you find to sit and talk about?' he said.

'I don't know,' I said. 'I don't remember. It doesn't sound like much to tell it.'

The burden of his words was lying there on my heart when I woke up in the morning. I went out by myself to the stable and led the horse to the door and put the saddle on her. If Puss were ill at ease for a day or two, he could look out the window in peace and see me riding high and mighty away. The day after tomorrow, I thought, or the next day, I'll sit down on the beach again and talk to the black boy. But when I rode out, I saw him seated idle there, under the boardwalk, heedless, looking away to the cool wide sea. He had been eating peanuts and the shells lay all around him. The dogs came running at the horse's heels, nipping the foam that lay along the tide.

The horse was as shy as a bird that morning, and when I drew her up beside the black boy, she tossed her head on high. Her mane went back and forth, from one side to the other, and a flight of joy in her limbs sent her forelegs like rockets into the air. The black boy stood up from the cold smooth sand, unsmiling, but a spark of wonder shone in his marble eyes. He put out his arm in the short tight sleeve of his coat and stroked her shivering shoulder.

'I was going to be a jockey once,' he said, 'but I changed my mind.'

I slid down on one side while he climbed up the other.

'I don't know as I can guide him right,' he said as I held her head. 'The kind of saddle you have, it gives you nothing to grip your knees around. I ride them with their bare skin.'

The black boy settled himself on the leather and put his feet in the stirrups. He was quiet and quick with delight, but he had no thought of smiling as he took the reins in his hand.

I stood on the beach with the dogs beside me, looking after the horse as she ambled down to the water. The black boy rode easily and straight, letting the horse stretch out and sneeze and canter. When they reached the jetty, he turned her casually and brought her loping back.

'Some folks licks hell out of their horses,' he said. 'I'd never raise a hand to one, unless he was to bite me or do something I didn't care for.'

He sat in the saddle at ease, as though in a rocker, stroking her shoulder with his hand spread open, and turning in the stirrups to smooth her shining flank.

'Jockeys make a pile of money,' I said.

'I wouldn't care for the life they have,' said the black boy. 'They have to watch their diet so careful.'

His fingers ran delicately through her hair and laid her soft mane back on her neck.

When I was up on the horse again, I turned her towards the boardwalk.

'I'm going to take her over the jetty,' I said. 'You'll see how she clears it. I'll take her up under the boardwalk to give her a good start.'

I struck her shoulder with the end of my crop, and she started towards the tough black beams. She was under it, galloping, when the dogs came down the beach like mad. They had chased a cat out of cover and were after it, screaming as they ran, with a wing of sand blowing wide behind them, and when the horse saw them under her legs, she jumped sideways in sprightliness and terror and flung herself against an iron arch.

For a long time I heard nothing at all in my head except the melody of someone crying, whether it was my dead mother holding me in comfort, or the soft wind grieving over me where I had fallen. I lay on the sand asleep; I could feel it running with my tears through my fingers. I was rocked in a cradle of love, cradled and rocked in sorrow.

'Oh, my little lamb, my little lamb pie!' Oh, sorrow, sorrow, wailed the wind, or the tide, or my own kin about me. 'Oh, lamb, oh, lamb!'

I could feel the long swift fingers of love untying the terrible knot of pain that bound my head. And I put my arms around him and lay close to his heart in comfort.

Puss was alive then, and when he met the black boy carrying me up to the house, he struck him square across the mouth.

Virginia Woolf

Lappin and Lapinova

They were married. The wedding march pealed out. The
pigeons fluttered. Small boys in Eton jackets threw rice; a fox
terrier sauntered across the path; and Ernest Thorburn led
his bride to the car through the small inquisitive crowd of complete
strangers which always collects in London to enjoy other people's
happiness or unhappiness. Certainly he looked handsome and she
looked shy. More rice was thrown, and the car moved off.

That was on Tuesday. Now it was Saturday. Rosalind had still to
get used to the fact that she was Mrs Ernest Thorburn. Perhaps
she never would get used to the fact that she was Mrs Ernest
Anybody, she thought, as she sat in the bow window of the hotel
looking over the lake to the mountains, and waited for her husband
to come down to breakfast. Ernest was a difficult name to get
used to. It was not the name she would have chosen. She would
have preferred Timothy, Antony, or Peter. He did not look like
Ernest either. The name suggested the Albert Memorial, mahogany
sideboards, steel engravings of the Prince Consort with his family –
her mother-in-law's dining-room in Porchester Terrace, in short.

But here he was. Thank goodness he did not look like Ernest –
no. But what did he look like? She glanced at him sideways. Well,
when he was eating toast he looked like a rabbit. Not that anyone
else would have seen a likeness to a creature so diminutive and
timid in this spruce, muscular young man with the straight nose,
the blue eyes, and the very firm mouth. But that made it all the
more amusing. His nose twitched very slightly when he ate. So
did her pet rabbit's. She kept watching his nose twitch; and then
she had to explain, when he caught her looking at him, why she
laughed.

'It's because you're like a rabbit, Ernest,' she said. 'Like a wild rabbit,' she added, looking at him. 'A hunting rabbit; a King Rabbit; a rabbit that makes laws for all the other rabbits.'

Ernest had no objection to being that kind of rabbit, and since it amused her to see him twitch his nose – he had never known that his nose twitched – he twitched it on purpose. And she laughed and laughed; and he laughed too, so that the maiden ladies and the fishing man and the Swiss waiter in his greasy black jacket all guessed right; they were very happy. But how long does such happiness last? they asked themselves; and each answered according to his own circumstances.

At lunch time, seated on a clump of heather beside the lake, 'Lettuce, rabbit?' said Rosalind, holding out the lettuce that had been provided to eat with the hard-boiled eggs. 'Come and take it out of my hand,' she added, and he stretched out and nibbled the lettuce and twitched his nose.

'Good rabbit, nice rabbit,' she said, patting him, as she used to pat her tame rabbit at home. But that was absurd. He was not a tame rabbit, whatever he was. She turned it into French. 'Lapin,' she called him. But whatever he was, he was not a French rabbit. He was simply and solely English – born at Porchester Terrace, educated at Rugby, now a clerk in His Majesty's Civil Service. So she tried 'Bunny' next, but that was worse. 'Bunny' was someone plump and soft and comic; he was thin and hard and serious. Still, his nose twitched. 'Lappin,' she exclaimed suddenly; and gave a little cry as if she had found the very word she looked for.

'Lappin, Lappin, King Lappin,' she repeated. It seemed to suit him exactly; he was not Ernest, he was King Lappin. Why? She did not know.

When there was nothing new to talk about on their long solitary walks – and it rained, as everyone had warned them that it would rain or when they were sitting over the fire in the evening, for it was cold and the maiden ladies had gone and the fishing man, and the waiter only came if you rang the bell for him, she let her fancy play with the story of the Lappin tribe. Under her hands – she was sewing; he was reading – they became very real, very vivid, very amusing. Ernest put down the paper and helped her. There were the black rabbits and the red; there were the enemy rabbits and the friendly. There were wood in which they lived and the outlying prairies and the swamp. Above

all there was King Lappin, who, far from having only the one trick –
that he twitched his nose – became as the days passed an animal of
the greatest character; Rosalind was always finding new qualities in
him. But above all he was a great hunter.

'And what', said Rosalind, on the last day of the honeymoon, 'did
the King do today?'

In fact they had been climbing all day; and she had worn a blister
on her heel; but she did not mean that.

'Today,' said Ernest, twitching his nose as he bit the end off
his cigar, 'he chased a hare.' He paused; struck a match, and
twitched again.

'A woman hare,' he added.

'A white hare!' Rosalind exclaimed, as if she had been expecting
this. 'Rather a small hare; silver grey; with big bright eyes?'

'Yes,' said Ernest, looking at her as she had looked at him, 'a
smallish animal; with eyes popping out of her head, and two little
front paws dangling.' It was exactly how she sat, with her sewing
dangling in her hands; and her eyes, that were so big and bright,
were certainly a little prominent.

'Ah, Lapinova,' Rosalind murmured.

'Is that what she's called?' said Ernest – 'the real Rosalind?' He
looked at her. He felt very much in love with her.

'Yes; that's what she's called,' said Rosalind. 'Lapinova.' And before
they went to bed that night it was all settled. He was King Lappin; she
was Queen Lapinova. They were the very opposite of each other; he
was bold and determined; she wary and undependable. He ruled over
the busy world of rabbits; her world was a desolate, mysterious place,
which she ranged mostly by moonlight. All the same, their territories
touched; they were King and Queen.

Thus when they came back from their honeymoon they possessed
a private world, inhabited, save for the one white hare, entirely by
rabbits. No one guessed that there was such a place, and that of
course made it all the more amusing. It made them feel, more
even than most young married couples, in league together against
the rest of the world. Often they looked slyly at each other when
people talked about rabbits and woods and traps and shooting. Or
they winked furtively across the table when Aunt Mary said that she
could never bear to see a hare in a dish – it looked so like a baby: or

when John, Ernest's sporting brother, told them what price rabbits were fetching that autumn in Wiltshire, skins and all. Sometimes when they wanted a gamekeeper, or a poacher or a Lord of the Manor, they amused themselves by distributing the parts among their friends. Ernest's mother, Mrs Reginald Thorburn, for example, fitted the part of the Squire to perfection. But it was all secret – that was the point of it; nobody save themselves knew that such a world existed.

Without that world, how, Rosalind wondered, that winter could she have lived at all? For instance, there was the golden-wedding party, when all the Thorburns assembled at Porchester Terrace to celebrate the fiftieth anniversary of that union which had been so blessed – had it not produced Ernest Thorburn? and so fruitful – had it not produced nine other sons and daughters into the bargain, many themselves married and also fruitful? She dreaded that party. But it was inevitable. As she walked upstairs she felt bitterly that she was an only child and an orphan at that; a mere drop among all those Thorburns assembled in the great drawing-room with the shiny satin wallpaper and the lustrous family portraits. The living Thorburns much resembled the painted; save that instead of painted lips they had real lips; out of which came jokes; jokes about schoolrooms, and how they had pulled the chair from under the governess; jokes about frogs, and how they had put them between the virgin sheets of maiden ladies. As for herself, she had never even made an apple-pie bed. Holding her present in her hand she advanced toward her mother-in-law sumptuous in yellow satin; and toward her father-in-law decorated with a rich yellow carnation. All round them on tables and chairs there were golden tributes; some nestling in cotton wool; others branching resplendent – candlesticks; cigar boxes; chains; each stamped with the goldsmith's proof that it was solid gold, hall-marked, authentic. But her present was only a little pinchbeck box pierced with holes; an old sand caster, an eighteenth-century relic, once used to sprinkle sand over wet ink. Rather a senseless present she felt – in an age of blotting paper; and as she proffered it, she saw in front of her the stubby black handwriting in which her mother-in-law when they were engaged had expressed the hope that 'My son will make you happy'. No, she was not happy. Not at all happy. She looked at Ernest, straight as a

69

ramrod with a nose like all the noses in the family portraits; a nose that never twitched at all.

Then they went down to dinner. She was half hidden by the great chrysanthemums that curled their red and gold petals into large tight balls. Everything was gold. A gold-edged card with gold initials intertwined recited the list of all the dishes that would be set one after another before them. She dipped her spoon in a plate of clear golden fluid. The raw white fog outside had been turned by the lamps into a golden mesh that blurred the edges of the plates and gave the pineapples a rough golden skin. Only she herself in her white wedding dress peering ahead of her with her prominent eyes seemed insoluble as an icicle.

As the dinner wore on, however, the room grew steamy with heat. Beads of perspiration stood out on the men's foreheads. She felt that her icicle was being turned to water. She was being melted; dispersed; dissolved into nothingness; and would soon faint. Then through the surge in her head and the din in her ears she heard a woman's voice exclaim, 'But they breed so!'

The Thorburns – yes; they breed so, she echoed; looking at all the round red faces that seemed doubled in the giddiness that overcame her; and magnified in the gold mist that enhaloed them. 'They breed so.' Then John bawled:

'Little devils! . . . shoot 'em! Jump on 'em with big boots! That's the only way to deal with 'em . . . rabbits!'

At that word, that magic word, she revived. Peeping between the chrysanthemums she saw Ernest's nose twitch. It rippled, it ran with successive twitches. And at that a mysterious catastrophe befell the Thorburns. The golden table became a moor with the gorse in full bloom; the din of voices turned to one peal of lark's laughter ringing down from the sky. It was a blue sky – clouds passed slowly. And they had all been changed – the Thorburns. She looked at her father-in-law, a furtive little man with dyed moustaches. His foible was collecting things – seals, enamel boxes, trifles from eighteenth-century dressing-tables which he hid in the drawers of his study from his wife. Now she saw him as he was – a poacher, stealing off with his coat bulging with pheasants and partridges to drop them stealthily into a three-legged pot in his smoky little cottage. That was her real father-in-law – a poacher.

And Celia, the unmarried daughter, who always nosed out other people's secrets, the little things they wished to hide – she was a white ferret with pink eyes, and a nose clotted with earth from her horrid underground nosings and pokings. Slung round men's shoulders, in a net, and thrust down a hole – it was a pitiable life – Celia's; it was none of her fault. So she saw Celia. And then she looked at her mother-in-law – whom they dubbed The Squire. Flushed, coarse, a bully – she was all that, as she stood returning thanks, but now that Rosalind – that is Lapinova – saw her, she saw behind her the decayed family mansion, the plaster peeling off the walls, and heard her, with a sob in her voice, giving thanks to her children (who hated her) for a world that had ceased to exist. There was a sudden silence. They all stood with their glasses raised; they all drank; then it was over.

'Oh, King Lappin!' she cried as they went home together in the fog, 'if your nose hadn't twitched just at the moment, I should have been trapped!'

'But you're safe,' said King Lappin, pressing her paw.

'Quite safe,' she answered.

And they drove back through the Park, King and Queen of the marsh, of the mist, and of the gorse-scented moor.

Thus time passed; one year; two years of time. And on a winter's night, which happened by a coincidence to be the anniversary of the golden-wedding party – but Mrs Reginald Thorburn was dead; the house was to let; and there was only a caretaker in residence – Ernest came home from the office. They had a nice little home; half a house above a saddler's shop in South Kensington, not far from the tube station. It was cold, with fog in the air, and Rosalind was sitting over the fire, sewing.

'What d'you think happened to me today?' she began as soon as he had settled himself down with his legs stretched to the blaze. 'I was crossing the stream when –'

'What stream?' Ernest interrupted her.

'The stream at the bottom, where our wood meets the black wood,' she explained.

Ernest looked completely blank for a moment.

'What the deuce are you talking about?' he asked.

'My dear Ernest!' she cried in dismay. 'King Lappin,' she added, dangling her little front paws in the firelight. But his nose did not twitch. Her hands – they turned to hands – clutched the stuff she was holding; her eyes popped half out of her head. It took him five minutes at least to change from Ernest Thorburn to King Lappin; and while she waited she felt a load on the back of her neck, as if somebody were about to wring it. At last he changed to King Lappin; his nose twitched; and they spent the evening roaming the woods much as usual.

But she slept badly. In the middle of the night she woke, feeling as if something strange had happened to her. She was stiff and cold. At last she turned on the light and looked at Ernest lying beside her. He was sound asleep. He snored. But even though he snored, his nose remained perfectly still. It looked as if it had never twitched at all. Was it possible that he was really Ernest; and that she was really married to Ernest? A vision of her mother-in-law's dining-room came before her; and there they sat, she and Ernest, grown old, under the engravings, in front of the sideboard . . . It was their golden-wedding day. She could not bear it.

'Lappin, King Lappin!' she whispered, and for a moment his nose seemed to twitch of its own accord. But he still slept. 'Wake up, Lappin, wake up!' she cried.

Ernest woke; and seeing her sitting bolt upright beside him he asked: 'What's the matter?'

'I thought my rabbit was dead!' she whimpered. Ernest was angry.

'Don't talk such rubbish, Rosalind,' he said. 'Lie down and go to sleep.'

He turned over. In another moment he was sound asleep and snoring.

But she could not sleep. She lay curled up on her side of the bed, like a hare in its form. She had turned out the light, but the street lamp lit the ceiling faintly, and the trees outside made a lacy network over it as if there were a shadowy grove on the ceiling in which she wandered, turning, twisting, in and out, round and round, hunting, being hunted, hearing the bay of hounds and horns; flying, escaping . . . until the maid drew the blinds and brought their early tea.

Next day she could settle to nothing. She seemed to have lost something. She felt as if her body had shrunk; it had grown small, and black and hard. Her joints seemed stiff too, and when she looked in the glass, which she did several times as she wandered about the flat, her eyes seemed to burst out of her head, like currants in a bun. The rooms also seemed to have shrunk. Large pieces of furniture jutted out at odd angles and she found herself knocking against them. At last she put on her hat and went out. She walked along the Cromwell Road; and every room she passed and peered into seemed to be a dining-room where people sat eating under steel engravings, with thick yellow lace curtains, and mahogany sideboards. At last she reached the Natural History Museum; she used to like it when she was a child. But the first thing she saw when she went in was a stuffed hare standing on sham snow with pink glass eyes. Somehow it made her shiver all over. Perhaps it would be better when dusk fell. She went home and sat over the fire, without a light, and tried to imagine that she was out alone on a moor; and there was a stream rushing; and beyond the stream a dark wood. But she could get no further than the stream. At last she squatted down on the bank on the wet grass, and sat crouched in her chair, with her hands dangling empty, and her eyes glazed, like glass eyes, in the firelight. Then there was the crack of a gun . . . she started as if she had been shot. It was only Ernest, turning his key in the door. She waited, trembling. He came in and switched on the light. There he stood tall, and handsome, rubbing his hands that were red with cold.

'Sitting in the dark?' he said.

'Oh, Ernest, Ernest!' she cried, starting up in her chair.

'Well, what's up now?' he asked briskly, warming his hands at the fire.

'It's Lapinova . . .' she faltered, glancing wildly at him out of her great startled eyes. 'She's gone, Ernest. I've lost her!'

Ernest frowned. He pressed his lips tight together. 'Oh, that's what's up, is it?' he said, smiling rather grimly at his wife. For ten seconds he stood there, silent; and she waited, feeling hands tightening at the back of her neck.

'Yes,' he said at length. 'Poor Lapinova . . .' He straightened his tie at the looking-glass over the mantelpiece.

'Caught in a trap,' he said, 'killed', and sat down and read the newspaper.

So that was the end of that marriage.

Edith Wharton

After Holbein

I

Anson Warley had had his moments of being a rather remarkable man; but they were only intermittent; they recurred
at ever-lengthening intervals; and between times he was
a small poor creature, chattering with cold inside, in spite of his
agreeable and even distinguished exterior.

He had always been perfectly aware of these two sides of himself
(which, even in the privacy of his own mind, he contemptuously
refused to dub a dual personality); and as the rather remarkable
man could take fairly good care of himself, most of Warley's attention
was devoted to ministering to the poor wretch who took longer and
longer turns at bearing his name, and was more and more insistent
in accepting the invitations which New York, for over thirty years,
had tirelessly poured out on him. It was in the interest of this
lonely fidgety unemployed self that Warley, in his younger days, had
frequented the gaudiest restaurants and the most glittering Palace
Hotels of two hcmispheres, subscribed to the most advanced literary
and artistic reviews, bought the pictures of the young painters
who were being the most vehemently discussed, missed few of
the showiest first nights in New York, London or Paris, sought
the company of the men and women – especially the women –
most conspicuous in fashion, scandal, or any other form of social
notoriety, and thus tried to warm the shivering soul within him at
all the passing bonfires of success.

The original Anson Warley had begun by staying at home in his
little flat, with his books and his thoughts, when the other poor
creature went forth; but gradually – he hardly knew when or how
– he had slipped into the way of going too, till finally he made the

74

bitter discovery that he and the creature had become one, except on the increasingly rare occasions when, detaching himself from all casual contingencies, he mounted to the lofty watershed which fed the sources of his scorn. The view from there was vast and glorious, the air was icy but exhilarating; but soon he began to find the place too lonely, and too difficult to get to, especially as the lesser Anson not only refused to go up with him but began to sneer, at first ever so faintly, then with increasing insolence, at this affectation of a taste for the heights.

'What's the use of scrambling up there, anyhow? I could understand it if you brought down anything worth while – a poem or a picture of your own. But just climbing and staring: what does it lead to? Fellows with the creative gift have got to have their occasional Sinaïs; I can see that. But for a mere looker-on like you, isn't that sort of thing rather a pose? You talk awfully well – brilliantly, even (oh, my dear fellow, no false modesty between you and *me*, please!). But who the devil is there to listen to you, up there among the glaciers? And sometimes, when you come down, I notice that you're rather – well, heavy and tongue-tied. Look out, or they'll stop asking us to dine! And sitting at home every evening – brr! Look here, by the way; if you've got nothing better for tonight, come along with me to Chrissy Torrance's – or the Bob Briggses' – or Princess Kate's; anywhere where there's lots of racket and sparkle, places that people go to in Rollses, and that are smart and hot and overcrowded, and you have to pay a lot – in one way or another – to get in.'

Once and again, it is true, Warley still dodged his double and slipped off on a tour to remote uncomfortable places, where there were churches or pictures to be seen, or shut himself up at home for a good bout of reading, or just, in sheer disgust at his companion's platitude, spent an evening with people who were doing or thinking real things. This happened seldomer than of old, however, and more clandestinely; so that at last he used to sneak away to spend two or three days with an archæologically-minded friend, or an evening with a quiet scholar, as furtively as if he were stealing to a lovers' tryst; which, as lovers' trysts were now always kept in the limelight, was after all a fair exchange. But he always felt rather apologetic to the other Warley about these escapades – and, if the truth were known, rather bored and restless before they were over. And in the back of his mind there lurked an increasing dread of missing something hot and noisy and overcrowded when he went off to one of his mountain-tops. 'After all, that highbrow business has been awfully overdone – now hasn't it?' the little Warley would insinuate, rummaging for his pearl studs, and consulting his flat evening watch as nervously as if it were a railway timetable. 'If only we haven't missed something really jolly by all this backing and filling . . .'

'Oh, you poor creature, you! Always afraid of being left out, aren't you? Well – just for once, to humour you, and because I happen to be feeling rather stale myself. But only to think of a sane man's wanting to go to places just because they're hot and smart and overcrowded!' And off they would dash together . . .

II

All that was long ago. It was years now since there had been two distinct Anson Warleys. The lesser one had made away with the other, done him softly to death without shedding of blood; and only a few people suspected (and they no longer cared) that the pale white-haired man, with the small slim figure, the ironic smile and the perfect evening clothes, whom New York still indefatigably invited, was nothing less than a murderer.

Anson Warley – Anson Warley! No party was complete without Anson Warley. He no longer went abroad now; too stiff in the joints; and there had been two or three slight attacks of dizziness . . . Nothing to speak of, nothing to think of, even; but somehow one dug one's self into one's comfortable quarters, and felt less and less like moving out of them, except to motor down to Long Island for weekends, or to Newport for a few visits in summer. A trip to the Hot Springs, to get rid of the stiffness, had not helped much, and the ageing Anson Warley (who really, otherwise, felt as young as ever) had developed a growing dislike for the promiscuities of hotel life and the monotony of hotel food.

Yes; he was growing more fastidious as he grew older. A good sign, he thought. Fastidious not only about food and comfort but about people also. It was still a privilege, a distinction, to have him to dine. His old friends were faithful, and the new people fought for him, and often failed to get him; to do so they had to offer very special inducements in the way of *cuisine*, conversation or beauty. Young beauty; yes, that would do it. He did like to sit and watch a lovely face, and call laughter into lovely eyes. But no dull dinners for *him*, not even if they fed you off gold. As to that he was as firm as the other Warley, the distant aloof one with whom he had – er, well, parted company, oh, quite amicably, a good many years ago . . .

On the whole, since that parting, life had been much easier and pleasanter; and by the time the little Warley was sixty-three he found himself looking forward with equanimity to an eternity of New York dinners.

Oh, but only at the right houses – always at the right houses; that was understood! The right people – the right setting – the right wines . . . He smiled a little over his perennial enjoyment of them; said 'Nonsense, Filmore,' to his devoted tiresome manservant, who was beginning to hint that really, every night, sir, and sometimes a dance afterward, was too much, especially when you kept at it for months on end; and Dr—

'Oh, damn your doctors!' Warley snapped. He was seldom ill-tempered; he knew it was foolish and upsetting to lose one's self-control. But Filmore began to be a nuisance, nagging him, preaching at him. As if he himself wasn't the best judge . . .

Besides, he chose his company. He'd stay at home any time rather than risk a boring evening. Damned rot, what Filmore had said about his going out every night. Not like poor old Mrs Jaspar, for instance . . . He smiled self-approvingly as he evoked her tottering image. 'That's the kind of fool Filmore takes me for,' he chuckled, his good-humour restored by an analogy that was so much to his advantage.

Poor old Evelina Jaspar! In his youth, and even in his prime, she had been New York's chief entertainer – 'leading hostess', the newspapers called her. Her big house in Fifth Avenue had been an entertaining machine. She had lived, breathed, invested and reinvested her millions, to no other end. At first her pretext had been that she had to marry her daughters and amuse her sons; but when sons and daughters had married and left her she had seemed hardly aware of it; she had just gone on entertaining. Hundreds, no, thousands of dinners (on gold plate, of course, and with orchids, and all the delicacies that were out of season) had been served in that vast pompous dining-room, which one had only to close one's eyes to transform into a railway buffet for millionaires, at a big junction, before the invention of restaurant trains . . .

Warley closed his eyes, and did so picture it. He lost himself in amused computation of the annual number of guests, of saddles of mutton, of legs of lamb, of terrapin, canvas-backs, magnums of champagne and pyramids of hot-house fruit that must have passed through that room in the last forty years.

And even now, he thought – hadn't one of old Evelina's nieces told him the other day, half bantering, half shivering at the avowal, that the poor old lady, who was gently dying of softening of the brain, still imagined herself to be New York's leading hostess, still sent out invitations (which of course were never delivered), still ordered terrapin, champagne and orchids, and still came down every evening to her great shrouded drawing-rooms, with her tiara askew on her purple wig, to receive a stream of imaginary guests?

Rubbish, of course – a macabre pleasantry of the extravagant Nelly Pierce, who had always had her joke at Aunt Evelina's expense . . . But Warley could not help smiling at the thought that those dull monotonous dinners were still going on in their hostess's clouded imagination. Poor old Evelina, he thought! In a way she was right. There was really no reason why that kind of standardized entertaining should ever cease; a performance so undiscriminating, so undifferentiated, that one could almost imagine, in the hostess's tired brain, all the dinners she had ever given merging into one Gargantuan pyramid of food and drink, with the same faces, perpetually the same faces, gathered stolidly about the same gold plate.

Thank heaven, Anson Warley had never conceived of social values in terms of mass and volume. It was years since he had dined at Mrs Jaspar's. He even felt that he was not above reproach in that respect. Two or three times, in the past, he had accepted her invitations (always sent out weeks ahead), and then chucked her at the eleventh hour for something more amusing. Finally, to avoid such risks, he had made it a rule always to refuse her dinners. He had even – he remembered – been rather funny about it once, when someone had told him that Mrs Jaspar couldn't understand . . . was a little hurt . . . said it couldn't be true that he always had another engagement the nights she asked him . . . 'True? Is the truth what she wants? All right! Then the next time I get a "Mrs Jaspar requests the pleasure" I'll answer it with a "Mr Warley declines the boredom". Think she'll understand that, eh?' And the phrase became a catchword in his little set that winter. '"Mr Warley declines the boredom" – good, good, *good!* 'Dear Anson, I do hope you won't decline the boredom of coming to lunch next Sunday to meet the new Hindu Yoghi' – or the new saxophone soloist, or that genius of a mulatto boy who plays Negro spirituals on a toothbrush; and so on and so on. He only hoped poor old Evelina never heard of it . . .

'Certainly I shall *not* stay at home tonight – why, what's wrong with me?' he snapped, swinging round on Filmore.

The valet's long face grew longer. His way of answering such questions was always to pull out his face; it was his only means of putting any expression into it. He turned away into the bedroom, and Warley sat alone by his library fire . . . Now what did the man see that was wrong with him, he wondered? He had felt a little confusion that morning, when he was doing his daily sprint around the Park (his exercise was reduced to that!); but it had been only a passing flurry, of which Filmore could of course know nothing. And as soon as it was over his mind had seemed more lucid, his eye keener, than ever; as sometimes (he reflected) the electric light in his library lamps would blaze up too brightly after a break in the current, and he would say to himself, wincing a little at the sudden glare on the page he was reading: 'That means that it'll go out again in a minute.'

Yes; his mind, at that moment, had been quite piercingly clear and perceptive; his eye had passed with a renovating glitter over every detail of the daily scene. He stood still for a minute under the leafless trees of the Mall, and looking about him with the sudden insight of age, understood that he had reached the time of life when Alps and cathedrals become as transient as flowers.

Everything was fleeting, fleeting . . . yes, that was what had given him the vertigo. The doctors, poor fools, called it the stomach, or high blood pressure; but it was only the dizzy plunge of the sands in the hourglass, the everlasting plunge that emptied one of heart and bowels, like the drop of an elevator from the top floor of a skyscraper.

Certainly, after that moment of revelation, he had felt a little more tired than usual for the rest of the day; the light had flagged in his mind as it sometimes did in his lamps. At Chrissy Torrance's, where he had lunched, they had accused him of being silent, his hostess had said that he looked pale; but he had retorted with a joke, and thrown himself into the talk with a feverish loquacity. It was the only thing to do; for he could not tell all these people at the lunch table that very morning he had arrived at the turn in the path from which mountains look as transient as flowers – and that one after another they would all arrive there too.

He leaned his head back and closed his eyes, but not in sleep. He did not feel sleepy, but keyed up and alert. In the next room he heard Filmore reluctantly, protestingly, laying out his evening clothes ... He had no fear about the dinner tonight; a quiet intimate little affair at an old friend's house. Just two or three congenial men, and Elfmann, the pianist (who would probably play), and that lovely Elfrida Flight. The fact that people asked him to dine to meet Elfrida Flight seemed to prove pretty conclusively that he was still in the running! He chuckled softly at Filmore's pessimism, and thought: 'Well, after all, I suppose no man seems young to his valet ... Time to dress very soon,' he thought; and luxuriously postponed getting up out of his chair ...

III

'She's worse than usual tonight,' said the day nurse, laying down the evening paper as her colleague joined her. 'Absolutely determined to have her jewels out.'

The night nurse, fresh from a long sleep and an afternoon at the movies with a gentleman friend, threw down her fancy bag, tossed off her hat and rumpled up her hair before old Mrs Jaspar's tall toilet mirror. 'Oh, I'll settle that – don't you worry,' she said brightly.

'Don't you fret her, though, Miss Cress,' said the other, getting wearily out of her chair. 'We're very well off here, take it as a whole, and I don't want her pressure rushed up for nothing.'

Miss Cress, still looking at herself in the glass, smiled reassuringly at Miss Dunn's pale reflection behind her. She and Miss Dunn got on very well together, and knew on which side their bread was buttered. But at the end of the day Miss Dunn was always fagged out and fearing the worst. The patient wasn't as hard to handle as all that. Just let her ring for her old maid, old Lavinia, and say: 'My sapphire velvet tonight with the diamond stars' – and Lavinia would know exactly how to manage her.

Miss Dunn had put on her hat and coat, and crammed her knitting, and the newspaper, into her bag, which, unlike Miss Cress's, was capacious and shabby; but she still loitered undecided on the threshold. 'I could stay with you till ten as easy as not ...' She looked almost reluctantly about the big high-studded dressing-room (everything in the house was high-studded), with its rich dusky carpet and curtains, and its monumental dressing-table draped with lace and laden with gold-backed brushes and combs, gold-stoppered toilet-bottles, and all the charming paraphernalia of beauty at her glass. Old Lavinia even renewed every morning the roses and carnations in the slim crystal vases between the powder boxes and the nail polishers. Since the family had shut down the hot-houses at the uninhabited country place on the Hudson, Miss Cress suspected that old Lavinia bought these flowers out of her own pocket.

'Cold out tonight?' queried Miss Dunn from the door.

'Fierce ... Reg'lar blizzard at the corners. Say, shall I lend you my fur scarf?' Miss Cress, pleased with the memory of her afternoon (they'd be engaged soon, she thought), and with the drowsy prospect of an evening in a deep armchair near the warm gleam of the dressing-room fire, was disposed to kindliness toward that poor thin Dunn girl, who supported her mother, and her brother's idiot twins. And she wanted Miss Dunn to notice her new fur.

'My! Isn't it too lovely? No, not for worlds, thank you ...' Her hand on the door-knob, Miss Dunn repeated: 'Don't you cross her now,' and was gone.

Lavinia's bell rang furiously, twice; then the door between the dressing-room and Mrs Jaspar's bedroom opened, and Mrs Jaspar herself emerged.

'Lavinia!' she called, in a high irritated voice; then, seeing the nurse, who had slipped into her print dress and starched cap, she added in a lower tone: 'Oh, Miss Lemoine, good evening.' Her first nurse, it appeared, had been called Miss Lemoine; and she gave the same name to all the others, quite unaware that there had been any changes in the staff.

'I heard talking, and carriages driving up. Have people begun to arrive?' she asked nervously. 'Where is Lavinia? I still have my jewels to put on.'

She stood before the nurse, the same petrifying apparition which always, at this hour, struck Miss Cress to silence. Mrs Jaspar was tall; she had been broad; and her bones remained impressive though the flesh had withered on them. Lavinia had encased her, as usual, in her low-necked purple velvet dress, nipped in at the waist in the old-fashioned way, expanding in voluminous folds about the hips and flowing in a long train over the darker velvet of the carpet. Mrs Jaspar's swollen feet could no longer be pushed into the high-heeled satin slippers which went with the dress; but her skirts were so long and spreading that, by taking short steps, she managed (so Lavinia daily assured her) entirely to conceal the broad round tips of her black orthopædic shoes.

'Your jewels, Mrs Jaspar? Why, you've got them on,' said Miss Cress brightly.

Mrs Jaspar turned her porphyry-tinted face to Miss Cress, and looked at her with a glassy incredulous gaze. Her eyes, Miss Cress thought, were the worst ... She lifted one old hand, veined and knobbed as a raised map, to her elaborate purple-black wig, groped among the puffs and curls and undulations (queer, Miss Cress thought, that it never occurred to her to look into the glass), and after an interval affirmed: 'You must be mistaken, my dear. Don't you think you ought to have your eyes examined?'

The door opened again, and a very old woman, so old as to make Mrs Jaspar appear almost young, hobbled in with sidelong steps. 'Excuse me, madam. I was downstairs when the bell rang.'

Lavinia had probably always been small and slight; now, beside her towering mistress, she looked a mere feather, a straw. Everything about her had dried, contracted, been volatilized into nothingness, except her watchful grey eyes, in which intelligence and comprehension burned like two fixed stars. 'Do excuse me, madam,' she repeated.

Mrs Jaspar looked at her despairingly. 'I hear carriages driving up. And Miss Lemoine says I have my jewels on; and I know I haven't.'

'With that lovely necklace!' Miss Cress ejaculated.

Mrs Jaspar's twisted hand rose again, this time to her denuded shoulders, which were as stark and barren as the rock from which the hand might have been broken. She felt and felt, and tears rose in her eyes . . .

'Why do you lie to me?' she burst out passionately.

Lavinia softly intervened. 'Miss Lemoine meant how lovely you'll be when you get the necklace on, madam.'

'Diamonds, diamonds,' said Mrs Jaspar with an awful smile.

'Of course, madam.'

Mrs Jaspar sat down at the dressing-table, and Lavinia, with eager random hands, began to adjust the *point de Venise* about her mistress's shoulders, and to repair the havoc wrought in the purple-black wig by its wearer's gropings for her tiara.

'Now you do look lovely, madam,' she sighed.

Mrs Jaspar was on her feet again, stiff but incredibly active. ('Like a cat she is,' Miss Cress used to relate.) 'I do hear carriages – or is it an automobile? The Magraws, I know, have one of those new-fangled automobiles. And now I hear the front door opening. Quick, Lavinia! My fan, my gloves, my handkerchief . . . how often have I got to tell you? I used to have a *perfect* maid –'

Lavinia's eyes brimmed. 'That was me, madam,' she said, bending to straighten out the folds of the long purple velvet train. ('To watch the two of 'em', Miss Cress used to tell a circle of appreciative friends, 'is a lot better than any circus.')

Mrs Jaspar paid no attention. She twitched the train out of Lavinia's vacillating hold, swept to the door, and then paused there as if stopped by a jerk of her constricted muscles. 'Oh, but my diamonds – you cruel woman, you! You're letting me go down without my diamonds!' Her ruined face puckered up in a grimace like a newborn baby's, and she began to sob despairingly. 'Everybody . . . Every . . . body's . . . against me . . .' she wept in her powerless misery.

Lavinia helped herself to her feet and tottered across the floor. It was almost more than she could bear to see her mistress in distress. 'Madam, madam – if you'll just wait till they're got out of the safe,' she entreated.

The woman she saw before her, the woman she was entreating and consoling, was not the old petrified Mrs Jaspar with porphyry face

83

and wig awry whom Miss Cress stood watching with a smile, but a young proud creature, commanding and splendid in her Paris gown of amber *moiré*, who, years ago, had burst into just such furious sobs because, as she was sweeping down to receive her guests, the doctor had told her that little Grace, with whom she had been playing all the afternoon, had a diphtheritic throat, and no one must be allowed to enter. 'Everybody's against me, everybody ...' she had sobbed in her fury; and the young Lavinia, stricken by such Olympian anger, had stood speechless, longing to comfort her, and secretly indignant with little Grace and the doctor ...

'If you'll just wait, madam, while I go down and ask Munson to open the safe. There's no one come yet, I do assure you ...'

Munson was the old butler, the only person who knew the combination of the safe in Mrs Jaspar's bedroom. Lavinia had once known it too, but now she was no longer able to remember it. The worst of it was that she feared lest Munson, who had been spending the day in the Bronx, might not have returned. Munson was growing old too, and he did sometimes forget about these dinner-parties of Mrs Jaspar's, and then the stupid footman, George, had to announce the names; and you couldn't be sure that Mrs Jaspar wouldn't notice Munson's absence, and be excited and angry. These dinner-party nights were killing old Lavinia, and she did so want to keep alive; she wanted to live long enough to wait on Mrs Jaspar to the last.

She disappeared, and Miss Cress poked up the fire, and persuaded Mrs Jaspar to sit down in an armchair and 'tell her who was coming'. It always amused Mrs Jaspar to say over the long list of her guests' names, and generally she remembered them fairly well, for they were always the same – the last people, Lavinia and Munson said, who had dined at the house, on the very night before her stroke. With recovered complacency she began, counting over one after another on her ring-laden fingers: 'The Italian Ambassador, the Bishop, Mr and Mrs Torrington Bligh, Mr and Mrs Fred Amesworth, Mr and Mrs Mitchell Magraw, Mr and Mrs Torrington Bligh ...' ('You've said them before,' Miss Cress interpolated, getting out her fancy knitting – a necktie for her friend – and beginning to count the stitches.) And Mrs Jasper, distressed and bewildered by the interruption, had to repeat over and over: 'Torrington Bligh, Torrington Bligh,' till the connection was re-established, and she went on again swimmingly with 'Mr and Mrs Fred Amesworth, Mr and Mrs Mitchell Magraw, Miss Laura Ladew, Mr Harold Ladew, Mr and Mrs Benjamin Bronx, Mr and Mrs Torrington Bl – no, I mean, Mr Anson Warley. Yes, Mr Anson Warley; that's it,' she ended complacently.

Miss Cress smiled and interrupted her counting. 'No, that's *not* it.'

'What do you mean, my dear – not it?'

'Mr Anson Warley. He's not coming.'

Mrs Jaspar's jaw fell, and she stared at the nurse's coldly smiling face. 'Not coming?'

'No. He's not coming. He's not on the list.' (That old list! As if Miss Cress didn't know it by heart! Everybody in the house did, except the booby, George, who heard it reeled off every other night by Munson, and who was always stumbling over the names, and having to refer to the written paper.)

'Not on the list?' Mrs Jaspar gasped.

Miss Cress shook her pretty head.

Signs of uneasiness gathered on Mrs Jaspar's face and her lip began to tremble. It always amused Miss Cress to give her these little jolts, though she knew Miss Dunn and the doctors didn't approve of her doing so. She knew also that it was against her own interests, and she did try to bear in mind Miss Dunn's oft-repeated admonition about not sending up the patient's blood pressure; but when she was in high spirits, as she was tonight (they would certainly be engaged), it was irresistible to get a rise out of the old lady. And she thought it funny, this new figure unexpectedly appearing among those time-worn guests. ('I wonder what the rest of 'em 'll say to him,' she giggled inwardly.)

'No; he's not on the list.' Mrs Jaspar, after pondering deeply, announced the fact with an air of recovered composure.

'That's what I told you,' snapped Miss Cress.

'He's not on the list; but he promised me to come. I saw him yesterday,' continued Mrs Jaspar, mysteriously.

'You *saw* him – where?'

She considered. 'Last night, at the Fred Amesworths' dance.'

'Ah,' said Miss Cress, with a little shiver; for she knew that Mrs Amesworth was dead, and she was the intimate friend of the trained nurse who was keeping alive, by dint of *piqûres* and high frequency, the inarticulate and inanimate Mr Amesworth. 'It's funny', she remarked to Mrs Jaspar, 'that you'd never invited Mr Warley before.'

'No, I hadn't; not for a long time. I believe he felt I'd neglected him; for he came up to me last night, and said he was so sorry he hadn't been able to call. It seems he's been ill, poor fellow. Not as young as he was! So of course I invited him. He was very much gratified.'

Mrs Jaspar smiled at the remembrance of her little triumph; but Miss Cress's attention had wandered, as it always did when the patient became docile and reasonable. She thought: 'Where's old Lavinia? I bet she can't find Munson.' And she got up and crossed the floor to look into Mrs Jaspar's bedroom, where the safe was.

There an astonishing sight met her. Munson, as she had expected, was nowhere visible; but Lavinia, on her knees before the safe, was in the act of opening it herself, her twitching hand slowly moving about the mysterious dial.

'Why, I thought you'd forgotten the combination!' Miss Cress exclaimed.

Lavinia turned a startled face over her shoulder. 'So I had, Miss. But I've managed to remember it, thank God. I *had* to, you see, because Munson's forgot to come home.'

'Oh,' said the nurse incredulously. ('Old fox,' she thought, 'I wonder why she's always pretended she'd forgotten it.') For Miss Cress did not know that the age of miracles is not yet past.

Joyous, trembling, her cheeks wet with grateful tears, the little old woman was on her feet again, clutching to her breast the diamond stars, the necklace of *solitaires,* the tiara, the earrings. One by one she spread them out on the velvet-lined tray in which they always used to be carried from the safe to the dressing-room; then, with rambling fingers, she managed to lock the safe again, and put the keys in the drawer where they belonged, while Miss Cress continued to stare at her in amazement. 'I don't believe the old witch is as shaky as she makes out,' was her reflection as Lavinia passed her, bearing the jewels to the dressing-room where Mrs Jaspar, lost in pleasant memories, was still computing: 'The Italian Ambassador, the Bishop, the Torrington Blighs, the Mitchell Magraws, the Fred Amesworths . . .'

Mrs Jaspar was allowed to go down to the drawing-room alone on dinner-party evenings because it would have mortified her too much to receive her guests with a maid or a nurse at her elbow; but Miss Cress and Lavinia always leaned over the stair-rail to watch her descent, and make sure it was accomplished in safety.

'She do look lovely yet, when all her diamonds is on,' Lavinia sighed, her purblind eyes bedewed with memories, as the bedizened wig and purple velvet disappeared at the last bend of the stairs. Miss Cress, with a shrug, turned back to the fire and picked up her knitting, while Lavinia set about the slow ritual of tidying up her mistress's room. From below they heard the sound of George's stentorian monologue: 'Mr and Mrs Torrington Bligh, Mr and Mrs Mitchell Magraw ... Mr Ladew, Miss Laura Ladew ...'

IV

Anson Warley, who had always prided himself on his equable temper, was conscious of being on edge that evening. But it was an irritability which did not frighten him (in spite of what those doctors always said about the importance of keeping calm) because he knew it was due merely to the unusual lucidity of his mind. He was in fact feeling uncommonly well, his brain clear and all his perceptions so alert that he could positively hear the thoughts passing through his manservant's mind on the other side of the door, as Filmore grudgingly laid out the evening clothes.

Smiling at the man's obstinacy, he thought: 'I shall have to tell them tonight that Filmore thinks I'm no longer fit to go into society.' It was always pleasant to hear the incredulous laugh with which his younger friends received any allusion to his supposed senility. 'What, *you*? Well, that's a good one!' And he thought it was, himself.

And then, the moment he was in his bedroom, dressing, the sight of Filmore made him lose his temper again. 'No; *not* those studs, confound it. The black onyx ones – haven't I told you a hundred times? Lost them, I suppose? Sent them to the wash again in a soiled shirt? That it?' He laughed nervously, and sitting down before his dressing-table began to brush back his hair with short angry strokes.

'Above all,' he shouted out suddenly, 'don't stand there staring at me as if you were watching to see exactly at what minute to telephone for the undertaker!'

'The under –? Oh, sir!' gasped Filmore.

'The – the – damn it, are you *deaf* too? Who said undertaker? I said taxi can't you hear what I say?'

'You want me to call a taxi, sir?'

'No; I don't. I've already told you so. I'm going to walk.' Warley straightened his tie, rose and held out his arms toward his dress-coat.

'It's bitter cold, sir; better let me call a taxi all the same.'

Warley gave a short laugh. 'Out with it, now! What you'd really like to suggest is that I should telephone to say I can't dine out. You'd scramble me some eggs instead, eh?'

'I wish you would stay in, sir. There's eggs in the house.'

'My overcoat,' snapped Warley.

'Or else let me call a taxi; now do, sir.'

Warley slipped his arms into his overcoat, tapped his chest to see if his watch (the thin evening watch) and his notecase were in their proper pockets, turned back to put a dash of lavender on his handkerchief, and walked with stiff quick steps toward the front door of his flat.

Filmore, abashed, preceded him to ring for the lift; and then, as it quivered upward through the long shaft, said again: 'It's a bitter cold night, sir; and you've had a good deal of exercise today.'

Warley levelled a contemptuous glance at him. 'Daresay that's why I'm feeling so fit,' he retorted as he entered the lift.

It *was* bitter cold; the icy air hit him in the chest when he stepped out of the overheated building, and he halted on the doorstep and took a long breath. 'Filmore's missed his vocation; ought to be nurse to a paralytic,' he thought. 'He'd love to have to wheel me about in a chair.'

After the first shock of the biting air he began to find it exhilarating, and walked along at a good pace, dragging one leg ever so little after the other. (The *masseur* had promised him that he'd soon be rid of that stiffness.) Yes – decidedly a fellow like himself ought to have a younger valet; a more cheerful one, anyhow. He felt like a young'un himself this evening; as he turned into Fifth Avenue he rather wished he could meet someone he knew, some man who'd say afterward at his club: 'Warley? Why, I saw him sprinting up Fifth Avenue the other night like a two-year-old; that night it was four or five below . . .' He needed a good counter-irritant for Filmore's gloom. 'Always have young people about you,' he thought as he walked along; and at the words his mind turned to Elfrida Flight, next to whom he would soon be sitting in a warm pleasantly lit dining-room – *where*?

It came as abruptly as that: the gap in his memory. He pulled up at it as if his advance had been checked by a chasm in the pavement at his feet. Where the dickens was he going to dine? And with whom was he going to dine? God! But things didn't happen in that way; a sound strong man didn't suddenly have to stop in the middle of the street and ask himself where he was going to dine ...

Perfect in mind, body and understanding.' The old legal phrase bobbed up inconsequently into his thoughts. Less than two minutes ago he had answered in every particular to that description; what was he now? He put his hand to his forehead, which was bursting; then he lifted his hat and let the cold air blow for a while on his overheated temples. It was queer, how hot he'd got, walking. Fact was, he'd been sprinting along at a damned good pace. In future he must try to remember not to hurry ... Hang it – one more thing to remember! ... Well, but what was all the fuss about? Of course, as people got older their memories were subject to these momentary lapses; he'd noticed it often enough among his contemporaries. And, brisk and alert though he still was, it wouldn't do to imagine himself totally exempt from human ills ...

Where was it he was dining? Why, somewhere farther up Fifth Avenue; he was perfectly sure of that. With that lovely ... that lovely ... No; better not make any effort for the moment. Just keep calm, and stroll slowly along. When he came to the right street corner of course he'd spot it; and then everything would be perfectly clear again. He walked on, more deliberately, trying to empty his mind of all thoughts. 'Above all,' he said to himself, 'don't worry.'

He tried to beguile his nervousness by thinking of amusing things. 'Decline the boredom –' He thought he might get off that joke tonight. 'Mrs Jaspar requests the pleasure – Mr Warley declines the boredom.' Not so bad, really; and he had an idea he'd never told it to the people ... what in hell *was* their name? ... the people he was on his way to dine with ... *Mrs Jaspar requests the pleasure.* Poor old Mrs Jaspar; again it occurred to him that he hadn't always been very civil to her in old times. When everybody's running after a fellow it's pardonable now and then to chuck a boring dinner at the last minute; but all the same as one grew older one understood better how an unintentional slight of that sort might cause offence, cause even pain. And he hated to cause people pain ... He thought perhaps he'd better call on Mrs Jaspar some afternoon. She'd be surprised! Or ring her up, poor old girl, and propose himself, just informally, for dinner. One dull evening wouldn't kill him – and how pleased she'd be! Yes – he thought decidedly ... When he got to be her age, he could imagine how much he'd like it if somebody still in the running should ring him up unexpectedly and say –

He stopped, and looked up, slowly, wonderingly, at the wide illuminated façade of the house he was approaching. Queer coincidence – it was the Jaspar house. And all lit up; for a dinner evidently. And that was queerer yet; almost uncanny; for here he was, in front of the door, as the clock struck a quarter past eight; and of course – he remembered it quite clearly now – it was just here, it was with Mrs Jaspar, that he was dining ... Those little lapses of memory never lasted more than a second or two. How right he'd been not to let himself worry. He pressed his hand on the door-bell.

'God,' he thought, as the double doors swung open, 'but it's good to get in out of the cold.'

V

In that hushed sonorous house the sound of the door-bell was as loud to the two women upstairs as if it had been rung in the next room.

Miss Cress raised her head in surprise, and Lavinia dropped Mrs Jaspar's other false set (the more comfortable one) with a clatter on the marble wash-stand. She stumbled across the dressing-room, and hastened out to the landing. With Munson absent, there was no knowing how George might muddle things ...

Miss Cress joined her. 'Who is it?' she whispered excitedly. Below, they heard the sound of a hat and a walking-stick being laid down on the big marble-topped table in the hall, and then George's stentorian drone: 'Mr Anson Warley.'

'It is – it *is*! I can see him – a gentleman in evening clothes,' Miss Cress whispered, hanging over the stair-rail.

'Good gracious – mercy me! And Munson not here! Oh, whatever,

whatever shall we do?' Lavinia was trembling so violently that she had to clutch the stair-rail to prevent herself from falling. Miss Cress thought, with her cold lucidity: 'She's a good deal sicker than the old woman.'

'What shall we do, Miss Cress? That fool of a George – he's showing him in! Who could have thought it?' Miss Cress knew the images that were whirling through Lavinia's brain: the vision of Mrs Jaspar's having another stroke at the sight of this mysterious intruder, of Mr Anson Warley's seeing her there, in her impotence and her abasement, of the family's being summoned, and rushing in to exclaim, to question, to be horrified and furious – and all because poor old Munson's memory was going, like his mistress's, like Lavinia's, and because he had forgotten that it was one of the *dinner nights*. Oh, misery . . . The tears were running down Lavinia's cheeks, and Miss Cress knew she was thinking: 'If the daughters send him off – and they will – where's he going to, old and deaf as he is, and all his people dead? Oh, if only he can hold on till she dies, and get his pension . . .'

Lavinia recovered herself with one of her supreme efforts. 'Miss Cress, we must go down at once, at once! Something dreadful's going to happen . . .' She began to totter toward the little velvet-lined lift in the corner of the landing.

Miss Cress took pity on her. 'Come along,' she said. 'But nothing dreadful's going to happen. You'll see.'

'Oh, thank you, Miss Cress. But the shock – the awful shock to her – of seeing that strange gentleman walk in.'

'Not a bit of it.' Miss Cress laughed as she stepped into the lift. 'He's not a stranger. She's expecting him.'

'Expecting him? Expecting Mr Warley?'

'Sure she is. She told me so just now. She says she invited him yesterday.'

'But, Miss Cress, what are you thinking of? Invite him – how? When you know she can't write nor telephone?'

'Well, she says she saw him; she saw him last night at a dance.'

'Oh, God,' murmured Lavinia, covering her eyes with her hands.

'At a dance at the Fred Amesworths' – that's what she said,' Miss Cress pursued, feeling the same little shiver run down her back as when Mrs Jaspar had made the statement to her.

91

'The Amesworths – oh, not the Amesworths?' Lavinia echoed, shivering too. She dropped her hands from her face, and followed Miss Cress out of the lift. Her expression had become less anguished, and the nurse wondered why. In reality, she was thinking, in a sort of dreary beatitude: 'But if she's suddenly got as much worse as this, she'll go before me, after all, my poor lady, and I'll be able to see to it that she's properly laid out and dressed, and nobody but Lavinia's hands'll touch her.'

'You'll see – if she was expecting him, as she says, it won't give her a shock, anyhow. Only, how did *he* know?' Miss Cress whispered, with an acuter renewal of her shiver. She followed Lavinia with muffled steps down the passage to the pantry, and from there the two women stole into the dining-room, and placed themselves noiselessly at its farther end, behind the tall Coromandel screen through the cracks of which they could peep into the empty room.

The long table was set, as Mrs Jaspar always insisted that it should be on these occasions; but old Munson not having returned, the gold plate (which his mistress also insisted on) had not been got out, and all down the table, as Lavinia saw with horror, George had laid the coarse blue and white plates from the servants' hall. The electric wall-lights were on, and the candles lit in the branching Sèvres candelabra – so much at least had been done. But the flowers in the great central dish of Rose Dubarry porcelain, and in the smaller dishes which accompanied it – the flowers, oh, shame, had been forgotten! They were no longer real flowers; the family had long since suppressed that expense; and no wonder, for Mrs Jaspar always insisted on orchids. But Grace, the youngest daughter who was the kindest, had hit on the clever device of arranging three beautiful clusters of artificial orchids and maiden hair, which had only to be lifted from their shelf in the pantry and set in the dishes – only, of course, that imbecile footman had forgotten, or had not known where to find them. And, oh, horror, realizing his oversight too late, no doubt to appeal to Lavinia, he had taken some old newspapers and bunched them up into something that he probably thought resembled a bouquet, and crammed one into each of the priceless Rose Dubarry dishes.

Lavinia clutched at Miss Cress's arm. 'Oh, look – look what he's done; I shall die of the shame of it . . . Oh, Miss, hadn't we better slip around to the drawing-room and try to coax my poor lady upstairs again, afore she ever notices?'

Miss Cress, peering through the crack of the screen, could hardly suppress a giggle. For at that moment the double doors of the dining-room were thrown open, and George, shuffling about in a baggy livery inherited from a long-departed predecessor of more commanding build, bawled out in his loud singsong: 'Dinner is served, madam.'

'Oh, it's too late,' moaned Lavinia. Miss Cress signed to her to keep silent, and the two watchers glued their eyes to their respective cracks of the screen.

What they saw, far off down the vista of empty drawing-rooms, and after an interval during which (as Lavinia knew) the imaginary guests were supposed to file in and take their seats, was the entrance, at the end of the ghostly cortège, of a very old woman, still tall and towering on the arm of a man somewhat smaller than herself, with a fixed smile on a darkly pink face, and a slim erect figure clad in perfect evening clothes, who advanced with short measured steps, profiting (Miss Cress noticed) by the support of the arm he was supposed to sustain. 'Well – I never!' was the nurse's inward comment.

The couple continued to advance, with rigid smiles and eyes staring straight ahead. Neither turned to the other, neither spoke. All their attention was concentrated on the immense, the almost unachievable effort of reaching that point, halfway down the long dinner table, opposite the big Dubarry dish, where George was drawing back a gilt armchair for Mrs Jaspar. At last they reached it, and Mrs Jaspar seated herself, and waved a stony hand to Mr Warley. 'On my right.' He gave a little bow, like the bend of a jointed doll, and with infinite precaution let himself down into his chair. Beads of perspiration were standing on his forehead, and Miss Cress saw him draw out his handkerchief and wipe them stealthily away. He then turned his head somewhat stiffly toward his hostess.

'Beautiful flowers,' he said, with great precision and perfect gravity, waving his hand toward the bunched-up newspaper in the bowl of Sèvres.

Mrs Jaspar received the tribute with complacency. 'So glad ... orchids ... From High Lawn ... every morning,' she simpered.

'Mar-vellous,' Mr Warley completed.

'I always say to the Bishop . . .' Mrs Jaspar continued.

'Ha – of course,' Mr Warley warmly assented.

'Not that I don't think . . .'

'Ha – rather!'

George had reappeared from the pantry with a blue crockery dish of mashed potatoes. This he handed in turn to one after another of the imaginary guests, and finally presented to Mrs Jaspar and her right-hand neighbour.

They both helped themselves cautiously, and Mrs Jaspar addressed an arch smile to Mr Warley. ''Nother month – no more oysters.'

'Ha – no more!'

George, with a bottle of Apollinaris wrapped in a napkin, was saying to each guest in turn: 'Perrier-Jouet, 'ninety-five.' (He had picked that up, thought Miss Cress, from hearing old Munson repeat it so often.)

'Hang it – well, then just a sip,' murmured Mr Warley.

'Old times,' bantered Mrs Jaspar; and the two turned to each other and bowed their heads and touched glasses.

'I often tell Mrs Amesworth . . .' Mrs Jaspar continued, bending to an imaginary presence across the table.

'Ha – *ha!*' Mr Warley approved.

George reappeared and slowly encircled the table with a dish of spinach. After the spinach the Apollinaris also went the rounds again, announced successively as Château Lafite, 'seventy-four, and 'the old Newbold Madeira'. Each time that George approached his glass, Mr Warley made a feint of lifting a defensive hand, and then smiled and yielded. 'Might as well – hanged for a sheep . . .' he remarked gaily; and Mrs Jaspar giggled.

Finally a dish of Malaga grapes and apples was handed. Mrs Jaspar, now growing perceptibly languid, and nodding with more and more effort at Mr Warley's pleasantries, transferred a bunch of grapes to her plate, but nibbled only two or three. 'Tired,' she said suddenly, in a whimper like a child's; and she rose, lifting herself up by the arms of her chair, and leaning over to catch the eye of an invisible lady, presumably Mrs Amesworth, seated opposite to her. Mr Warley was on his feet too, supporting himself by resting one hand on the table in a jaunty attitude. Mrs Jaspar waved to him to be reseated.

'Join us – after cigars,' she smilingly ordained; and with a great and concentrated effort he bowed to her as she passed toward the double doors which George was throwing open. Slowly, majestically, the purple velvet train disappeared down the long enfilade of illuminated rooms, and the last door closed behind her.

'Well, I do believe she's enjoyed it!' chuckled Miss Cress, taking Lavinia by the arm to help her back to the hall. Lavinia, for weeping, could not answer.

VI

Anson Warley found himself in the hall again, getting into his fur-lined overcoat. He remembered suddenly thinking that the rooms had been intensely overheated, and that all the other guests had talked very loud and laughed inordinately. 'Very good talk though, I must say,' he had to acknowledge.

In the hall, as he got his arms into his coat (rather a job, too, after that Perrier-Jouet) he remembered saying to somebody (perhaps it was to the old butler): 'Slipping off early – going on; 'nother engagement,' and thinking to himself the while that when he got out into the fresh air again he would certainly remember where the other engagement was. He smiled a little while the servant, who seemed a clumsy fellow, fumbled with the fastening of the door. 'And Filmore, who thought I wasn't well enough to dine out! Damned ass! What would he say if he knew I was going on?'

The door opened, and with an immense sense of exhilaration Mr Warley issued forth from the house and drew in a first deep breath of night air. He heard the door closed and bolted behind him, and continued to stand motionless on the step, expanding his chest, and drinking in the icy draught.

''Spose it's about the last house where they give you 'ninety-five Perrier-Jouet,' he thought; and then: 'Never heard better talk either ...'

He smiled again with satisfaction at the memory of the wine and the wit. Then he took a step forward, to where a moment before the pavement had been – and where now there was nothing.

Rahila Gupta

Untouchable

A chill wind was lashing streaks of pink across her cheeks. She kept her mind on the delicate buds softening the harsh skeleton of the apple blossom trees, a glimmer of spring holding the cold air in check. No visible sunsets here. She knew the day was drawing to a close by the pink glow behind the filigree of distant leafless trees. The satisfaction of having earned another £18 today, stacking shelves at the local supermarket, gave her that impenetrable aura that makes people going home from work so unapproachable. Yes, she would be just in time for *Neighbours*. A hot cup of tea, a bath, and then time to cook for her daughter and son-in-law.

It was a nice arrangement. She ended up cooking only two or three times a week. What a relief! Balu did more than his fair share, letting Roopa skip her turn if she had had a particularly tiring day at work. What a wonderful man he was. His curries were a little too spicy for her taste but when she got handed her dinner on a plate, the spice turned to honey in her mouth. If they knew about all this back home, many tongues would slice her happiness in half. Fancy letting your son-in-law cook for you, then warm up your food and even serve it.

Ranjit would have said that Balu should be wearing bangles but then that was Ranjit for you. How long she had endured him, his tantrums, his women, his drinking. Not a word could she utter, not a voice raised above a whisper – I keep you well, don't I, buy you saris and earrings for *Diwali*, what I do with my money is my business, he would rage. And most painful of all, Roopa idolized him. The gloss had hardened with his death. Not even the truth could dent it. She didn't know about the women, didn't know why her mum had gone to such great lengths to find male servants – in short supply because the growing industrial centres around Delhi were creaming them away for factory work.

The hardest thing of all – to lie in bed waiting for him to come home, imagining his hands tenderly caressing some other form – a tenderness which, if it had been reserved for her, would have taken the bite out of their lives, would have left her with some self-respect to scrape together and continue. And on those nights, when he jumped on her, liquor fumes filling the darkness, ramming her insides with a hardness that seemed filled with revenge, dragging her entrails out with each withdrawal, any residual passion in her would evaporate in the bitter knowledge that he had been unable to flush himself somewhere else that night.

Oh-hh . . . Balu was back early . . . his shoes were lying there behind the door . . . her heart leapt to her mouth . . . she rushed into the living-room . . . watching the early evening news, his face profiled by the white glow of the TV . . . he turned and smiled, his handsome face suffused with warmth. He was so fair . . .

'Wh– what are you doing at home?'

'The cat was off today, so all the mice scuttled home early. Sit down, I'll get you a cup of tea.'

'N – no. I can do it. I'll get you a cup.'

'I insist,' he said and walked into the kitchen.

She put her feet up on the sofa and lay back against the cushion. Watching the news was a small price to pay when she could watch it in his company.

The tea was hot, milky and sweet – just as she liked it. When Roopa made it, it was either too black or she skimped on the sugar – three spoons, she said, very unhealthy. What did the poor child know? She had to tear herself away to go into the bathroom when she realized that Roopa would soon be home and she hadn't even started cooking. She luxuriated in the hot shower, staring at her loose and flaccid tummy, her drooping breasts and the vast expanse of her back in the mirror opposite until it vanished in the steam clouding up the glass. Six pregnancies were bound to leave their mark. She still had her long black hair though, the envy of all her sisters, stretching down well below her sagging hips, only four inches short of her knees. Yes, she had trapped many a surreptitious glance in those silken tresses. She would leave it loose, today. Balu wouldn't mind. OK, so you should only bare your head in the company of other women. But this was England.

She put *kaajal* in her eyes, combed her long black hair, and returned to the lounge. She draped herself carefully on the settee, bringing her hair round to the front and spreading it across her left breast, she let it fall to the ground.

'Drying your hair, are you?'

'Yes,' she muttered nervously. He notices everything, but she hadn't washed it.

Suddenly, the door opened, Roopa was home. She hadn't heard the front door. She sat bolt upright and started plaiting her hair. Roopa threw a 'Hello, Ma' over her shoulder as she stooped to peck Balu on the cheek.

'Where's my cup of tea, then?' she demanded.

'Hang on a minute. The news will be over soon ... doesn't your mum look a mere slip of a girl today with her hair hanging loose?'

'She's got more than hair hanging loose. Honestly, Mum, at your age.'

She went into the kitchen, burning inside. So Balu thinks I look like a young girl. One of these days, he is bound to scream at Roopa, she treats him so badly, I must have a quiet word with her. The kids, today, they don't know when they're lucky. So difficult to find such a gem of a man. So what if he goes to the pub every night and spends a tenner. He never gets violent, that's the main thing. She heard the front door closing. That's Balu off to the pub, now. Roopa is probably

in a mood. She would catch her in half an hour when she had calmed
down a bit.

'Ouch,' said Roopa as a sizzling *jeera* shot out of the frying pan and
caught her on the arm as she headed for the broom to sweep the
kitchen floor.

'Let me finish the cooking before you start all that.'

'It's unhealthy, all your long hair falling out and lying on the
kitchen floor. Occasionally I get one in my dinner and my stomach
turns.'

'Look, there's no need to be in a mood just because Balu has gone
to the pub. You know, Papa used to drink . . .'

'Who's talking about Balu? I never saw Papa drunk and anyway
two wrongs don't make a right.'

'Roopa, *beti*, remember the old saying, "Dal eaten in someone else's
house is equivalent to the chicken cooked at home." Balu is a good
man, don't keep nagging him about housework and whether he takes
six months to put the bookshelf up. OK, so he likes a drink or two
in the evening. You've got a lot of freedom to do what you want. I
know it's not my business, but I don't think you should accept a lift
from that Billy chap from work. You're a married woman. Even the
clothes you wear, short skirts, low necklines . . .'

'Oh Mum,' Roopa expostulated. The broom went flying across the
kitchen, knocking a bottle of milk on to the floor. Roopa's mum
scuttled across to clear up the broken glass.

'Leave it alone,' Roopa screamed. 'What do you know about the
modern world? You with your hair dangling down talk to me about
low necklines. You've never been out to work, so how would you
know? You've lived such a protected life, the only men in your life
were uncles and brothers and until you married Papa, you probably
never met a strange man before . . .'

'Yes, protected it certainly was . . . violated in the four walls of
my own house . . . protected from the kindness of the outside
world,' her voice cracked, tears streamed down her face, her eyes
glazed over. How could she tell Roopa about the protection she had
received? . . .

. . . Uncle Tejpal, giving her a mustard oil massage to protect her four-year-old skin from the chapping effect of the winter air. On the terrace at the top of her childhood house, every Sunday, broad searching fingers, massaging long and hard, tickling her tummy, moving downwards, playing horsy, sitting naked across his *dhoti* clad thighs while she giggled at the strange stirrings under his muslin *dhoti*, the horse's mane, she had to grip it firmly in her little hands, otherwise she would fall off as the horse rocked harder and harder, yukks, it was all wet, Uncle Tejpal had done a *susu*, where's the horse's mane gone, she would fall off if she couldn't hold on, no, the horse was tired, Uncle Tejpal slipped his kurta over his *dhoti*, stood up and stretched. Let's play horsy, Uncle, she stood there stamping her feet. No, he shooed her away with a careless gesture of his arm ... then Uncle Tejpal stopped coming to the house ... until the time, when she was only six and her sixteen-year-old cousin came to stay in his summer holidays ... the sun was so hot, you could faint if you stayed in it longer than five minutes. He would follow her everywhere she went but especially when she was leaning against the window and looking out at the monkeys on the rooftops across the road, then he would insist on looking out of the same tiny window, pressing hard against her till the sweat poured down her thighs, go away, it's so hot, find another window, and when the monkeys moved out of sight, Raju suggested playing doctor and patient ... prodding and poking ... talcum powder on her back while the doctor marked out the area for surgery with a pen ... egg white ... gummy and slithery ... alien to her body ... she saw the horse's mane for the first time – fascinating, not at all as she had imagined it, hiding under the folds of white muslin ... egg white running slowly on a black granite floor ... he running for a cloth ... using her doll's dress ... the egg white that had made her sense of wholeness slip away ...

Guilt jerked her slouched frame into frightened alertness as she felt Roopa's hand on her shoulder. 'Sorry, Ma, you have a way of getting under my skin. Tell me ...'

'I'm going to bed,' said Roopa's mum. She trudged wearily upstairs, treading carefully in the minefields of her distant past. It felt such a load – all that undisclosed history, if only she could talk about it. She switched on the telly in her room and got under the covers. Normally even halfway through a film or play, her attention could be drawn unwaveringly. But not tonight. Could not keep the stray edges of her mind tucked into the uncomplicated little compartments that she was used to. Could not muffle the sound of her mother's piercing '*Shaitan, shaitan*' echoing through the past . . . shame etched across her soul . . . *mataji* telling her at thirteen, stop running around, hair hanging loose, barefooted and wild, come straight home from school, no hanging around eating *chaat* off wayside stalls, only another three years left to your 'betrothal', it wouldn't be Raju or Uncle Tejpal, would it . . . no, no, no . . . she would have to atone . . . eyes lowered, legs together, legs covered, no more dresses . . . paying for past sins . . . blood at thirteen, gripes in her tummy . . . *didi*, her elder sister explaining . . . when you get married . . . my God, she had indulged from age four . . . Ranjit, fifteen years older, appears . . . *mataji* is impressed . . . she must submit . . . Balu, fifteen years younger . . . what's the difference . . .

Next Monday when Balu would be off work, she would develop this searing pain in her tummy at lunch time so that even Mrs Lal, her supervisor, would have to relent; she would come home and find a way of raising the subject. Yes, Monday was only four days away . . .

The loneliness lifted like a shroud falling away. She didn't even notice the biting cold which made her clench her chest all the way to work so that it took her five minutes of deep and hard breathing to free it. She arranged her tins any which way with a song in her heart and a defiant over-her-shoulder look at Mrs Lal. She was followed everywhere by Balu offering her tea even as she munched her dry hard chapattis. She made her peace with Roopa and refused to be goaded by her taunts. She wrote to her sisters in the village about the wonders of London. Did they know that you could get a hot cup of tea from a machine? Did they know that staircases would move

101

from top to bottom and the other way round and you only had to stand still to get from one floor to the next?

The next four days went past in such a hurry that they became one of those inexplicable holes in the memory. The television was on all the time. When she was not cooking or having a bath, she just remembered meticulously avoiding both Roopa and Balu. Roopa would come up to her room to start a conversation and it just irritated her because she would be forced to concentrate and reply appropriately and the effort of doing that would chase Balu away. Then it would take minutes or even a quarter of an hour before she could invite Balu in and pin him down in a favourite corner of her mind. Actually bumping into Balu on her forays out of the room was not very satisfying unless he had something kindly to say which would then give her hours of satisfaction chewing over every nuance of meaning and tone.

Monday was a drag. She could have picked up half a dozen tins and thrown them at Mrs Lal or one of those incessant crying snotty-nosed babies who seemed to live in supermarkets. At lunch time, she went through her routine and Mrs Lal ungraciously gave her the rest of the day off. Trying not to rush to her coat, looking suitably pained, she hobbled out of the shop. Once round the corner, she walked as quickly as she could. Suddenly, she was plagued by doubt – what did he do on his day off, would he be asleep, would he be repairing his car, would he be out shopping or at the library? What would she say? The question that had never occurred to her in the last four days made her suddenly stop still in the middle of the pavement and sent a shooting pain through her ankle as some murderous mum pushed a buggy right into her heel. There's no escaping a snotty-nosed kid.

When she got home she went straight to bed, her heart beating madly, her mind flapping blankly. She was so lost inside herself that at first she didn't even hear the knocking. It was Balu.
  'What's the matter? Aren't you well? Have you eaten?'

102

She shook her head from side to side. Before she could protest, Balu disappeared into the kitchen and brought her some lunch on a tray. She decided to take the plunge. She patted her bed and gestured to him to sit down. He sat right on the edge of the bed.

'Sit properly. I won't eat you up. Here, let me feed you,' she said, scooping the rice and meat up in her fingers.

'I've had my food. If there's anything else you need, let me know.'

She giggled. 'Don't you want to have it?', she persisted in a whisper.

'I told you, I have eaten,' Balu said standing up. She caught his hand and as his fingers wriggled out of hers, she let out a strangled noise, somewhere between a cry and a nervous laugh. She knew she had lost the moment as he stomped out of the room.

She could hear him pace the floor downstairs. She would have to make things clear. As she entered the living-room, Balu, stuttering, rounded on her: 'I don't know how to put this ... have I misunderstood something ... but are you ... are you inviting me to go to ... to sleep with you?'

'Balu, I know you are unhappy with Roopa. Although she's my own, I can see you don't like the way ...'

'It is none of your business, woman. Can't you see what you have done? If Roopa got to hear of this, she would throw you out on the streets but it would tear the lining out of her. Roopa wanted so much for you to come. She worked overtime to save the money, and this is how you repay her. How can someone your age behave like this?'

'You were so nice ...' her voice broke, 'no man has shown me so much kindness. I just wanted to be rocked and cradled and soothed ... wipe away the forty-five years of misery and suffering,' she crooned, wrapping her arms around her chest and rocking from side to side, 'wipe away the dirt, make me whole again, touch me so that I feel no pain, there has been no touch without the pain ... even you don't understand, oh, that the earth would open up so that I can bury my shame ... put me away ... I am dirt, I have been touched ... I am nothing ... send me back, oh God, what have I done ...'

Balu sat there with his head between his hands, unable to feel the total revulsion with which he had started this discussion. Suddenly he stood up and walked decisively to the front door.

'Don't ring Roopa,' she screamed between her sobs.

He came back two hours later to find her lying in a heap on the living-room sofa, staring blankly at the ceiling, puffy eyed and beyond reach. What explanation would he give to Roopa? The walk in the park had not helped to clear his mind. Senile dementia . . . senile dementia . . . was the only explanation he could find.

He tried to shake her into conversation. 'I think you need treatment. You are sick . . . sick in the mind . . . we can't help you . . . you must go back to Delhi next week, tell Roopa that one of your sisters is very ill . . . I won't tell Roopa anything if you agree to go back.'

She looked at him blankly. 'Whatever you think is best . . .' she muttered in a broken whisper.

Alice Munro

❦

Simon's Luck

R ose gets lonely in new places; she wishes she had invitations.
She goes out and walks the streets and looks in the lighted
windows at all the Saturday-night parties, the Sunday-night
family suppers. It's no good telling herself she wouldn't be long
inside there, chattering and getting drunk, or spooning up the
gravy, before she'd wish she was walking the streets. She thinks
she could take on any hospitality. She could go to parties in rooms
hung with posters, lit by lamps with Coca-Cola shades, everything
crumbly and askew; or else in warm professional rooms with lots
of books, and brass rubbings, and maybe a skull or two; even in
the recreation rooms she can just see the tops of, through the
basement windows: rows of beer steins, hunting horns, drinking
horns, guns. She could go and sit on Lurex-threaded sofas under
hangings of black velvet displaying mountains, galleons, polar bears
executed in brushed wool. She would like very much to be dishing
up a costly *cabinet de diplomate* out of a cut-glass bowl in a rich
dining-room with a big gleaming belly of sideboard behind her,
and a dim picture of horses feeding, cows feeding, sheep feeding,
on badly painted purple grass. Or she could do as well with batter
pudding in the eating nook of a kitchen in a little stucco house by
the bus stop, plaster pears and peaches decorating the wall, ivy
curling out of little brass pots. Rose is an actress; she can fit
in anywhere.

She does get asked to parties. About two years ago, she was at a
party in a high-rise apartment building in Kingston. The windows
looked out on Lake Ontario and Wolfe Island. Rose didn't live in
Kingston. She lived up-country; she had been teaching drama for
two years at a community college. Some people were surprised that
she would do this. They did not know how little money an actress

105

might make; they thought that being well-known automatically meant being well-off.

She had driven down to Kingston just for this party, a fact which slightly shamed her. She had not met the hostess before. She had known the host last year, when he was teaching at the community college and living with another girl.

The hostess, whose name was Shelley, took Rose into the bedroom to put down her coat. Shelley was a thin, solemn-looking girl, a true blonde, with nearly white eyebrows, hair long and thick and straight as if cut from a block of wood. It seemed that she took her waif style seriously. Her voice was low and mournful, making Rose's own voice, her greeting of a moment ago, sound altogether too sprightly in her own ears.

In a basket at the foot of the bed a tortoiseshell cat was suckling four tiny, blind kittens.

'That's Tasha,' the hostess said. 'We can look at her kittens but we can't touch them, else she wouldn't feed them anymore.'

She knelt down by the basket, crooning, talking to the mother cat with an intense devotion that Rose thought affected. The shawl around her shoulders was black, rimmed with jet beads. Some beads were crooked, some were missing. It was a genuine old shawl, not an imitation. Her limp, slightly yellowed, eyelet-embroidered dress was genuine too, though probably a petticoat in the first place. Such clothes took looking for.

On the other side of the spool bed was a large mirror, hung suspiciously high, and tilted. Rose tried to get a look at herself when the girl was bent over the basket. It is very hard to look in the mirror when there is another, and particularly a younger, woman in the room. Rose was wearing a flowered cotton dress, a long dress with a tucked bodice and puffed sleeves, which was too short in the waist and too tight in the bust to be comfortable. There was something wrongly youthful or theatrical about it; perhaps she was not slim enough to wear that style. Her reddish-brown hair was dyed at home. Lines ran both ways under her eyes, trapping little diamonds of darkened skin.

Rose knew by now that when she found people affected, as she did this girl, and their rooms coyly decorated, their manner of living irritating (that mirror, the patchwork quilt, the Japanese

106

erotic drawings over the bed, the African music coming from the living-room), it was usually because she, Rose, hadn't received and was afraid she wouldn't receive the attention she wanted, hadn't penetrated the party, felt that she might be doomed to hang around on the fringes of things, making judgements.

She felt better in the living-room, where there were some people she knew, and some faces as old as her own. She drank quickly at first, and before long was using the newborn kittens as a springboard for her own story. She said that something dreadful had happened to her cat that very day.

'And the worst of it is,' she said, 'I never liked my cat much. It wasn't my idea to have a cat. It was his. He followed me home one day and insisted on being taken in. He was just like some big sneering hulk of an unemployable, set on convincing me I owed him a living. Well, he always had a fondness for the clothes dryer. He liked to jump in when it was warm, as soon as I'd taken the clothes out. Usually I just have one load but today I had two, and when I reached in to take the second load out, I thought I felt something. I thought, what do I have that's fur?'

People moaned or laughed, in a sympathetically horrified way. Rose looked around at them appealingly. She felt much better. The living-room, with its lake view, its careful decor (a jukebox, barbershop mirrors, turn-of-the-century advertisements – *Smoke, for your throat's sake* – old silk lampshades, farmhouse bowls and jugs, primitive masks and sculptures), no longer seemed so hostile. She took another drink of her gin and knew there was a limited time coming now when she would feel light and welcome as a hummingbird, convinced that many people in the room were witty and many were kind, and some were both together.

'Oh, *no*, I thought. But it was. It was. Death in the dryer.'

'A warning to all pleasure seekers,' said a little sharp-faced man at her elbow, a man she had known slightly for years. He taught in the English department of the university, where the host taught now, and the hostess was a graduate student.

'That's terrible,' said the hostess, with her cold, fixed look of sensitivity. Those who had laughed looked a bit abashed, as if they thought they might have seemed heartless. 'Your cat. That's terrible. How could you come tonight?'

As a matter of fact the incident had not happened today at all; it had happened last week. Rose wondered if the girl meant to put her at a disadvantage. She said sincerely and regretfully that she hadn't been very fond of the cat and that had made it seem worse, somehow. That's what she was trying to explain, she said.

'I felt as if maybe it was my fault. Maybe if I'd been fonder, it wouldn't have happened.'

'Of course it wouldn't,' said the man beside her. 'It was warmth he was seeking in the dryer. It was love. Ah, Rose!'

'Now you won't be able to fuck the cat anymore,' said a tall boy Rose hadn't noticed before. He seemed to have sprung up, right in front of her. 'Fuck the dog, fuck the cat, I don't know what you do, Rose.'

She was searching for his name. She had recognized him as a student, or former student.

'David,' she said. 'Hello, David.' She was so pleased at coming up with the name that she was slow in registering what he had said.

'Fuck the dog, fuck the cat,' he repeated, swaying over her.

'I beg your pardon,' Rose said, and put on a quizzical, indulgent, charming expression. The people around her were finding it as hard to adjust to what the boy said as she was. The mood of sociability, sympathy, expectation of goodwill was not easy to halt; it rolled on in spite of signs that there was plenty here it wasn't going to be able to absorb. Almost everyone was still smiling, as if the boy was telling an anecdote or playing a part, the point of which would be made clear in a moment. The hostess cast down her eyes and slipped away.

'Beg yours,' said the boy in a very ugly tone. 'Up yours, Rose.' He was white and brittle-looking, desperately drunk. He had probably been brought up in a gentle home, where people talked about answering Nature's call and blessed each other for sneezing.

A short, strong man with black curly hair took hold of the boy's arm just below the shoulder.

'Move it along,' he said, almost maternally. He spoke with a muddled European accent, mostly French, Rose thought, though she was not good about accents. She did tend to think, in spite of knowing better, that such accents spring from a richer and more complicated masculinity than the masculinity to be found in North America and in places like Hanratty, where she had grown up. Such an accent promised masculinity tinged with suffering, tenderness, and guile.

108

The host appeared in a velvet jumpsuit and took hold of the other arm, more or less symbolically, at the same time kissing Rose's cheek, because he hadn't seen her when she came in. 'Must talk to you,' he murmured, meaning he hoped he wouldn't have to, because there was so much tricky territory; the girl he had lived with last year, for one thing, and a night he had spent with Rose toward the end of term, when there had been a lot of drinking and bragging and lamenting about faithlessness, as well as some curiously insulting though pleasurable sex. He was looking very brushed and tended, thinner but softened, with his flowing hair and suit of bottle-green velvet. Only three years younger than Rose, but look at him. He had shed a wife, a family, a house, a discouraging future, set himself up with new clothes and new furniture and a succession of student mistresses. Men can do it.

'My, my,' Rose said and leaned against the wall: 'What was that all about?'

The man beside her, who had smiled all the time and looked into his glass, said, 'Ah, the sensitive youth of our time! Their grace of language, their depth of feeling! We must bow before them.'

The man with the black curly hair came back, didn't say a word, but handed Rose a fresh drink and took her glass.

The host came back too.

'Rose baby. I don't know how he got in. I said no bloody students. There's got to be some place safe from them.'

'He was in one of my classes last year,' Rose said. That really was all she could remember. She supposed they were thinking there must be more to it.

'Did he want to be an actor?' said the man beside her. 'I'll bet he did. Remember the good old days when they all wanted to be lawyers and engineers and business executives? They tell me that's coming back. I hope so. I devoutly hope so. Rose, I bet you listened to his problems. You must never do that. I bet that's what you did.'

'Oh, I suppose.'

'They come along looking for a parent-substitute. It's banal as can be. They trail around worshiping you and bothering you and then bam! It's parent-substitute rejecting time!'

Rose drank, and leaned against the wall, and heard them take up the theme of what students expected nowadays, how they broke

109

down your door to tell you about their abortions, their suicide attempts, their creativity crises, their weight problems. Always using the same words: personhood, values, rejection.

'I'm not rejecting you, you silly bugger, I'm flunking you!' said the little sharp man, recalling a triumphant confrontation he had had with one such student. They laughed at that and at the young woman who said, 'God, the difference when I was at university! You wouldn't have mentioned an abortion in a professor's office any more than you would have shit on the floor. *Shat* on the floor.'

Rose was laughing too, but felt smashed, under the skin. It would be better, in a way, if there were something behind this such as they suspected. If she had slept with that boy. If she had promised him something, if she had betrayed him, humiliated him. She could not remember anything. He had sprung out of the floor to accuse her. She must have done something, and she could not remember it. She could not remember anything to do with her students; that was the truth. She was solicitous and charming, all warmth and acceptance; she listened and advised; then she could not get their names straight. She could not remember a thing she had said to them.

A woman touched her arm. 'Wake up,' she said, in a tone of sly intimacy that made Rose think she must know her. Another student? But no, the woman introduced herself.

'I'm doing a paper on female suicide,' she said. 'I mean the suicide of female artists.' She said she had seen Rose on television and was longing to talk to her. She mentioned Diane Arbus, Virginia Woolf, Sylvia Plath, Anne Sexton, Christiane Pflug. She was well informed. She looked like a prime candidate herself, Rose thought: emaciated, bloodless, obsessed. Rose said she was hungry, and the woman followed her out to the kitchen.

'And too many actresses to count –' the woman said. 'Margaret Sullavan –'

'I'm just a teacher now.'

'Oh, nonsense. I'm sure you are an actress to the marrow of your bones.'

The hostess had made bread: glazed and braided and decorated loaves. Rose wondered at the pains taken here. The bread, the pâté, the hanging plants, the kittens, all on behalf of a most precarious and temporary domesticity. She wished, she often wished, that she could take such pains, that she could make ceremonies, impose herself, make bread.

She noticed a group of younger members of the faculty – she would have thought them students, except for what the host had said about students not being let in – who were sitting on the counters and standing in front of the sink. They were talking in low, serious voices. One of them looked at her. She smiled. Her smile was not returned. A couple of others looked at her, and went on talking. She was sure they were talking about her, about what had happened in the living-room. She urged the woman to try some bread and pâté. Presumably that would keep her quiet, so that Rose could overhear what was being said.

'I never eat at parties.'

The woman's manner toward her was turning dark and vaguely accusing. Rose had learned that this was a department wife. Perhaps it had been a political move, inviting her. And promising her Rose; had that been part of the move?

'Are you always so hungry?' the woman said. 'Are you never ill?'

'I am when there's something this good to eat,' Rose said. She was only trying to set an example, and could hardly chew or swallow, in her anxiety to hear what was being said of her. 'No, I'm not often ill,' she said. It surprised her to realize that was true. She used to get sick with colds and flu and cramps and headaches; those definite ailments had now disappeared, simmered down into a low, steady hum of uneasiness, fatigue, apprehension.

Fucked-up jealous establishment.

Rose heard that, or thought she heard it. They were giving her quick, despising looks. Or so she thought; she could not look directly at them. *Establishment*. That was Rose. Was it? Was that Rose? Was that Rose who had taken a teaching job because she wasn't getting enough acting jobs to support herself, was granted the teaching job because of her experience on stage and television, but had to accept a cut in pay because she lacked degrees? She wanted to go over and tell them that. She wanted to state her case. The years of work, the exhaustion, the traveling, the high school auditoriums, the nerves, the boredom, the never knowing where your next pay was coming from. She wanted to plead with them, so they would forgive her and love her and take her on their side. It was their side she wanted to

111

be on, not the side of the people in the living-room who had taken up her cause. But that was a choice made because of fear, not on principle. She feared them. She feared their hardhearted virtue, their cool despising faces, their secrets, their laughter, their obscenities.

She thought of Anna, her own daughter. Anna was seventeen. She had long fair hair and wore a fine gold chain around her throat. It was so fine you had to look closely to make sure it was a chain, not just a glinting of her smooth bright skin. She was not like these young people but she was equally remote. She practiced ballet and rode her horse every day, but she didn't plan to ride in competitions or be a ballerina. Why not?

'Because it would be silly.'

Something about Anna's style, the fine chain, her silences, made Rose think of her grandmother, Patrick's mother. But then, she thought, Anna might not be so silent, so fastidious, so unforthcoming, with anybody but her mother.

The man with the black curly hair stood in the kitchen doorway giving her an impudent and ironic look.

'Do you know who that is?' Rose said to the suicide woman. 'The man who took the drunk away?'

'That's Simon. I don't think the boy was drunk, I think he's on drugs.'

'What does he do?'

'Well, I expect he's a student of sorts.'

'No,' said Rose. 'That man – Simon?'

'Oh, Simon. He's in the classics department. I don't think he's always been a teacher.'

'Like me,' Rose said, and turned the smile she had tried on the young people on Simon. Tired and adrift and witless as she was, she was beginning to feel familiar twinges, tidal promises.

If he smiles back, things will start to be all right.

He did smile, and the suicide woman spoke sharply.

'Look, do you come to a party just to meet men?'

When Simon was fourteen, he and his older sister and another boy, a friend of theirs, were hidden in a freight car, traveling from occupied to unoccupied France. They were on their way to Lyons, where they

112

would be looked after, redirected to safe places, by members of an organization that was trying to save Jewish children. Simon and his sister had already been sent out of Poland, at the beginning of the war, to stay with French relatives. Now they had to be sent away again.

The freight car stopped. The train was standing still, at night somewhere out in the country. They could hear French and German voices. There was some commotion in the cars ahead. They heard the doors grinding open, heard and felt the boots striking on the bare floors of those cars. An inspection of the train. They lay down under some sacks, but did not even try to cover their faces; they thought there was no hope. The voices were getting closer and they heard the boots on the gravel beside the track. Then the train began to move. It moved so slowly that they did not notice for a moment or so, and even then thought it was just a shunting of the cars. They expected it to stop, so that the inspection could continue. But the train kept moving. It moved a little faster, then faster; it picked up its ordinary speed, which was nothing very great. They were moving, they were free of the inspection, they were being carried away. Simon never knew what had happened. The danger was past.

Simon said that when he realized they were safe he suddenly felt that they would get through, that nothing could happen to them now, that they were particularly blessed and lucky. He took what happened for a lucky sign.

Rose asked him, had he ever seen his friend and his sister again?

'No. Never. Not after Lyons.'

'So, it was lucky only for you.'

Simon laughed. They were in bed, in Rose's bed in an old house, on the outskirts of a crossroads village; they had driven there straight from the party. It was April, the wind was cold, and Rose's house was chilly. The furnace was inadequate. Simon put a hand to the wallpaper behind the bed, made her feel the draft.

'What it needs is some insulation.'

'I know. It's awful. And you should see my fuel bills.'

Simon said she should get a wood stove. He told her about various kinds of firewood. Maple, he said, was a lovely wood to burn. Then he held forth on different kinds of insulation. Styrofoam, Micafil, fiberglass. He got out of bed and padded around naked, looking at the walls of her house. Rose shouted after him.

'Now I remember. It was a grant.'

'What? I can't hear you.'

She got out of bed and wrapped herself in a blanket. Standing at the top of the stairs, she said, 'That boy came to me with an application for a grant. He wanted to be a playwright. I just this minute remember.'

'What boy?' said Simon. 'Oh.'

'But I recommended him. I know I did.' The truth was she recommended everybody. If she could not see their merits, she believed it might just be a case of their having merits she was unable to see.

'He must not have got it. So he thought I shafted him.'

'Well, suppose you had,' said Simon, peering down the cellarway. 'That would be your right.'

'I know. I'm a coward about that lot. I hate their disapproval. They are so virtuous.'

'They are not virtuous at all,' said Simon. 'I'm going to put my shoes on and look at your furnace. You probably need the filters cleaned. That is just their style. They are not much to be feared, they are just as stupid as anybody. They want a chunk of the power. Naturally.'

'But would you get such venomous' – Rose had to stop and start the word again – 'such *venomousness*, simply from ambition?'

'What else?' said Simon, climbing the stairs. He made a grab for the blanket, wrapped himself up with her, pecked her nose. 'Enough of that, Rose. Have you no shame? I'm a poor fellow come to look at your furnace. Your basement furnace. Sorry to bump into you like this, ma'am.' She already knew a few of his characters. This was The Humble Workman. Some others were The Old Philosopher, who bowed low to her, Japanese style, as he came out of the bathroom, murmuring *memento mori, memento mori*, and, when appropriate, The Mad Satyr, nuzzling and leaping, making triumphant smacking noises against her navel.

At the crossroads store she bought real coffee instead of instant, real cream, bacon, frozen broccoli, a hunk of local cheese, canned crabmeat, the best-looking tomatoes they had, mushrooms, long-grained rice. Cigarettes as well. She was in that state of happiness which seems perfectly natural and unthreatened. If asked, she would have said it was because of the weather – the day was bright, in spite of the harsh wind – as much as because of Simon.

'You must've brought home company,' said the woman who kept the store. She spoke with no surprise or malice or censure, just a comradely sort of envy.

'When I wasn't expecting it.' Rose dumped more groceries on the counter. 'What a lot of bother they are. Not to mention expense. Look at that bacon. And cream.'

'I could stand a bit of it,' the woman said.

Simon cooked a remarkable supper from the resources provided, while Rose did nothing much but stand around watching, and change the sheets.

'Country life,' she said. 'It's changed, or I'd forgotten. I came here with some ideas about how I would live. I thought I would go for long walks on deserted country roads. And the first time I did, I heard a car coming tearing along on the gravel behind me. I got well off. Then I heard shots. I was terrified. I hid in the bushes and a car came roaring past, weaving all over the road – and they were shooting out of the windows. I cut back through the fields and told the woman at the store I thought we should call the police. She said oh, yes, weekends the boys get a case of beer in the car and they go out shooting groundhogs. Then she said, what were you doing up that road anyway? I could see she thought going for walks by yourself was a lot more suspicious than shooting groundhogs. There were lots of things like that. I don't think I'd stay, but the job's here and the rent's cheap. Not that she isn't nice, the woman in the store. She tells fortunes. Cards and teacups.'

Simon said that he had been sent from Lyons to work on a farm in the mountains of Provence. The people there lived and farmed very much as in the Middle Ages. They could not read or write or speak French. When they got sick they waited either to die or to get better. They had never seen a doctor, though a veterinarian came once a year to inspect the cows. Simon ran a pitchfork into his foot, the wound became infected, he was feverish and had the greatest difficulty in persuading them to send for the veterinarian, who was then in the next village. At last they did, and the veterinarian came and gave Simon a shot with a great horse needle, and he got better. The household was bewildered and amused to see such measures taken on behalf of human life.

He said that while he was getting better he taught them to play cards. He taught the mother and the children; the father and the grandfather were too slow and unwilling, and the grandmother was kept shut up in a cage in the barn, fed scraps twice a day.

'Is that true? Is it possible?'

They were at the stage of spreading things out for each other: pleasures, stories, jokes, confessions.

'Country life!' said Simon. 'But here it is not so bad. This house could be made very comfortable. You should have a garden.'

'That was another idea I had, I tried to have a garden. Nothing did very well. I was looking forward to the cabbages, I think cabbages are beautiful, but some worm got into them. It ate up the leaves till they looked like lace, and then they all turned yellow and lay on the ground.'

'Cabbages are a very hard thing to grow. You should start with something easier.' Simon left the table and went to the window. 'Point me out where you had your garden.'

'Along the fence. That's where they had it before.'

'That is no good, it's too close to the walnut tree. Walnut trees are bad for the soil.'

'I didn't know that.'

'Well, it's true. You should have it nearer the house. Tomorrow I will dig up a garden for you. You'll need a lot of fertilizer. Now. Sheep manure is the very best fertilizer. Do you know anyone around here who has sheep? We will get several sacks of sheep manure and draw up a plan of what to plant, though it's too early yet, there could still be frost. You can start some things indoors, from seed. Tomatoes.'

'I thought you had to go back on the morning bus,' Rose said. They had driven up in her car.

'Monday is a light day. I will phone up and cancel. I'll tell the girls in the office to say I have a sore throat.'

'Sore throat?'

'Something like that.'

'It's good that you're here,' said Rose truthfully. 'Otherwise I'd be

116

spending my time thinking about that boy. I'd be trying not to, but it would keep coming at me. In unprotected moments. I would have been in a state of humiliation.'

'That's a pretty small thing to get into a state of humiliation about.'

'So I see. It doesn't take much with me.'

'Learn not to be so thin-skinned,' said Simon, as if he were taking her over, in a sensible way, along with the house and garden. 'Radishes. Leaf lettuce. Onions. Potatoes. Do you eat potatoes?'

Before he left they drew up a plan of the garden. He dug and worked the soil for her, though he had to content himself with cow manure. Rose had to go to work, on Monday, but kept him in her mind all day. She saw him digging in the garden. She saw him naked peering down the cellarway. A short, thick man, hairy, warm, with a crumpled comedian's face. She knew what he would say when she got home. He would say, 'I hope I done it to your satisfaction, mum,' and yank a forelock.

That was what he did, and she was so delighted she cried out, 'Oh Simon, you idiot, you're the man for my life!' Such was the privilege, the widespread sunlight of the moment, that she did not reflect that saying this might be unwise.

In the middle of the week she went to the store, not to buy anything, but to get her fortune told. The woman looked in her cup and said, 'Oh, you! You've met the man who will change everything.'

'Yes, I think so.'

'He will change your life. Oh, Lord. You won't stay here. I see fame. I see water.'

'I don't know about that. I think he wants to insulate my house.'

'The change has begun already.'

'Yes. I know it has. Yes.'

She could not remember what they had said about Simon coming again. She thought that he was coming on the weekend. She expected him, and she went out and bought groceries, not at the local store this time but at a supermarket several miles away. She hoped the woman at the store wouldn't see her carrying the grocery bags into the house. She had wanted fresh vegetables and steak and imported black cherries, and Camembert and pears. She had bought wine, too, and a pair of sheets covered with stylish garlands of blue and yellow flowers. She was thinking her pale haunches would show up well against them.

On Friday night she put the sheets on the bed and the cherries in a blue bowl. The wine was chilling, the cheese was getting soft. Around nine o'clock came the loud knock, the expected joking knock on the door. She was surprised that she hadn't heard his car.

'Felt lonesome,' said the woman from the store. 'So I just thought I'd drop in and – oh-oh. You're expecting your company.'

'Not really,' Rose said. Her heart had started thumping joyfully when she heard the knock and was thumping still. 'I don't know when he's arriving here,' she said. 'Maybe tomorrow.'

'Bugger of a rain.'

The woman's voice sounded hearty and practical, as if Rose might need distracting or consoling.

'I just hope he isn't driving in it, then,' Rose said.

'No sir, you wouldn't want him driving in it.'

The woman ran her fingers through her short grey hair, shaking the rain out, and Rose knew she ought to offer her something. A glass of wine? She might become mellow and talkative, wanting to stay and finish the bottle. Here was a person Rose had talked to, plenty of times, a friend of sorts, somebody she would have claimed to like, and she could hardly be bothered to acknowledge her. It would have been the same at that moment with anyone who was not Simon. Anyone else seemed accidental and irritating.

Rose could see what was coming. All the ordinary delights, consolations, diversions, of life would be rolled up and packed away; the pleasure found in food, lilacs, music, thunder in the night, would vanish. Nothing would do anymore but to lie under Simon, nothing would do but to give way to pangs and convulsions.

She decided on tea. She thought she might as well put the time to use by having another go at her future.

'It's not clear,' the woman said.

'What's not?'

'I'm not able to get anything in focus tonight. That happens. No, to be honest, I can't locate him.'

'Can't locate him?'

'In your future. I'm beat.'

Rose thought she was saying this out of ill-will, out of jealousy.

'Well, I'm not just concerned about him.'

'Maybe I could do better if you had a possession of his, just let me have it to hang on to. Anything he had his hands on, do you have that?'

'Me,' said Rose. A cheap boast, at which the fortune-teller was obliged to laugh.

'No, seriously.'

'I don't think so. I threw his cigarette butts out.'

After the woman had gone, Rose sat up waiting. Soon it was midnight. The rain came down hard. The next time she looked it was twenty to two. How could time so empty pass so quickly? She put out the lights because she didn't want to be caught sitting up. She undressed, but couldn't lie down on the fresh sheets. She sat on in the kitchen, in the dark. From time to time she made fresh tea. Some light from the street light at the corner came into the room. The village had bright new mercury vapor lights. She could see that light, a bit of the store, the church steps across the road. The church no longer served the discreet and respectable Protestant sect that had built it, but proclaimed itself a Temple of Nazareth, also a Holiness Center, whatever that might be. Things were more askew here than Rose had noticed before. No retired farmers lived in these houses; in fact there were no farms to retire from, just the poor fields covered with juniper. People worked thirty or forty miles away, in factories, in the Provincial Mental Hospital, or they didn't work at all, they lived a mysterious life on the borders of criminality or a life of orderly craziness in the shade of the Holiness Center. People's lives were surely more desperate than they used to be, and what could be more desperate than a woman of Rose's age, sitting up all night in her dark kitchen waiting for her lover? And this was a situation she had created, she had done it all herself, it seemed she never learned any lessons at all. She had turned Simon into the peg on which her hopes

119

were hung and she could never manage now to turn him back into himself.

The mistake was in buying the wine, she thought, and the sheets and the cheese and the cherries. Preparations court disaster. She hadn't realized that till she opened the door and the commotion of her heart turned from merriment to dismay, like the sound of a tower full of bells turned comically (but not for Rose) into a rusty foghorn.

Hour after hour in the dark and the rain she foresaw what could happen. She could wait through the weekend, fortifying herself with excuses and sickening with doubt, never leaving the house in case the phone might ring. Back at work on Monday, dazed but slightly comforted by the real world, she would get up the courage to write him a note, in care of the classics department.

'I was thinking we might plant the garden next weekend. I have bought a great array of seeds (a lie, but she would buy them, if she heard from him). Do let me know if you're coming, but don't worry if you've made other plans.'

Then she would worry: did it sound too offhand, with that mention of other plans? Wouldn't it be too pushy, if she didn't tack that on? All her confidence, her lightness of heart, would have leaked away, but she would try to counterfeit it.

'If it's too wet to work in the garden we could always go for a drive. Maybe we could shoot some groundhogs. Best, Rose.'

Then a further time of waiting, for which the weekend would have been only a casual trial run, a haphazard introduction to the serious, commonplace, miserable ritual. Putting her hand into the mailbox and drawing the mail out without looking at it, refusing to leave the college until five o'clock, putting a cushion against the telephone to block her view of it; pretending inattention. Watch-pot thinking. Sitting up late at night, drinking, never getting quite sick enough of this foolishness to give up on it because the waiting would be interspersed with such green and springlike reveries, such convincing arguments as to his intentions. These would be enough, at some point, to make her decide that he must have been taken ill, he would never have deserted her otherwise. She would phone the Kingston Hospital, ask about his condition, be told that he was not a patient. After that would come the day she went into

120

the college library, picked up back copies of the Kingston paper, searched the obituaries to discover if he had by any chance dropped dead. Then, giving in utterly, cold and shaking, she would call him at the university. The girl in his office would say he was gone. Gone to Europe, gone to California; he had only been teaching there for a single term. Gone on a camping trip, gone to get married.

Or she might say, 'Just a minute, please,' and turn Rose over to him, just like that.

'Yes?'

'Simon?'

'Yes.'

'It's Rose.'

'Rose?'

It wouldn't be as drastic as that. It would be worse.

'I've been meaning to call you,' he would say, or, 'Rose, how *are* you?' or even, 'How is that garden?'

Better lose him now. But going by the phone she put her hand on it, to see if it was warm, maybe, or to encourage it.

Before it began to get light Monday morning she packed what she thought she would need into the back of the car, and locked the house, with the Camembert still weeping on the kitchen counter; she drove off in a westerly direction. She meant to be gone a couple of days, until she came to her senses and could face the sheets and the patch of readied earth and the place behind the bed where she had put her hand to feel the draft. (Why did she bring her boots and her winter coat, if this was the case?) She wrote a letter to the college – she could lie beautifully in letters, though not on the phone – in which she said that she had been called to Toronto by the terminal illness of a dear friend. (Perhaps she didn't lie so beautifully after all, perhaps she overdid it.) She had been awake almost the whole weekend, drinking, not so very much, but steadily. *I'm not having any of it*, she said out loud, very seriously and emphatically, as she loaded the car. And as she crouched in the front seat, writing the letter, which she could more comfortably have written in the house, she thought how many crazy letters she had written, how many overblown excuses she had found, having to leave a place, or being afraid to leave a place, on account of some man. Nobody knew the extent of her foolishness, friends who had known her twenty years didn't know half of the flights she had been on, the money she had spent, and the risks she had taken.

Here she was, she thought a bit later, driving a car, shutting down the windshield wipers as the rain finally let up on a Monday morning at ten o'clock, stopping for gas, stopping to get a transfer of money, now that the banks were open; she was competent and cheery, she remembered what to do, who would guess what mortifications, memories of mortification, predictions, were beating in her head? The most mortifying thing of all was simply hope, which burrows so deceitfully at first, masks itself cunningly, but not for long. In a week's time it can be out trilling and twittering and singing hymns at heaven's gate. And it was busy even now, telling her that Simon might be turning into her driveway at this very moment, might be standing at her door with his hands together, praying, mocking, apologizing. *Memento mori.*

Even so, even if that were true, what would happen some day, some morning? Some morning she could wake up and she would know by his breathing that he was awake beside her and not touching her, and that she was not supposed to touch him. So much female touching is asking (this is what she would have learned, or learned again, from him); women's tenderness is greedy, their sensuality is dishonest. She would lie there wishing she had some plain defect, something her shame could curl around and protect. As it was, she would have to be ashamed of, burdened by, the whole physical fact of herself, the whole outspread naked digesting putrefying fact. Her flesh could seem disastrous; thick and porous, grey and spotty. His body would not be in question, it never would be; he would be the one who condemned and forgave and how could she ever know if he would forgive her again? *Come here*, he could tell her, or *go away*. Never since Patrick had she been the free person, the one with that power; maybe she had used it all up, all that was coming to her.

Or she might hear him at a party, saying, 'And then I knew I'd be all right, I knew it was a lucky sign.' Telling his story to some tarty unworthy girl in a leopard-spotted silk, or – far worse – to a gentle long-haired girl in an embroidered smock, who would lead him by the hand, sooner or later, through a doorway into a room or landscape where Rose couldn't follow.

Yes, but wasn't it possible nothing like that would happen, wasn't it possible there'd be nothing but kindness, and sheep manure, and deep spring nights with the frogs singing? A failure to appear, on the first weekend, or to telephone, might have meant nothing but a different timetable; no ominous sign at all. Thinking like this, every twenty miles or so, she slowed, even looked for a place to turn around. Then she did not do it, she speeded up, thinking she would drive a little further to make sure her head was clear. Thoughts of herself sitting in the kitchen, images of loss, poured over her again. And so it was, back and forth, as if the rear end of the car was held by a magnetic force, which ebbed and strengthened, ebbed and strengthened again, but the strength was never quite enough to make her turn, and after a while she became almost impersonally curious, seeing it as a real physical force and wondering if it was getting weaker, as she drove, if at some point far ahead the car and she would leap free of it, and she would recognize the moment when she left its field.

So she kept driving. Muskoka; the Lakehead; the Manitoba border. Sometimes she slept in the car, pulled off to the side of the road for an hour or so. In Manitoba it was too cold to do that; she checked into a motel. She ate in roadside restaurants. Before she entered a restaurant she combed her hair and made up her face and put on that distant, dreamy, shortsighted look women wear when they think some man may be watching them. It was too much to say that she really expected Simon to be there, but it seemed she did not entirely rule him out.

The force did weaken, with distance. It was as simple as that, though the distance, she thought afterward, would have to be covered by car, or by bus, or bicycle; you couldn't get the same results by flying. In a prairie town within sight of the Cypress Hills she recognized the change. She had driven all night until the sun came up behind her and she felt calm and clearheaded as you do at such times. She went into a café and ordered coffee and fried eggs. She sat at the counter looking at the usual things there are behind café counters – the coffeepots and the bright, probably stale pieces of lemon and raspberry pie, the thick glass dishes they put ice cream or jello in. It was those dishes that told her of her changed state. She could not have said she found them shapely, or eloquent, without misstating the case. All she could have said was that she saw them in a way that wouldn't be possible to a person in any stage of love. She felt their solidity with a convalescent gratitude whose weight settled comfortably into her brains and feet. She realized then that she had come into this café without the least farfetched idea of Simon, so it seemed the world had stopped being a stage where she might meet him, and gone back to being itself. During that bountifully clear half hour before her breakfast made her so sleepy she had to get to a motel, where she fell asleep with her clothes on and the curtains open to the sun, she thought how love removes the world for you, and just as surely when it's going well as when it's going badly. This shouldn't have been, and wasn't, a surprise to her; the surprise was that she so much wanted, required, everything to be there for her, thick and plain as ice-cream dishes, so that it seemed to her it might not be the disappointment, the losses, the dissolution, she had been running from, any more than the opposite of those things: the celebration and shock of love, the dazzling alteration. Even if that was safe, she couldn't accept it. Either way you were robbed of something – a private balance spring, a little dry kernel of probity. So she thought.

She wrote to the college that while in Toronto attending the deathbed of her friend she had run into an old acquaintance who had offered her a job on the west coast, and that she was going there immediately. She supposed they could make trouble for her but she also supposed, rightly, that they would not bother, since the terms of her employment, and particularly her pay, were not quite regular. She wrote to the agency from which she rented the house; she wrote to the woman at the store, good luck and goodbye. On the Hope-Princeton highway she got out of the car and stood in the cool rain of the coastal mountains. She felt relatively safe, and exhausted, and sane, though she knew she had left some people behind who would not agree with that.

Luck was with her. In Vancouver she met a man she knew who was casting a new television series. It was to be produced on the west coast and concerned a family, or pseudo-family, of eccentrics and drifters using an old house on Salt Spring Island as their home or headquarters. Rose got the role of the woman who owned the house, the pseudo-mother. Just as she had said in the letter; a job on the west coast, possibly the best job she had ever had. Some special

124

make-up techniques, ageing techniques, had to be used on her face; the make-up man joked that if the series was a success, and ran for a few years, these techniques would not be necessary.

A word everybody at the coast was using was *fragile*. They spoke of feeling fragile today, of being in a fragile state. Not me, Rose said, I am getting a distinct feeling of being made of old horsehide. The wind and sun on the prairies had browned and roughened her skin. She slapped her creased brown neck, to emphasize the word *horsehide*. She was already beginning to adopt some of the turns of phrase, the mannerisms, of the character she was to play.

A year or so later Rose was out on the deck of one of the BC ferries, wearing a dingy sweater and a headscarf. She had to creep around among the lifeboats, keeping an eye on a pretty young girl who was freezing in cut-off jeans and a halter. According to the script, the woman Rose played was afraid this young girl meant to jump off the boat because she was pregnant.

Filming this scene, they collected a sizeable crowd. When they broke and walked toward the sheltered part of the deck, to put on their coats and drink coffee, a woman in the crowd reached out and touched Rose's arm.

'You won't remember me,' she said, and in fact Rose did not remember her. Then this woman began to talk about Kingston, the couple who had given the party, even about the death of Rose's cat. Rose recognized her as the woman who had been doing the paper on suicide. But she looked quite different; she was wearing an expensive beige pantsuit, a beige and white scarf around her hair; she was no longer fringed and soiled and stringy and mutinous-looking. She introduced a husband, who grunted at Rose as if to say that if she expected him to make a big fuss about her, she had another think coming. He moved away and the woman said, 'Poor Simon. You know he died.'

Then she wanted to know if they were going to be shooting any more scenes. Rose knew why she asked. She wanted to get into the background or even the foreground of these scenes so that she could call up her friends and tell them to watch her. If she called the people who had been at that party she would have to say that she knew the series was utter tripe but that she had been persuaded to be in a scene, for the fun of it.

'Died?'

The woman took off her scarf and the wind blew her hair across her face.

'Cancer of the pancreas,' she said, and turned to face the wind so that she could put the scarf on again, more to her satisfaction. Her voice seemed to Rose knowledgeable and sly. 'I don't know how well you knew him,' she said. Was that to make Rose wonder how well *she* knew him? That slyness could ask for help, as well as measure victories; you could be sorry for her perhaps, but never trust her. Rose was thinking this instead of thinking about what she had told her. 'So sad,' she said, businesslike now, as she tucked her chin in, knotting the scarf. 'Sad. He had it for a long time.'

Somebody was calling Rose's name; she had to go back to the scene. The girl didn't throw herself into the sea. They didn't have things like that happening in the series. Such things always threatened to happen but they didn't happen, except now and then to peripheral and unappealing characters. People watching trusted that they would be protected from predictable disasters, also from those shifts of emphasis that throw the story line open to question, the disarrangements which demand new judgements and solutions, and throw the windows open on appropriate unforgettable scenery.

Simon's dying struck Rose as that kind of disarrangement. It was preposterous, it was unfair, that such a chunk of information should have been left out, and that Rose even at this late date could have thought herself the only person who could seriously lack power.

Elizabeth Bowen

Sunday Afternoon

'So here you are!' exclaimed Mrs Vesey to the newcomer who joined the group on the lawn. She reposed for an instant her light, dry fingers on his. 'Henry has come from London,' she added. Acquiescent smiles from the others round her showed that the fact was already known – she was no more than indicating to Henry the role that he was to play. 'What are your experiences? – Please tell us. But nothing dreadful: we are already feeling a little sad.'

'I am sorry to hear that,' said Henry Russel, with the air of one not anxious to speak of his own affairs. Drawing a cane chair into the circle, he looked from face to face with concern. His look travelled on to the screen of lilac, whose dark purple, pink-silver, and white plumes sprayed out in the brilliance of the afternoon. The late May Sunday blazed, but was not warm: something less than a wind, a breath of coldness, fretted the edge of things. Where the lilac barrier ended, across the sun-polished meadows, the Dublin mountains continued to trace their hazy, today almost colourless line. The coldness had been admitted by none of the seven or eight people who, in degrees of elderly beauty, sat here full in the sun, at this sheltered edge of the lawn: they continued to master the coldness, or to deny it, as though with each it were some secret *malaise*. An air of fastidious, stylized melancholy, an air of being secluded behind glass, characterized for Henry these old friends in whose shadow he had grown up. To their pleasure at having him back among them was added, he felt, a taboo or warning – he was to tell a little, but not much. He could feel with a shock, as he sat down, how insensibly he had deserted, these last years, the aesthetic of living that he had got from them. As things were, he felt over him their suspended charm. The democratic smell of the Dublin bus, on which he had made the outward journey to join

127

them, had evaporated from his person by the time he was halfway up Mrs Vesey's chestnut avenue. Her house, with its fanlights and tall windows, was a villa in the Italian sense, just near enough to the city to make the country's sweetness particularly acute. Now, the sensations of wartime, that locked his inside being, began as surely to be dispelled – in the influence of this eternalized Sunday afternoon.

'Sad?' he said, 'that is quite wrong.'

'These days, our lives seem unreal,' said Mrs Vesey – with eyes that penetrated his point of view. 'But, worse than that, this afternoon we discover that we all have friends who have died.'

'Lately?' said Henry, tapping his fingers together.

'Yes, in all cases,' said Ronald Cuffe – with just enough dryness to show how much the subject had been beginning to tire him. 'Come, Henry, we look to you for distraction. To us, these days, you are quite a figure. In fact, from all we have heard of London, it is something that you should be alive. Are things there as shocking as they say – or are they more shocking?' he went on, with distaste.

'Henry's not sure,' said someone, 'he looks pontifical.'

Henry, in fact, was just beginning to twiddle this far-off word 'shocking' round in his mind, when a diversion caused some turning of heads. A young girl stepped out of a window and began to come their way across the lawn. She was Maria, Mrs Vesey's niece. A rug hung over her bare arm: she spread out the rug and sat down at her aunt's feet. With folded arms, and her fingers on her thin pointed elbows, she immediately fixed her eyes on Henry Russel. 'Good afternoon,' she said to him, in a mocking but somehow intimate tone.

The girl, like some young difficult pet animal, seemed in a way to belong to everyone there. Miss Ria Store, the patroness of the arts who had restlessly been refolding her fur cape, said: 'And where have *you* been, Maria?'

'Indoors.'

Someone said, 'On this beautiful afternoon?'

'Is it?' said Maria, frowning impatiently at the grass.

'Instinct', said the retired judge, 'now tells Maria it's time for tea.'

'No, this does,' said Maria, nonchalantly showing her wrist with the watch on it. 'It keeps good time, thank you, Sir Isaac.' She returned her eyes to Henry. 'What have you been saying?'

'You interrupted Henry. He was just going to speak.'

'*Is* it so frightening?' Maria said.

'The bombing?' said Henry. 'Yes. But as it does not connect with the rest of life, it is difficult, you know, to know what one feels. One's feelings seem to have no language for anything so preposterous. As for thoughts —'

'At that rate,' said Maria, with a touch of contempt, 'your thoughts would not be interesting.'

'Maria,' said somebody, 'that is no way to persuade Henry to talk.'

'About what is important,' announced Maria, 'it seems that no one can tell one anything. There is really nothing, till one knows it oneself.'

'Henry is probably right', said Ronald Cuffe, 'in considering that this – this outrage is *not* important. There is no place for it in human experience; it apparently cannot make a place of its own. It will have no literature.'

'Literature!' said Maria. 'One can see, Mr Cuffe, that *you* have always been safe!'

'Maria,' said Mrs Vesey, 'you're rather pert.'

Sir Isaac said, 'What does Maria expect to know?'

Maria pulled off a blade of grass and bit it. Something calculating and passionate appeared in her; she seemed to be crouched up inside herself. She said to Henry sharply: 'But you'll go back, of course?'

'To London? Yes – this is only my holiday. Anyhow, one cannot stay long away.'

Immediately he had spoken Henry realized how subtly this offended his old friends. Their position was, he saw, more difficult than his own, and he could not have said a more cruel thing. Mrs Vesey, with her adept smile that was never entirely heartless, said: 'Then we must hope your time here will be pleasant. Is it so very short?'

'And be careful, Henry,' said Ria Store, 'or you will find Maria stowed away in your baggage. And there would be an embarrassment, at an English port! We can feel her planning to leave us at any time.'

Henry said, rather flatly: 'Why should not Maria travel in the ordinary way?'

'Why should Maria travel at all? There is only one journey now – into danger. We cannot feel that that is necessary for her.'

Sir Isaac added: 'We fear, however, that this is the journey Maria wishes to make.'

Maria, curled on the lawn with the nonchalance of a feline creature, through this kept her eyes cast down. Another cold puff came through the lilac, soundlessly knocking the blooms together. One woman, taken quite unawares, shivered – then changed this into a laugh. There was an aside about love from Miss Store, who spoke with a cold, abstracted knowledge – 'Maria has no experience, none whatever; she hopes to meet heroes – she meets none. So now she hopes to find heroes across the sea. Why, Henry, she might make a hero of you.'

'It is not that,' said Maria, who had heard. Mrs Vesey bent down and touched her shoulder; she sent the girl into the house to see if tea were ready. Presently they all rose and followed – in twos and threes, heads either erect composedly or else deliberately bowed in thought. Henry knew the idea of summer had been relinquished: they would not return to the lawn again. In the dining-room – where the white walls and the glass of the pictures held the reflections of summers – burned the log fire they were so glad to see. With her shoulder against the mantelpiece stood Maria, watching them take their places at the round table. Everything Henry had heard said had fallen off her – in these few minutes all by herself she had started in again on a fresh phase of living that was intact and pure. So much so, that Henry felt the ruthlessness of her disregard for the past, even the past of a few minutes ago. She came forward and put her hands on two chairs – to show she had been keeping a place for him.

Lady Ottery, leaning across the table, said: 'I must ask you – we heard you had lost everything. But that cannot be true?'

Henry said, unwillingly: 'It's true that I lost my flat, and everything in my flat.'

'*Henry,*' said Mrs Vesey, 'all your beautiful things?'

'Oh dear,' said Lady Ottery, overpowered, 'I thought that could not be possible. I ought not to have asked.'

Ria Store looked at Henry critically. 'You take this too calmly. What has happened to you?'

'It was some time ago. And it happens to many people.'

'But not to everyone,' said Miss Store. 'I should see no reason, for instance, why it should happen to me.'

'One cannot help looking at you,' said Sir Isaac. 'You must forgive our amazement. But there was a time, Henry, when I think we all used to feel that we knew you well. If this is not a painful question, at this juncture, why did you not send your valuables out of town? You could have even shipped them over to us.'

'I was attached to them. I wanted to live with them.'

'And now,' said Miss Store, 'you live with nothing, for ever. Can you really feel that that is life?'

'I do. I may be easily pleased. It was by chance I was out when the place was hit. You may feel – and I honour your point of view – that I should have preferred, at my age, to go into eternity with some pieces of glass and jade and a dozen pictures. But, in fact, I am very glad to remain. To exist.'

'On what level?'

'On any level.'

'Come, Henry,' said Ronald Cuffe, 'that is a cynicism one cannot like in you. You speak of your age: to us, of course, that is nothing. You are at your maturity.'

'Forty-three.'

Maria gave Henry an askance look, as though, after all, he were not a friend. But she then said: 'Why should he wish he was dead?' Her gesture upset some tea on the lace cloth, and she idly rubbed it up with her handkerchief. The tug her rubbing gave to the cloth shook a petal from a Chinese peony in the centre bowl on to a plate of cucumber sandwiches. This little bit of destruction was watched by the older people with fascination, with a kind of appeasement, as though it were a guarantee against something worse.

'Henry is not young and savage, like you are. Henry's life is – or was – an affair of attachments,' said Ria Store. She turned her eyes, under their lids, on Henry. 'I wonder how much of you *has* been blown to blazes.'

'I have no way of knowing,' he said. 'Perhaps you have?'

'Chocolate cake?' said Maria.

'Please.'

For chocolate layer cake, the Vesey cook had been famous since Henry was a boy of seven or eight. The look, then the taste, of the brown segment linked him with Sunday afternoons when he had been brought here by his mother; then, with a phase of his adolescence when he had been unable to eat, only able to look round. Mrs Vesey's beauty, at that time approaching its last lunar quarter, had swum on him when he was about nineteen. In Maria, child of her brother's late marriage, he now saw that beauty, or sort of physical genius, at the start. In Maria, this was without hesitation, without the halting influence that had bound Mrs Vesey up – yes and bound Henry up, from his boyhood, with her – in a circle of quizzical half-smiles. In revenge, he accused the young girl who moved him – who seemed framed, by some sort of anticipation, for the new catastrophic *outward* order of life – of brutality, of being without spirit. At his age, between two generations, he felt cast out. He felt Mrs Vesey might not forgive him for having left her for a world at war.

Mrs Vesey blew out the blue flame under the kettle, and let the silver trapdoor down with a snap. She then gave exactly one of those smiles – at the same time, it was the smile of his mother's friend. Ronald Cuffe picked the petal from the sandwiches and rolled it between his fingers, waiting for her to speak.

'It is cold, *indoors*,' said Mrs Vesey. 'Maria, put another log on the fire – Ria, you say the most unfortunate things. We must remember Henry has had a shock. – Henry, let us talk about something better. You work in an office, then, since the war?'

'In a Ministry – in an office, yes.'

'Very hard? – Maria, that is all you would do if you went to England: work in an office. This is not like a war history, you know.'

Maria said: 'It is not in history yet.' She licked round her lips for the rest of the chocolate taste, then pushed her chair a little back from the table. She looked secretively at her wrist-watch. Henry wondered what the importance of time could be.

He learned what the importance of time was when, on his way down the avenue to the bus, he found Maria between two chestnut trees. She slanted up to him and put her hand on the inside of his elbow. Faded dark-pink stamen from the flowers above them had moulted down on to her hair. 'You have ten minutes more, really,' she said. 'They sent you off ten minutes before your time. They are frightened someone would miss the bus and come back; then

132

everything would have to begin again. As it is always the same, you would not think it would be so difficult for my aunt.'

'Don't talk like that; it's unfeeling; I don't like it,' said Henry, stiffening his elbow inside Maria's grasp.

'Very well, then: walk to the gate, then back. I shall be able to hear your bus coming. It's true what they said – I'm intending to go away. They will have to make up something without me.'

'Maria, I can't like you. Everything you say is destructive and horrible.'

'Destructive? – I thought you didn't mind.'

'I still want the past.'

'Then how weak you are,' said Maria. 'At tea I admired you. The past – things done over and over again with more trouble than they were ever worth? – However, there's no time to talk about that. Listen, Henry: I must have your address. I suppose you *have* an address now?' She stopped him, just inside the white gate with the green drippings: here he blew stamen off a page of his notebook, wrote on the page and tore it out for her. 'Thank you,' said Maria, 'I might turn up – if I wanted money, or anything. But there will be plenty to do: I can drive a car.'

Henry said: 'I want you to understand that I won't be party to this – *in any way.*'

She shrugged and said. 'You want *them* to understand' – and sent a look back to the house. Whereupon, on his entire being, the suspended charm of the afternoon worked. He protested against the return to the zone of death, and perhaps never ever seeing all this again. The cruciform lilac flowers, in all their purples, and the colourless mountains behind Mrs Vesey's face besought him. The moment he had been dreading, returning desire, flooded him in this tunnel of avenue, with motors swishing along the road outside and Maria standing staring at him. He adored the stoicism of the group he had quitted – with their little fears and their great doubts – the grace of the thing done over again. He thought, with nothing left but our brute courage, we shall be nothing but brutes.

'What is the matter?' Maria said. Henry did not answer: they turned and walked to and fro inside the gates. Shadow played over her dress and hair: feeling the disenchantedness of his look at her she asked again, uneasily, 'What's the matter?'

'You know,' he said, 'when you come away from here, no one will care any more that you are Maria. You will no longer be Maria, as a matter of fact. Those looks, those things that are said to you – they make you, you silly little girl. You are you only inside their spell. You may think action is better – but who will care for you when you only act? You will have an identity number, but no identity. Your whole existence has been in contradistinction. You may think you want an ordinary fate – but there is no ordinary fate. And that extraordinariness in the fate of each of us is only recognized by your aunt. I admit that her view of life is too much for me – that is why I was so stiff and touchy today. But where shall we be when nobody has a view of life?'

'You don't expect me to understand you, do you?'

'Even your being a savage, even being scornful – yes, even that you have got from them. – Is that my bus?'

'At the other side of the river: it has still got to cross the bridge. – Henry –' she put her face up. He touched it with kisses thoughtful and cold. 'Goodbye,' he said, 'Miranda.'

'– Maria –'

'Miranda. This is the end of *you*. Perhaps it is just as well.'

'I'll be seeing you –'

'You'll come round my door in London – with your little new number chained to your wrist.'

'The trouble with you is, you're half old.'

Maria ran out through the gates to stop the bus, and Henry got on to it and was quickly carried away.

Katherine Mansfield

Life of Ma Parker

When the literary gentleman, whose flat old Ma Parker cleaned every Tuesday, opened the door to her that morning, he asked after her grandson. Ma Parker stood on the doormat inside the dark little hall, and she stretched out her hand to help her gentleman shut the door before she replied. 'We buried 'im yesterday, sir,' she said quietly.

'Oh, dear me! I'm sorry to hear that,' said the literary gentleman in a shocked tone. He was in the middle of his breakfast. He wore a very shabby dressing-gown and carried a crumpled newspaper in one hand. But he felt awkward. He could hardly go back to the warm sitting-room without saying something – something more. Then because these people set such store by funerals he said kindly, 'I hope the funeral went off all right.'

'Beg parding, sir?' said old Ma Parker huskily.

Poor old bird! She did look dashed. 'I hope the funeral was a – a – success,' said he. Ma Parker gave no answer. She bent her head and hobbled off to the kitchen, clasping the old fish bag that held her cleaning things and an apron and a pair of felt shoes. The literary gentleman raised his eyebrows and went back to his breakfast.

'Overcome, I suppose,' he said aloud, helping himself to the marmalade.

Ma Parker drew the two jetty spears out of her toque and hung it behind the door. She unhooked her worn jacket and hung that up too. Then she tied her apron and sat down to take off her boots. To take off her boots or to put them on was an agony to her, but it had been an agony for years. In fact, she was so accustomed to the pain that her face was drawn and screwed up ready for the twinge before she'd

135

so much as untied the laces. That over, she sat back with a sigh and softly rubbed her knees . . .

'Gran! Gran!' Her little grandson stood on her lap in his button boots. He'd just come in from playing in the street.

'Look what a state you've made your gran's skirt into – you wicked boy!'

But he put his arms round her neck and rubbed his cheek against hers.

'Gran, gi' us a penny!' he coaxed.

'Be off with you; Gran ain't got no pennies.'

'Yes, you 'ave.'

'No, I ain't.'

'Yes, you 'ave. Gi' us one!'

Already she was feeling for the old, squashed, black leather purse.

'Well, what'll you give your gran?'

He gave a shy little laugh and pressed closer. She felt his eyelid quivering against her cheek. 'I ain't got nothing,' he murmured . . .

The old woman sprang up, seized the iron kettle off the gas stove and took it over to the sink. The noise of the water drumming in the kettle deadened her pain, it seemed. She filled the pail, too, and the washing-up bowl.

It would take a whole book to describe the state of that kitchen. During the week the literary gentleman 'did' for himself. That is to say, he emptied the tea-leaves now and again into a jam jar set aside for that purpose, and if he ran out of clean forks he wiped over one or two on the roller towel. Otherwise, as he explained to his friends, his 'system' was quite simple, and he couldn't understand why people made all this fuss about housekeeping.

'You simply dirty everything you've got, get a hag in once a week to clean up, and the thing's done.'

The result looked like a gigantic dustbin. Even the floor was littered with toast crusts, envelopes, cigarette ends. But Ma Parker bore him no grudge. She pitied the poor young gentleman for having no one to look after him. Out of the smudgy little window you could see an immense expanse of sad-looking sky, and whenever there were clouds they looked very worn, old clouds, frayed at the edges, with holes in them, or dark stains like tea.

While the water was heating, Ma Parker began sweeping the floor. 'Yes,' she thought, as the broom knocked, 'what with one thing and another I've had my share. I've had a hard life.'

Even the neighbours said that of her. Many a time, hobbling home with her fish bag, she heard them, waiting at the corner, or leaning over the area railings, say among themselves, 'She's had a hard life, has Ma Parker.' And it was so true she wasn't in the least proud of it. It was just as if you were to say she lived in the basement-back at Number 27. A hard life! ...

At sixteen she'd left Stratford and come up to London as kitching-maid. Yes, she was born in Stratford-on-Avon. Shakespeare, sir? No, people were always arsking her about him. But she'd never heard his name until she saw it on the theatres.

Nothing remained of Stratford except that 'sitting in the fireplace of a evening you could see the stars through the chimney', and 'Mother always 'ad 'er side of bacon 'anging from the ceiling.' And there was something – a bush, there was – at the front door, that smelt ever so nice. But the bush was very vague. She'd only remembered it once or twice in the hospital, when she'd been taken bad.

That was a dreadful place – her first place. She was never allowed out. She never went upstairs except for prayers morning and evening. It was a fair cellar. And the cook was a cruel woman. She used to snatch away her letters from home before she'd read them, and throw them in the range because they made her dreamy ... And the beedles! Would you believe it? – until she came to London she'd never seen a black beedle. Here Ma always gave a little laugh, as though – not to have seen a black beedle! Well! It was as if to say you'd never seen your own feet.

When that family was sold up she went as 'help' to a doctor's house, and after two years there, on the run from morning till night, she married her husband. He was a baker.

'A baker, Mrs Parker!' the literary gentleman would say. For occasionally he laid aside his tomes and lent an ear, at least, to this product called Life. 'It must be rather nice to be married to a baker!' Mrs Parker didn't look so sure.

'Such a clean trade,' said the gentleman.

Mrs Parker didn't look convinced.

'And didn't you like handing the new loaves to the customers?'

'Well, sir,' said Mrs Parker, 'I wasn't in the shop above a great deal. We had thirteen little ones and buried seven of them. If it wasn't the 'ospital it was the infirmary, you might say!'

'You might, *indeed*, Mrs Parker!' said the gentleman, shuddering, and taking up his pen again.

Yes, seven had gone, and while the six were still small her husband was taken ill with consumption. It was flour on the lungs, the doctor told her at the time . . . Her husband sat up in bed with his shirt pulled over his head, and the doctor's finger drew a circle on his back.

'Now, if we were to cut him open *here*, Mrs Parker,' said the doctor, 'you'd find his lungs chock-a-block with white powder. Breathe, my good fellow!' And Mrs Parker never knew for certain whether she saw or whether she fancied she saw a great fan of white dust come out of her poor dear husband's lips . . .

But the struggle she'd had to bring up those six little children and keep herself to herself. Terrible it had been! Then, just when they were old enough to go to school, her husband's sister came to stop with them to help things along, and she hadn't been there more than two months when she fell down a flight of steps and hurt her spine. And for five years Ma Parker had another baby – and such a one for crying! – to look after. Then young Maudie went wrong and took her sister Alice with her; the two boys emigrimated, and young Jim went to India with the army, and Ethel, the youngest, married a good-for-nothing little waiter who died of ulcers the year little Lennie was born. And now little Lennie – my grandson . . .

The piles of dirty cups, dirty dishes, were washed and dried. The ink-black knives were cleaned with a piece of potato and finished off with a piece of cork. The table was scrubbed, and the dresser and the sink that had sardine tails swimming in it . . .

He'd never been a strong child – never from the first. He'd been one of those fair babies that everybody took for a girl. Silvery fair curls he had, blue eyes, and a little freckle like a diamond on one side of his nose. The trouble she and Ethel had had to rear that child! The things out of the newspapers they tried him with! Every Sunday morning Ethel would read aloud while Ma Parker did her washing.

> DEAR SIR, – Just a line to let you know my little Myrtil was laid out for dead ... After four bottils ... gained 8 lbs. in 9 weeks, *and is still putting it on.*

And then the egg cup of ink would come off the dresser and the letter would be written, and Ma would buy a postal order on her way to work next morning. But it was no use. Nothing made little Lennie put it on. Taking him to the cemetery, even, never gave him a colour; a nice shake-up in the bus never improved his appetite.

But he was Gran's boy from the first ...

'Whose boy are you?' said old Ma Parker, straightening up from the stove and going over to the smudgy window. And a little voice so warm, so close, it half stifled her – it seemed to be in her breast under her heart – laughed out, and said, 'I'm Gran's boy!'

At that moment there was a sound of steps, and the literary gentleman appeared, dressed for walking.

'Oh, Mrs Parker, I'm going out.'

'Very good, sir.'

'And you'll find your half-crown in the tray of the inkstand.'

'Thank you, sir.'

'Oh, by the way, Mrs Parker,' said the literary gentleman quickly, 'you didn't throw away any cocoa last time you were here – did you?'

'No, sir.'

'*Very* strange. I could have sworn I left a teaspoonful of cocoa in the tin.' He broke off. He said softly and firmly, 'You'll always tell me when you throw things away – won't you, Mrs Parker?' And he walked off very well pleased with himself, convinced, in fact, he'd shown Mrs Parker that under his apparent carelessness he was as vigilant as a woman.

The door banged. She took her brushes and cloths into the bedroom. But when she began to make the bed, smoothing, tucking, patting, the thought of little Lennie was unbearable. Why did he have to suffer so? That's what she couldn't understand. Why should a little angel child have to arsk for his breath and fight for it? There was no sense in making a child suffer like that.

... From Lennie's little box of a chest there came a sound as though something was boiling. There was a great lump of something bubbling in his chest that he couldn't get rid of. When he coughed, the sweat sprang out on his head; his eyes bulged, his hands waved, and the great lump bubbled as a potato knocks in a saucepan. But what was more awful than all was when he didn't cough he sat against the pillow and never spoke or answered, or even made as if he heard. Only he looked offended.

'It's not your poor old gran's doing it, my lovey,' said old Ma Parker, patting back the damp hair from his scarlet ears. But Lennie moved his head and edged away. Dreadfully offended with her he looked – and solemn. He bent his head and looked at her sideways as though he couldn't have believed it of his gran.

But at the last ... Ma Parker threw the counterpane over the bed. No, she simply couldn't think about it. It was too much – she'd had too much in her life to bear. She'd borne it up till now, she'd kept herself to herself, and never once had she been seen to cry. Never by a living soul. Not even her own children had seen Ma break down. She'd kept a proud face always. But now! Lennie gone – what had she? She had nothing. He was all she'd got from life, and now he was took too. Why must it all have happened to me? she wondered. 'What have I done?' said old Ma Parker. 'What have I done?'

As she said those words she suddenly let fall her brush. She found herself in the kitchen. Her misery was so terrible that she pinned on her hat, put on her jacket and walked out of the flat like a person in a dream. She did not know what she was doing. She was like a person so dazed by the horror of what has happened that he walks away – anywhere, as though by walking away he could escape ...

It was cold in the street. There was a wind like ice. People went flitting by, very fast; the men walked like scissors; the women trod like cats. And nobody knew – nobody cared. Even if she broke down, if at last, after all these years, she were to cry, she'd find herself in the lock-up as like as not.

But at the thought of crying it was as though little Lennie leapt in his gran's arms. Ah, that's what she wants to do, my dove. Gran wants to cry. If she could only cry now, cry for a long time, over everything beginning with her first place and the cruel cook, going on to the doctor's, and then the seven little ones, death of her husband, the children's leaving her, and all the years of misery that led up to Lennie. But to have a proper cry over all these things would take a long time. All the same, the time for it had come. She must do it. She couldn't put it off any longer; she couldn't wait any more ... Where could she go?

'She's had a hard life, has Ma Parker.' Yes, a hard life, indeed! Her chin began to tremble; there was no time to lose. But where? Where?

She couldn't go home; Ethel was there. It would frighten Ethel out of her life. She couldn't sit on a bench anywhere; people would come arsking her questions. She couldn't possibly go back to the gentleman's flat; she had no right to cry in strangers' houses. If she sat on some steps a policeman would speak to her.

Oh, wasn't there anywhere where she could hide and keep herself to herself and stay as long as she liked, not disturbing anybody, and nobody worrying her? Wasn't there anywhere in the world where she could have her cry out – at last?

Ma Parker stood, looking up and down. The icy wind blew out her apron into a balloon. And now it began to rain. There was nowhere.

141

Pauline Melville

Tuxedo

Everybody knows that Tuxedo has good ideas about as often as a hen has teeth. Which is why Tuxedo is on his own this particular night, crouching with his ear to the tumbrils of a small safe behind the counter of the video shop. The snag is that Tuxedo is not built for crouching lower than a pool table. His left foot has cramp and his blue satin boxer shorts are twisted in his crotch causing him aggravation. On top of all this, twiddling the knobs on the safe is getting him nowhere and he is overcome by a craving for sweet potato pie.

Anybody, from the Frontline to the Backline, could tell you that Tuxedo is jinxed. Take one instance. Yesterday Tuxedo buys a second-hand car for three hundred and fifty, cash. This guy gives him all the documents but when he gets home the log book turns out to be an old parking summons and the car is clearly hotter than Tina Turner; if Tuxedo thinks he has just laid his hands on some pure Jamaican sensimilla, you can bet your bottom dollar that it will turn out to be home-grown from Kensal Rise; even the all-night Kentucky Fried Chicken runs out of corn on the cob as soon as Tuxedo steps through the portals. Anybody could tell you that the day Tuxedo gets lucky will be the day it snows ink. Which is why he has this near-permanent frowning glare on his face, a wicked screw that most people mistake for hostility when in fact it's the anxious stare of one who knows that God has been up most of the night laying traps for him, sometimes in the shape of things, mostly in the shape of people.

* * *

Tuxedo glares at the safe:

'Come on, you bastard,' he mutters, then adds: 'It's all right, God, it's the safe I'm talking to, not you.'

Of one thing, Tuxedo is certain. God is white. Once, when he was younger, he had listened to his militant cousin explain how white people had tricked the world into believing that Jesus was white when he was really black and so it followed that God was black too, or at least brown, more likely brown seeing that he was from the Middle East. Tuxedo told all this to his mother who gave him several licks for daring to call God 'a dutty half-breed'. In the end, Tuxedo came to his own conclusion, simple and to the point. If God isn't white, how come black people have such a hard time?

Anyway, Tuxedo is in this office which is short of space what with the desk and the metal filing cabinets. The light is on because Tuxedo doesn't much like the dark ever since the school caretaker accidentally locked him in the boiler room where he was hiding because he couldn't remember the lyrics of the seven-times table. Since then, Tuxedo gets jittery in the dark. So he is tackling his first safe, solo, with the light on in the back of Edwards Electronic and TV Rental shop. As it happens, he has only discovered the safe by chance, stubbing his toe against it while he is in the back of the shop looking for some Vaseline.

The reason Tuxedo is looking for Vaseline is this. He has broken into the shop to get a video recorder for Dolores Burton, his current mainsqueeze. Now all the episodes of *Hill Street Blues* would lead you to believe that during the commission of these minor felonies, people break out in a nervous sweat. Just when the music gets tense and trembly and the camera goes into close-up, you can see sweat streaming down their faces. Not so Tuxedo. His face goes all dry and cracky, especially the lips, which prompts him to put down the video recorder and look in the back of the shop on the offchance of finding some Vaseline or even a little Johnson's baby oil to rub in his face. And this is precisely what he is doing when the safe attracts the attention of his big toe.

* * *

143

Outside, the August night is warm. The street is still strewn with litter from the market and the sweet glutinous smell of rotting vegetables hangs in the air. The street lamps cast a bilious glow over the row of shops. Parked outside the video shop is Tuxedo's getaway car, a powder-blue Vauxhall Chevette, the same one he got yesterday. The choice of this particular model, he considers to be a stroke of genius. Any passing beast would think it belonged to an estate agent or a lady doctor. Not that many lady doctors park their cars outside a video shop at three in the morning with the driver's door open and the sound cassette pumping out into the night air:

> 'Trouble you de trouble mi – no I
> I woudda jus' flash me ting.'

The car chants away rhythmically to itself. A few doors down, the burglar alarm in the chemist's shop shrills monotonous and unattended. Tuxedo twists the knobs on the safe impatiently. Nobody is about.

Nobody is about, that is, except Frankie Formosa, known to his girlfriends as 'Mr Too Handsome to Work', who happens to stroll around the corner on his way back from picking up a ten pound draw from Mr Mighty's Ace Shebeen. He is draining the last drop from a can of vanilla nutriment so he doesn't at first spot the car. But just as he throws the empty can into the gutter, he sights up the means of transport that would save him a fifteen-minute walk back to Ladbroke Grove. Besides, there is no one around to admire him walking through the streets in his new Tachini tracksuit and trainers to match. Don't think that Frankie is in any way unfit enough for such a walk. Frankie is always super-plus fit when he comes out of jail because he spends all his time there in the gym. Although this time he could not get all the exercise he wanted on account of a little squirt called Mouth-Mouth. Mouth-Mouth is Frankie's sister's boyfriend and it is sheer bad luck that he turns up in jail at the same time as Frankie because Frankie did not really want it known that he was inside for such a minor offence as driving round the streets without a licence and had put it about that he was in jail for the more prestigious and universally popular offence of assaulting a policeman. Then Mouth-Mouth comes in and spills the beans which meant that it was Mouth-Mouth who got assaulted and Frankie had to continue getting what exercise he could in the restricting confines of the punishment block.

So Frankie pulls to a halt on the opposite side of the road to the Chevette.

'Yuh free to look but don' you dare stare,' chants the car happily. But Frankie is not staring. He is giving quick looks up and down the street checking out whether Fate has actually come up trumps and offered him a deserted street and an unlocked car at one and the same time. He crosses back towards the car. On the pavement are large fragments of glass from the plate-glass door. The door itself swings carelessly on its hinges and although there is a light on in the back, nobody seems to be there. This is because Tuxedo is bent double on the floor having about as much luck with the combination on the safe as he did with his seven-times table. Frankie waits for a moment or two in the doorway of the Ace Liquor Mart.

> 'When something good – we say it Bad.
> Bubble you de bubble mi – yes I
> I woudda jus' dip an' run een.'

The car has now given up all pretensions of good breeding and is singing in a gruff, suggestive voice to the accompanying sounds of a deep thumping bass and whistling bullets. Frankie peeps out warily from the doorway. Nobody in sight. He slips round the front of the car and slides into the driver's seat, shutting the door gently behind him. Ten seconds later, Frankie Formosa is heading smoothly towards the block of flats in Notting Hill Gate which the council uses to house, temporarily, people they don't like.

Tuxedo has cramp. He shifts and stands up. He abandons the attempt to open the safe in the shop and decides to take it home with him along with the video cassette recorder. That will impress Dolores. On the desk is a grubby cream telephone and Tuxedo is sorely tempted to give Dolores a bell just to show how cool his nerve is under pressure. Sensing, however, that time, like most things, is not on his side, he resists the impulse. Which is just as well because

Dolores has long time since taken her tail off to Ozo's Club where she is sandwiched between two gentlemen both with wet-look hairstyles smothered in Dax pomade and each competing with the other as to who can buy her one of the over-priced drinks at the bar.

Life never deals out a hand of entirely bum cards. Mr George Evans, proprietor and manager of Edwards Electronics, is a man for whom the notion of good salesmanship is twinned with the notion of well-greased hair. In the third drawer of the desk, Tuxedo comes across Mr Evans's king-size jar of Vaseline pure petroleum jelly. And it is while he is rubbing it on his face that he becomes aware of a change of sounds from outside. The raunchy upful beat from his car has been replaced by the disjointed, mechanical, crackling voices that spurt so unexpectedly from the radios policemen wear on their chests. Tuxedo steps cautiously from the lighted office holding up the jar of Vaseline like a candle. In the darkened exterior of the shop he makes out three silhouettes, one of them pushing away broken glass with its foot.

Wappen Bappen – Tuxedo is under arrest.

It takes him five seconds to decide against pleading racial harassment and on his face as he walks sheepishly to the door is the same expression of disgust, disbelief and exasperation as when he misses an easy shot in the snooker hall. This expression changes when he reaches the street. His delicate pale blue ladies' saloon car has metamorphosed into a big, businesslike Rover with jazzy red and blue markings and a revolving blue light on top, for all the world like it is the Metropolitan Police mobile disco.

'Just a minute. Just a minute,' says Tuxedo in pure bewilderment before accepting the invitation from two of the police to step in the back of the car. The third one remains behind reasoning seriously with his radio.

* * *

146

The night sky has that purplish haze and Tuxedo catches sight of it between the faded, peeling, white house fronts. He is gazing up in that direction because he is conducting one of his silent conversations with the Almighty as the car cruises along:

'You bastard. Yes guy, it's you I'm talkin' to. Nuff trouble you give me. Spiteful I call it. Fucking spite.' Tuxedo talks to God in the same way he talks to the police, in his London accent, saving the Jamaican for his mates. Then suddenly he remembers the small packet of herb in his underpants. Casually, he slips his hand into the elasticated waistband of his boxer shorts. The move goes unnoticed. He slips his hand further down and starts fishing imperceptibly for the tiny packet of ganga secreted in his yellow underpants. All the while, he stares morosely out of the car window. One discreet cough and Tuxedo has in his mouth about two square inches of *The Voice* newspaper, umpteen seeds and bits of stick as well as several heads and leaves of ganga.

'Lock the fucker in the cell if he won't talk.' Detective Sergeant Blake sounds weary. Tuxedo's mother has taught him never to speak with his mouth full. 'Check with the owner what's missing from the shop.' Tuxedo is taken downstairs and put in the fourth cell along the row.

One hour later, Mr Evans of Edwards Electronics has checked and double-checked and confirmed to the remaining policeman that the only item missing from the premises is the pot of Vaseline. Tuxedo is sprawling on a hard bed with the grey blanket wrapped round him and one big smile on his face. He has discovered that he can talk to God Jamaica-style like one black man to another. It makes God feel more like one of the boys:

'Is wha' mi a go do? Oonoo help mi nuh? Is jus' one lickle degi-degi ting me a tek, one lickle pot of cream fi oil mi face. Mi a hear seh yuh work in mysterious ways. Show mi nuh. Don' gwaan bad about it. Remember Tuxedo don' business wid violence.'

The more Tuxedo chats in this confidential manner, the more he realizes that things are not nearly as bad as they might be. He could have been caught with the stolen Chevette, the video machine, the office safe and a bunch of weed. As it is, there is only the Vaseline

147

to be reckoned with. A little fine probably. Dolores will no doubt kick up because her favourite tape has gone with the car. Tuxedo thinks of Dolores for a minute, tucked up under the candlewick bedspread, her right hand under her jaw, which is how she sleeps, and wonders if there is any sweet potato pie left in the fridge. Tuxedo wants to get back to Dolores and hug her up for a while. He gets this rush of warmth towards her which spills over and includes God. On the whole, events have not turned out too badly:

'Yes mi baas,' says Tuxedo to God. 'Now me see how it is yuh work dis ting out fi me in the best possible way.'

In the charge room, Detective Sergeant Blake is getting confused as he tries to take down Tuxedo's statement:

'So you broke into the TV shop . . .'

'To get some Vaseline,' adds Tuxedo, helpfully.

'Why didn't you go into the chemist's?'

'The chemist's was shut,' says Tuxedo.

Detective Sergeant Blake decides to charge Tuxedo quickly and go home. Tuxedo has much the same idea. Once charged, he asks if it is OK for him to go now and get ready to appear in court in the morning in case the magistrates do not fully appreciate the vision of him appearing before them in his boxer shorts.

'You're not going anywhere,' says Blake tetchily. 'We haven't been able to establish that the address you gave is the correct one. So you will stay here and we will take you to court in the morning.'

'Phone my girlfriend. She's at home,' protests Tuxedo.

'We've already tried phoning twice and a constable has called round there. There's nobody there.'

Mystified, Tuxedo allows himself to be led back to cell number four.

'What's the time?' he asks anxiously, as the policeman is about to bang the door to.

'Half-past four.'

Where is Dolores? Why isn't she asleep in bed the one night he needs her to be in? Where the hell is Dolores?

Tuxedo is mightily vex. He walks up and down the cell for a bit then looks at the window which is set high up in the wall. The top is curved, the bars are painted cream, the panes are of unbreakable, dingy plastic. Behind them the sun is beginning to rise. He crosses the room and stands on tiptoe to look out.

'White bastard!' he yells at the pale, dawn sky.

Grace Paley

Samuel

Some boys are very tough. They're afraid of nothing. They are the ones who climb a wall and take a bow at the top. Not only are they brave on the roof, but they make a lot of noise in the darkest part of the cellar where even the super hates to go. They also jiggle and hop on the platform between the locked doors of the subway cars.

Four boys are jiggling on the swaying platform. Their names are Alfred, Calvin, Samuel, and Tom. The men and the women in the cars on either side watch them. They don't like them to jiggle or jump but don't want to interfere. Of course some of the men in the cars were once brave boys like these. One of them had ridden the tail of a speeding truck from New York to Rockaway Beach without getting off, without his sore fingers losing hold. Nothing happened to him then or later. He had made a compact with other boys who preferred to watch: Starting at Eighth Avenue and Fifteenth Street, he would get to some specified place, maybe Twenty-third and the river, by hopping the tops of the moving trucks. This was hard to do when one truck turned a corner in the wrong direction and the nearest truck was a couple of feet too high. He made three or four starts before succeeding. He had gotten this idea from a film at school called *The Romance of Logging*. He had finished high school, married a good friend, was in a responsible job and going to night school.

These two men and others looked at the four boys jumping and jiggling on the platform and thought, It must be fun to ride that way, especially now the weather is nice and we're out of the tunnel and way high over the Bronx. Then they thought, These kids do seem to be acting sort of stupid. They *are* little. Then they thought of some of the brave things they had done when they were boys and jiggling didn't seem so risky.

150

The ladies in the car became very angry when they looked at the four boys. Most of them brought their brows together and hoped the boys could see their extreme disapproval. One of the ladies wanted to get up and say, Be careful you dumb kids, get off that platform or I'll call a cop. But three of the boys were Negroes and the fourth was something else she couldn't tell for sure. She was afraid they'd be fresh and laugh at her and embarrass her. She wasn't afraid they'd hit her, but she was afraid of embarrassment. Another lady thought, Their mothers never know where they are. It wasn't true in this particular case. Their mothers all knew that they had gone to see the missile exhibit on Fourteenth Street.

Out on the platform, whenever the train accelerated, the boys would raise their hands and point them up to the sky to act like rockets going off, then they rat-tat-tatted the shatterproof glass pane like machine guns, although no machine guns had been exhibited.

For some reason known only to the motorman, the train began a sudden slowdown. The lady who was afraid of embarrassment saw the boys jerk forward and backward and grab the swinging guard chains. She had her own boy at home. She stood up with determination and went to the door. She slid it open and said, 'You boys will be hurt. You'll be killed. I'm going to call the conductor if you don't just go into the next car and sit down and be quiet.'

Two of the boys said, 'Yes'm', and acted as though they were about to go. Two of them blinked their eyes a couple of times and pressed their lips together. The train resumed its speed. The door slid shut, parting the lady and the boys. She leaned against the side door because she had to get off at the next stop.

The boys opened their eyes wide at each other and laughed. The lady blushed. The boys looked at her and laughed harder. They began to pound each other's back. Samuel laughed the hardest and pounded Alfred's back until Alfred coughed and the tears came. Alfred held tight to the chain hook. Samuel pounded him even harder when he saw the tears. He said, 'Why you bawling? You a baby, huh?' and laughed. One of the men whose boyhood had been more watchful than brave became angry. He stood up straight and looked at the boys for a couple of seconds. Then he walked in a citizenly way to the end of the car, where he pulled the emergency cord. Almost at once, with a terrible hiss, the

151

pressure of air abandoned the brakes and the wheels were caught and held.

People standing in the most secure places fell forward, then backward. Samuel had let go of his hold on the chain so he could pound Tom as well as Alfred. All the passengers in the cars whipped back and forth, but he pitched only forward and fell head first to be crushed and killed between the cars.

The train had stopped hard, halfway into the station, and the conductor called at once for the trainmen who knew about this kind of death and how to take the body from the wheels and brakes. There was silence except for passengers from other cars who asked, What happened! What happened! The ladies waited around wondering if he might be an only child. The men recalled other afternoons with very bad endings. The little boys stayed close to each other, leaning and touching shoulders and arms and legs.

When the policeman knocked at the door and told her about it, Samuel's mother began to scream. She screamed all day and moaned all night, though the doctors tried to quiet her with pills.

Oh, oh, she hopelessly cried. She did not know how she could ever find another boy like that one. However, she was a young woman and she became pregnant. Then for a few months she was hopeful. The child born to her was a boy. They brought him to be seen and nursed. She smiled. But immediately she saw that this baby wasn't Samuel. She and her husband together have had other children, but never again will a boy exactly like Samuel be known.

Shena Mackay

Evening Surgery

A Chopin prelude was strained through the speaker that stood on a little shelf on the surgery wall above a garish oil painting that shone in the cruel neon striplight that picked out the lines and blemishes and red-hawed eyes of the patients on the black vinyl benches. Mavis Blizzard, senior receptionist, was proud of that picture; it had been painted by one of 'her' old ladies, a purblind resident of Peacehaven House for the Elderly, which she visited regularly, cheering up the old girls, surreptitiously putting right the great holes and loops that shaky fingers made in bits of knitting, jollying them along when they grew tearful over old snapshots that she had persuaded them to show. No matter that the picture was upside down, the artist had now lost her sight completely; it would hang as a testament to their friendship. From time to time the name of one of the four doctors flashed on a board, a buzzer sounded and a patient departed; the telephone rang, Mavis answered it, and greeted favoured customers by name when they came through the door; her two minions busied themselves among files and coffee cups; although they wore blue overalls like Mavis's own, they seemed interchangeable, merged into one subdued lady in glasses, for she was the star of the surgery. Sounds of passing cars came through the glittering black panes of the window, people coughed, pages turned. The music stopped abruptly, then an orchestral selection from *South Pacific* washed softly over the surgery.

'That's better!' announced Mavis Blizzard brightly. 'We'd all have been asleep in a minute. Dr Frazer's choice. Much too highbrow for my taste.'

She was leaning out of the hatch behind which she operated and enveloped her audience in a conspiratorial wink. As she opened her eye she couldn't believe that the young woman in the corner was

153

almost glaring at her. She had a quick read of her notes before sending them in to Doctor. An invisible hand had placed a cup of coffee at her elbow; she clattered the pink cup with a red waxy smear on its rim on to the saucer.

'Well, I won't be sorry to get home tonight. I've been on my feet since six o'clock this morning and my poor hubby will have to get his own tea tonight. It's his Church Lads' Band night. They're practising some carols to entertain the old folks at my senior citizens' party, bless them,' she announced to one of her sidekicks or to the surgery at large.

If there were any who thought that her husband had had a lucky reprieve, they were rifling through the *Reader's Digest or Woman and Home* and registered nothing.

The telephone rang.

'Hello, you're through to surgery appointments.'

Her voice grew louder.

'Of course, Mr Jackson. Is it urgent, only Doctor's very booked up tomorrow? What seems to be the trouble? Pardon? Oh, your waterworks, Mr Jackson.'

Someone sniggered behind the *Tatler*, others squirmed on the squeaky vinyl at this public shaming. It was enough to send two girls into fits; they snorted through their noses. The old man beside them moved an inch or two away from their cropped, hennaed heads, their earrings, their dark red mouths.

'You'll be old yourselves someday and it won't seem so funny then,' he said. The comic they hid behind shook in disbelief. Mavis Blizzard rolled her eyes; her own daughter was a Queen's Guide.

'– well,' she went on, 'Doctor's got a late surgery on Thursday. We could squeeze you in then at eleven forty-five. That's eleven forty-five on Thursday then. Not at all. See you Thursday then. Byee' – by which time the unfortunate man might be damned or drowned.

'Deaf as a post, bless him,' she explained.

'Next Patient for Dr Frazer' flashed up on the board. The woman in the corner jumped up, tossing her magazine on to the table, upsetting the neat pile. Mavis watched her disappearing jeans disapprovingly. She prided herself on getting on with all sorts, you had to in this job, but this one she definitely did not trust.

* * *

The woman walked into the consulting room. The doctor rose.

'Cathy! How've you been?'

'Bloody awful. You?'

'The same.'

She sat down. He took her hand across the desk.

'It's good to see you.'

'Yes.'

She was staring at the desk, twisting a paperclip with her other hand. There was so much to say, and nothing. They sat in silence. Then, as if suddenly aware of the briefness of their time together, he came round to her side of the desk.

When Mrs Blizzard had to come in to fetch a file the patient was buttoning her shirt. Dr Frazer stood beside her. Nothing unusual about that. So why did she feel as if she was fighting her way through an electric storm? The stethoscope lay on the desk.

'Come and see me again if the pain persists,' said Dr Frazer.

'OK,' she replied casually, without so much as a thank you or goodbye. Mavis rolled her eyes at the doctor, expecting a confirmatory twinkle at this rudeness, but he was grinning like a fool at the closing door.

'Well, really!' she said.

He pressed the buzzer as she went out. Nobody appeared. He was just going to buzz again when Mavis led in a frail old lady and helped her on to the chair.

'Let's make you comfy. I'll just pop this cushion behind your back.'

What a kind soul she is, the doctor thought. He realized that he hated her.

'Well, Miss Weatherby, let's have a look at you.' What's left of you, he almost said.

She struck the cushion to the floor with a tiny, surprisingly strong, gloved hand.

'I want you to give me a certificate, Doctor.'

'What kind of certificate?'

'A certificate to confirm that I am unfit; not well enough to attend her senior citizens' party!'

He had to fumble in his desk drawer, but she had seen his face.

'You can laugh, you don't have to go!'

She was laughing too, but tears glittered in her eyes.

'Neither do you, surely?'

'She's threatening to collect me in her car. I'll have to wear a paper hat and sing carols to the accompaniment of her husband's appalling boys' band, and then her daughter will hide behind the door and shake a bell and she will say, 'Hark! What's that I hear? Can it be sleighbells?' and her husband will leap into the room in a red plastic suit and give us bathcubes.'

'Couldn't you pretend a prior engagement?'

'She's managed to ferret out that I have no family or friends. She wants me to move into Peacehaven as soon as there's a coffin, I mean a bed.'

'I'm afraid I can't really give you a certificate, but I'll have a word if you like, about the party . . .', wondering how he could.

'It wouldn't do any good. I'll just have to turn out the lights and lie in bed until she's gone.'

'No you won't. Come and spend the evening with us. I can't promise any paper hats or bathcubes, but it would be nice if you did. OK?'

'OK,' she managed.

As she left he saw that her legs had shrunk to two sticks around which her stockings hung like pale, deflated balloons. Time unravels us, he thought, like old, colourless silk flags in churches, which have outlasted their cause.

At home, Mary's eyes, which lately a vague unhappiness had turned a darker blue, dimmed and were brighter, like mussels washed by a little wave, when he told her of Miss Weatherby's plight.

'Of course she must come. But why does she hate Mavis? She's so kind.'

'She's a ghoul. She feeds on illness and disease and death!' he burst out.

'But . . .' Mary closed her mouth. She went to the sideboard and poured him a drink, as she gave it to him he took her hand and kissed it. 'Thank you,' he said.

* * *

156

When Catherine opened the gate of the little terraced house she shared with her daughter and son she saw the room as a stranger might, through the unpulled curtains, lit from within like a candle whose wick has burned down below its rim; the paper moon suspended from the ceiling, the bowl of satsumas, the old chairs, the television glowing softly like a tank of tropical fish; the familiar tenderized and made strange by the darkness.

At seven o'clock in the morning a soapy fragment of moon was dissolving in the damp sky; birds assembled in the trees to wait for their breakfast, black shapes against the blue that slowly suffused the cloud; Catherine sat on the back step. She was glad that he could not see her in the old summer dress she was wearing as a nightdress, Lucy's clogs and her ex-husband's ropey bathrobe; her eyes stung as she looked along the length of her cigarette, such a lot to get through, her mouth felt thick and dry; behind her in the kitchen the washing machine threw a last convulsion and gave a little sob, like a child who has fallen asleep crying. Paul would be back from his paper round in a minute. She went in and ran a bath. As she lay in the water, left disagreeably tepid by the washing machine's excesses, she saw how she had failed with her husband, whose robe huddled in a heap on the floor; she had never let him see that she needed him. Because she had known that he would fail her. But if she had. She recalled Hardy's poem 'Had you but wept'. Such watery half-thoughts as float past when people are alone and naked vanished with the bubbles down the plughole.

She put the kettle on, switched on the radio, woke Lucy, made tea, made toast, made two packed lunches, flung the washing over the line, a jumble of socks and jeans and shirts that would not dry in the damp air, tested Lucy on her Latin while she combed her hair and coaxed some moribund mascara on to her lashes; the phone rang – for Lucy; wrote a note for Paul, who had been absent the day before; the phone rang again; Paul, eating the remains of yesterday's pudding from the fridge, dropped the bowl on the floor, Lucy ironed a PE shirt and the pop music on the radio crackled like an electric drill so she turned it up. No doubt, Catherine thought sourly, the Frazers are sitting down to muesli and motets. Someone called; the children left.

She found a splinter of glass on the floor near the sink and held it up to the light from the window. If one just stared at pretty glass fragments or soap bubbles or the sediment round the taps or studied the patterns left by spilled pudding on the tiles. Is that what it's like to be mad; or sane? But if everyone did there would be no glass, no iridescent bubbles in the washing-up bowl. Even as these thoughts drifted through her mind the glass splinter was in the pedal bin, a cloth was attacking the bleary taps. As she attempted to leave the house a plant pulled her back with a pale parched reproachful frond. 'I'll water you tonight,' she promised, but had to run back for the watering can and then run down the road, as usual, to the bookshop where she worked.

Her legs ached. With every book token, every cookery book, every DIY handbook, every copy of *Old Surrey in Pictures, Bygone Surrey, Views of Old Guildford, Views of Old Reigate, Views of Old Dorking,* every *Wine Bibber's Guide* that she sold she felt less Christmassy. How stupid and greedy the customers were, flapping cheque books at her and Pat, the other assistant, slapping fivers down on the counter so that they had to pick them up, taking all the change so that she had to go to the bank twice for more.

'Isn't Christmas shopping murder? Isn't it hell?' the customers said. 'I'll be glad when it's all over!'

Greetings flew from throats that sounded as if they were already engorged with mincemeat. No doubt several books were slipped into shopping bags.

'It must be lovely working here – all these lovely books!' people told them. 'I could browse for hours!'

'Oh, yes!' Pat agreed mistily, not seeing the floor which muddy feet had reduced to a football pitch and which she would not clean. She was twenty-nine and wore little girl shoes, and dresses which she made herself; Cathy thought that she must be too embarrassed to take her own measurements, because they never fitted very well. She spent her lunch hours in the stockroom eating packets of pale meat sandwiches and drinking tisanes, reading childrens' books and lives of the saints. Mr Hermitage, the shop's owner, who was bowing and gesticulating like a puppet in his velvet suit in the back of the shop, and who was too mean to employ a cleaner, did not like to ask Pat to wash the floor so Catherine's less spiritual hands were calloused by the mop.

158

When she got the chance Catherine went into the little kitchen behind the stockroom and put on the kettle and lit a cigarette. There was nowhere to sit so she leaned on the sink.

'I won't go to the surgery tonight,' she told herself. 'I mustn't. I know it's wrong. It's stealing. I'm not going to go.'

Mr Hermitage came in rubbing his hands.

'Coffee! That's good!'

His body contrived to brush against hers, as it always did.

'Sorry,' he said, patting her as if it had been an accident, as he always did.

She carried her coffee and a cup of cowslip tea for Pat into the shop, taking a gulp on the way to drown the smell of nicotine. Six or seven people stood at the counter, impatient at the speed of the two robots behind it. Pat rolled panic-stricken eyes at her; she was up to her ankles in spoiled wrapping paper. The sellotape sneered and snarled. As Catherine reached into the till Pat pressed the cash total button and the drawer slammed on her fingers. She yelled and swore. The customers looked offended; shop assistants' fingers don't have feelings, especially at Christmas time. Catherine waited for her nails to turn black. Now she would have to go to the surgery. Alas, her fingers remained red and painful, but could not justify medical treatment. Her hopes abated with the swelling.

She arrived home late that evening and dumped her heavy carrier bag. It had taken ages to do the money; it had been twelve pounds short. Pat had been flustered into making several over-rings; customers had asked for books and then changed their minds after they had been rung up, there was an unsigned cheque. Catherine's face ached with smiling at browsers and buyers; she had eaten nothing all day. There was a warm smell of cooking.

'Dinner's almost ready,' said Lucy.

'I've made you a cup of tea, Mum,' said Paul.

She did not let herself notice the potato peelings in the sink, the spilled sugar, the tea bag on the floor, which he had thrown at the pedal bin, and missed, the muddy rugby boots on the draining board.

'You're dear, kind children,' she said. She unbent her cold fingers one by one.

'Mum? ... Are you all right? I mean, you're not ill or anything are you?'

'Of course I'm not. Why?'

'It's just that you look so sad. You never smile. And you went to the doctor's.'

'It's just the Christmas rush in the shop. You've no idea what hell it is.'

Catherine felt ashamed. She saw that she was dragging them into into her own abyss.

'Nobody's going out tonight, are they? And nobody's coming round? Good.'

She wanted to draw them to her, to spend the sort of family evening they had enjoyed before this madness had overtaken her; the curtains closed, the gas fire blooming like a bed of lupins, the telly on; the sort of evening you thought nothing of.

Halfway through 'Top of the Pops' the phone rang.

'I'll get it!' Catherine grabbed the receiver with crossed fingers.

'Hello, could I speak to Lucy, please?'

Dumbly she handed it over. They had agreed that he should not ring or come to the house. And yet . . .

Later the door-bell rang; Catherine clamped herself to her chair.

'Door, Paul.'

A male voice at the door. She stopped herself from running to the mirror and glued her eyes to her book, looking up slowly as Paul slouched back, behind him John Frazer metamorphosed into a tall boy, through a sort of grey drizzle.

'Hi. I've come to copy Paul's maths.'

'Oh. How about some coffee, Paul?' Or a quadruple gin. Or a cup of hemlock.

As the boys went to the kitchen Catherine said to Lucy, 'Actually I don't feel very well. I keep getting headaches. The doctor gave me something for them, but it doesn't seem to work. I think I'd better go back tomorrow . . . so don't worry if I'm a bit late . . . Well, I suppose I'd better get on with the ironing.'

'Would you like me to do it?'

'Of course, but I'd rather you did your homework.'

Anyway it would kill an hour or so.

* * *

160

The case of a certain Dr Randal and a Mrs Peacock had, naturally, aroused much interest among the receptionists in the surgery. Mr Peacock had brought an action against the doctor, accusing him of the seduction of his wife, and it had become a minor *cause célèbre*, partly because there were those who thought that the rules should be changed, partly because there had been no meaty scandal of late, no politicians floundering in the soup. Dressed like their namesakes, he in flashy tie and cufflinks, she in drab brown tweed plumage, an invisible blanket of shame over her bowed head, the Peacocks strutted and scurried across evening television screens and stared greyly from the newspaper in Mavis Blizzard's hand.

'Of course, it's the woman I blame in a case like this; a doctor's in such a vulnerable position ... It's the children I feel sorry for. And his poor wife! What she must be going through.'

Mrs Peacock must be pecked to pieces by the rest of the flock; her brown feathers, torn by Mavis's sharp bill, drifted about the surgery.

'And she's not even pretty!'

'Must have hidden charms,' came with a timid snort from behind Mavis.

'Ssh.'

If their words were not, as she suspected, directed at Catherine, they none the less pierced the magazine she was using as a shield and managed to wound.

Mavis slotted in a cassette of Christmas carols and hummed along with it. A sickly fragrance of bathcubes emanated from her sanctum; she was wrapping them for her senior citizens' party, in between answering the phone and all her other tasks. Her daughter, Julie, who had come in to give her a hand, nudged her.

'That's Paul Richards's mother. He goes to our school. He's really horrible. This afternoon he and his friends turned on all the taps in the cloakroom and flooded it. They were having a fight with the paper towels. You never saw such a mess! Water all over the place, other people's belongings getting soaked! I wouldn't like to be them tomorrow morning!' she concluded with satisfaction.

A little boy, about two years old, was running round the table, bumping into people's knees, falling over their feet. His mother grew tired of apologizing and held him captive. He screamed and would not be pacified. She had to let him go.

'What's all this then? What's all the noise about?'

Mavis Blizzard had emerged and was advancing in a sort of crouch in her blue overall on the startled child, who backed into his mother's knees.

'We can't have you disturbing all my ladies and gentlemen, can we? Let's see if I've got anything in my pockets for good little boys, shall we?'

He clenched his hands behind his back. Mavis winked at his mother and dangled a sweet. The child gave a sob and flung himself on his mother banging his hard, hot head on her lip. A red weal sprang up immediately and the glassy eyes spilled over. The child joined a loud grizzling to her silent tears.

'I think we'd better let this little fellow see Doctor next, don't you?' Mavis looked round. 'That is, if nobody objects?'

Nobody objected. The mother jerked to her feet a silent girl in glasses who had kept her head bent over a comic throughout, and ran the gauntlet with her and the crying boy and a heavy shopping bag.

'Poor kid,' remarked Mavis as she returned to her hatch. 'She does find it hard to cope, bless her. My heart bleeds for these one-parent families. Not that I'm one to make judgements, live and let live, and lend a helping hand where you can, that's my motto.'

For a moment they were all bathed in her tolerance.

'Drat that phone! Blessed thing never stops, does it?' Evidently she forgot that most of her audience had been guilty . . .

'Hello, you're through to the surgery, can I help you? Of course. I'll drop the prescription in myself on my way home. No, it's no trouble at all. Save you turning out on your poor old legs in this nasty weather. No, it's hardly out of my way at all, and I shall be late home anyway. We've got a full house tonight!' She uttered the noise which served her for a laugh.

Catherine looked at her watch; the appointments were running ten minutes late. She reached for another magazine and saw a jar of carnations on the windowsill, slender stems in the beaded water, like cranes' green delicate legs. As the bubbles streamed to the surface and clustered round the birds' knees she wished she had not come; she wished she was at home cooking the evening meal. It was absurd; it was making neither of them happy.

'You said to come back if the pain persists. It persists.'

'Thank you for coming tonight. I've missed you so much.'

To her dismay she was crying. He scorned the box of pink tissues provided by Mavis for patients who wept and gave her his own white handkerchief. Even as she dried her eyes she realized that it had been laundered by his wife; it didn't help.

'It's not enough,' she said. 'At first it was enough just to know that you were on the same planet. Then I thought, if only we could be alone for five minutes, then it was an hour, then an evening ... it's almost worse than nothing.'

The door handle squeaked. Instinctively she leaped from his arms to the couch and turned her face to the wall as Mavis came in.

'Mrs Blizzard! I wish you wouldn't barge in when I'm with a patient!'

'You forget that I'm a trained nurse,' she bridled. 'Dr Macbeth always asks me to be present when he's examining a female patient. I'm sorry to have disturbed you!'

She slammed the door behind her.

'I know it's not enough,' he said quickly. 'Can you get out one evening? Meet me somewhere?'

'Yes.' So that was that. How easily principles, resolutions not to hurt anybody died.

He leaned over the couch and kissed her; she felt the silky hair on the back of his neck, his ear; she felt his hand run gently down her body, on her thigh.

'Don't, don't,' she said, but she didn't take his hand away.

'An urgent call for you, Dr Frazer,' squawked Mavis through the intercom.

Catherine slid off the couch and found the floor with trembling legs. Her face was burning.

'Just a minute,' he put his hand over the receiver. 'I love you. See you tomorrow morning? About eleven? We'll arrange something.'

Outside in the street she found his handkerchief in her hand and buried her face in it and, looking up, saw the stars over its white edge. As she lay in bed that night she put her hand where his hand had been.

163

He was late. She pushed her trolley up and down the aisles of Safeway's, putting in something from time to time for appearances' sake, waiting, loitering, buffeted, causing obstructions.

'I'm sorry.'

She whirled round. The smile withered on her face. A little girl was seated in his trolley. He rolled his eyes towards his wife's back, at the deli counter. As Mary turned to them he said, 'How are you?'

'As well as can be expected.'

She blundered to the checkout with her almost empty trolley.

'. . . a patient,' she heard him explain, betray.

After crying for a while in the precinct she had to go to Sainsbury's to finish her shopping and trudge home to transform herself from lovesick fool into mother. Loud music hit her as she opened the front door. An open biscuit tin stood on the kitchen table, seven or eight coffee cups had been placed thoughtfully in the sink; she had to wash them before she could start on the potatoes. Several pairs of muddy shoes lay about the floor. Teenage laughter came from the bedrooms. Not jealousy. Not bitterness. Just pain. Like the dull knife blade stabbing a potato. The telephone rang. Feet thudded towards it.

'She's not in.'

'I am in!' She shouted and ran to the telephone.

'Cathy?' Her ex-husband.

'Oh, it's you.'

She had to stop herself from hurling the receiver at the wall.

'Cathy, I was wondering about Christmas . . .'

'Yes?'

'Well, I just . . . I mean, what are you doing?'

'Oh, this and that. One or two parties. The children have lots of things on. We're going to my parents' on Boxing Day, all the family will be there. I suppose we'll go to church on Christmas Day. Why?'

She longed to be beyond the tinsel and crackers, in the greyness of January where melancholy was the norm.

'Well, I just wondered. I mean, it's a bit of a bleak prospect – the kids and all . . .'

'You mean you want to come here. You may as well. It makes

no difference to me. Why not? It will make everything just about perfect.'

She replaced the receiver, not wanting to wonder about whatever desperation had driven him to call, unable to contemplate any pain but her own.

At last the three of them sat down to lunch.

'Mum?'

'What?'

'We are going to get a tree, aren't we?'

She looked at her children, her babies; Lucy's long hair glittering in the electric light, Paul's pretty spikes. She determined to stop being such a pain.

'Of course we are. We always do, don't we? I thought we might go this afternoon.'

'Great.'

'You'll come, won't you, Paul?'

'Well, you'll need me to carry it, if we get a big one, won't you?'

At nine o'clock that night John was called to Miss Weatherby's house. A neighbour, taking his dog for a stroll, had been alarmed by her milk-bottle on the step, her newspaper jutting from the door, and had found the old lady very ill. Had she had any family, John might have comforted them: she died in my arms; but she had none. He drove away feeling infinitely sad. There was only one person he wanted to tell about it; to lie in her arms and be comforted, to have wiped away the memory of the one card on Miss Weatherby's mantelpiece which said, 'A Merry Xmas From Your Unigate Milkman'. He stopped at an off-licence and bought a bottle of whisky. What a shabby figure he had cut, with furtive meetings in the surgery and Safeway's. Why hadn't he telephoned her this morning after the fiasco in Safeway's? OK, so he hadn't been alone for a minute, but he could have made some excuse to get out to a call-box, couldn't he? Why on earth did she put up with him? There could be only one reason. She loved him. He switched on the radio. Music flooded the car. He was singing as he drove into her road. Soft pink and green and yellow stars, Christmas tree lights, glowed against black windows. He was touched by these talismans in little human habitations. But when he reached her house he couldn't park. A line of cars stretched along each side of the street. He caught

165

the poignant sparkle of her Christmas tree in a gap in the curtains. He found a space in the next road and walked back. The terraced house seemed to be jumping up and down between its neighbours, blazing with loud music. A volley of laughter hit him. He turned and walked away. He dumped the bottle in its fragile tissue paper in a litter-bin.

As Catherine cleared away the remains of last night's impromptu party from the carpet the telephone rang faintly through the Hoover's noise. She switched off. Only the radio. She switched on again. The phone rang again. Nothing. At last she decided that the ringing was conjured up by her own longing or was some electrical malevolence. The phantom telephone drilled out a shameful memory; last night, among her friends, as the party wore on, alcohol sharpened her loneliness until she dialled his number. Even as she did so she told herself that she would hate herself in the morning. She did. A woman's sleepy voice had answered. She hung up. Boring into their bedroom. Disturbing pink sheets; dreams.

She couldn't read, couldn't watch television, couldn't listen to the radio. She had to admit relief when the children went out that afternoon; when you are a mother, you can't scream that you are dying of loneliness and boredom, that your soul is rotting within you. Let his shadow fall across the glass in the door. Let the telephone ring. She stood at the window for a long time staring at sodden leaves and apples, then she grabbed her coat and went to borrow a dog from a neighbour, a patchy-skinned mongrel called Blue.

Ducks pulled melancholy trails across the dingy lake. It was no better here. When she first met John, people's faces, pavements, skies were irradiated, familiar buildings blossomed with pretty cornices and swags of flowers. Now how ugly and pointless everybody seemed, the whole of Creation a dreary mistake. Damp seeped into her boots, her coat hung open in the cold wind, her bare hands were purple and scratched from the sticks that the fawning Blue laid at her feet to be flung. She glared at the parents trundling past with their prams and tricycles, forgetting that she had been happy once doing that. She found a bench out of the wind and huddled in the corner; the wind whipped the flame from her lighter as she tried to light a cigarette. Ignited, it tasted dirty, the smoke blew into her hair. Without realizing it she was rocking slowly back and forth on the bench, head hunched between her shoulders. If only she had never gone to that party in the summer.

'Do you know Dr Frazer?' someone had asked.

'Actually, I'm one of your patients.'

'Oh, I'm sorry . . . I should have recognized you . . .'

'It's all right, we've never met. I'm never ill.'

'That's a pity.'

She had not met his wife, who was at the far end of the room in a group round the fire, but now, Oh God, wasn't that them coming round the corner? There was no escape.

'Hello.'

The family surrounded her bench. Blue jumped up at John; she saw him wince as the claws raked his thigh. He threw a stick; Blue bolted after it.

'I'm sorry. Your trousers. They're all muddy.'

'Don't worry about those old things! I'm always trying to get him to throw them out, but somehow he always retrieves them!'

Mary gave her a wifely smile; it might as well have been a dead leaf falling or the crisp bag bowling down the path. Mary shivered.

Blue was back with the stick, grinning through frilled red gums.

'I didn't know you had a dog.'

'It's not mine. He belongs to a friend.'

The three children in knitted hats, and Mary, grew impatient. Catherine stood up.

'Goodbye then. Come on Blue.'

John bent over the dog, stroking it inordinately. 'Goodbye, Beautiful.' Fondling its ears.

As Catherine walked away she heard a child's voice say, 'Dad, can we have a dog?'

'Don't you think your mother has enough to do?' his voice snapped, as she had never heard it. Good. I hope your bloody afternoon's ruined. Intruding on her in her ratty fake fur coat, jeans frayed with mud, smoking a cigarette on a park bench, with a borrowed dog; flaunting his family, his wife in her neat tweed coat and matching blue woolly hat. Well, that's that then. It's over. Good. Him in that anorak of horrifying orange. They were welcome to each other. To complete the afternoon's entertainment Mavis Blizzard was bearing down the path pushing part of an old man, wrapped in a tartan rug, in a wheelchair.

When John arrived at the surgery on Monday morning Julie Blizzard was there with her mother.

'Morning, Doctor,' said Mavis.

'Morning, Doctor,' parroted the clone.

He searched his frosty brain for a pleasantry.

'I suppose you'll be leaving school soon, Julie? Any idea of what you want to do?'

'I'm going to work with underprivileged children.'

'They will be,' he muttered as he went through. Then he turned back. 'By the way, Miss Weatherby died on Saturday night.' Or escaped, he might have added.

'Oh dear, the poor soul,' said Mavis absentmindedly. Miss Weatherby merited a small sigh then Mavis added, 'It's the weather, I expect. You know what they say, a green December fills the churchyard. I've got to go over to the hospital myself this afternoon to visit an old boy, that is if he's lasted the night, I'd better check with Sister first. He's blind and his wife's . . .'

'Doctor,' called Julie after him as he turned away rudely, 'you'll get a surprise when you go into your consulting room!'

Grey, rainy light filtered through white paper cut-out Santas and snowflakes pasted on the window. He punched the black couch where soon a procession of flesh in various stages of decay would stretch out for his inspection, and none of it that which he wanted to see.

Catherine ducked down behind the counter as Mavis Blizzard entered the shop with much jangling of the bell and shook sleety pearls from her plastic hood. When she emerged it was to confront Mary, who gave her a vague smile, as if she thought she ought to know her, and went distractedly from one row of books to another. A pair of wet gloves was placed over Mary's eyes. She gave a little scream. Mavis uncurled her black playful fingers.

'Oh, Mavis! You made me jump!'

As she served people and found and wrapped books Catherine managed to catch snatches of conversation.

'. . . peaky. Down in the dumps.'

'. . . Nothing really . . .'

'I always start my Christmas shopping in the January sales. Just a few last minute things.'

'. . . he's just tired, I suppose . . . so bad tempered . . . I can't seem to do anything right . . .'

'You poor little fool,' thought Catherine, 'confiding in that old harridan.'

She stared icily at Mavis as she paid for her book, a reduced volume of freezer recipes, putting the change down on the counter rather than into her hand, but could not kill the thought; I first liked him because he was so kind and now he is less kind because of me.

It was way past the end of Pat's lunch hour. Catherine went into the kitchen and found her, sandwich drooping in her hand, enthralled by the life of a modern saint. She lifted her eyes dreamily from the page.

'Do you know,' she said dreamily, 'she drank the water in which the lepers had washed their feet!'

'I think I'm going to throw up,' said Catherine.

She saw that the sink was clogged with cowslip flowers. Then, at a brawling sound from the street, they both ran back into the shop. A gang of teenagers was rampaging down the pavement, school blazers inside out, garlands of tinsel round their necks and in their hair, which some of them had daubed pink or green. Catherine's eyes blurred at their youth, their faces pink with cold, the flying tinsel. One detached himself and banged on the window.

'Hello, Mum!'

She managed a weak salute.

'Disgusting! No better than animals!' said a customer's voice.

'At least they're alive!' Catherine retorted, because for the moment they were young animals, and not fossicking among freezer recipes and jokey books about golf and fishing.

'I thought she was such a nice girl,' the customer complained to another as they went out.

'It's the other one who's a nice girl,' her friend explained.

* * *

169

'If Blizzard answers, I'll hang up,' Catherine decided as she dialled surgery appointments. One of the underlings took the call. Hers was the last appointment of the evening. She couldn't believe the little scene that was being enacted in the waiting room. Mavis evidently had caught a woman in the act of tearing a recipe from one of the magazines.

'But it is dated 1978 . . .', the culprit was quavering in her own defence.

'That's not the point. It's the principle of the thing!'

Mavis thrust a pen and a sheet torn from a notepad at her.

'Here, you can copy it out, if you like. If everybody did that . . .'

It was impossible to see from the woman's bent head if she was writing ground almonds or ground glass, but when her turn to go in came her face was stained a deep red.

Mavis had only Catherine with whom to exchange a triumphant glance; their eyes met for an instant before she retreated to her sanctum, which, Catherine was amazed to see, was decked with Christmas cards.

'Next Patient for Dr Frazer.'

Catherine went in.

'I knew it! I knew it! I knew something was going on! What do you think I am? Stupid?'

John and Catherine were frozen together as in a freak snow-storm.

'It's disgusting! It's smutty! It's . . .'

'I realize that's how it must seem to you, but really, I assure you . . .'

Catherine felt his fingers slide from her breast.

'That's how it appears to me and that's how it is. What do you take me for?' I'm not stupid you know.' She turned on Catherine.

'You come here night after night and yet there's never any-thing written on your card, never any prescription. How do you explain that? Just because you couldn't hold your own husband you try to pinch someone else's! Well, you're not so clever as you think you are, or you, Dr Frazer! Perhaps you'd care to read this?'

She flung an evening paper on the desk. The verdict in the Randal and Peacock case. The condemned pair would not look.

'Guilty, of course. It's his wife I feel sorry for. And the children. What they must be going through! I'd hate Mary to suffer what that poor woman's –'

'You wouldn't!'

'I –' She had to duck as a paperweight flew past her head and crashed into the door, then Catherine was struggling into her coat.

'Don't go,' he said, but she was gone, blundering through the empty surgery in tears.

A trombone belched outside the window.

'Oh my Gawd, the mince pies!'

Mavis ran from the room as the broken notes of 'Silent Night' brayed. Les Blizzard and his Church Lads' Band had mustered outside to give the doctors a carol.

Someone had rescued Mavis's mince pies, her annual surprise to the doctors, from the little oven she had installed in the office; they were only slightly blackened. The festivities took place in Dr Macbeth's, the senior partner's, room. John looked round: the three receptionists in their blue overalls, Johnson sucking burnt sugar from a painful tooth and trying to smile, Baines eyeing the bottle, Macbeth, eyes moist with sweet sherry, mincemeat in his white moustache, giving a convincing performance as a lovable old family practitioner, which of course he was. The window, like his own, was decorated with white paper cut-outs. Macbeth raised his glass to Mavis.

'I have heard the Mavis singing.
His love song to the morn.
I have –'

'*Her* love song, surely,' corrected Mavis, reducing his song to a gulp of sherry.

John drained his glass.

'Well, Happy Christmas, everybody. I must be off.'

'But Doctor, you haven't pulled your cracker! You can't break up the party yet!'

Mavis was waving the coloured goad in his face. He grasped the

171

end and pulled. 'What is it?' scrabbling among their feet. 'Oh, it's a lucky charm. There, put on your hat!'

She crammed a purple crown on his head; it slipped over his eyes. As he pushed it up, to his horror, he saw a sprig of mistletoe revolving on a thread from the light.

'Ho ho ho,' rumbled Macbeth.

Under cover of the crackers' explosions John muttered, 'Do you think you could remove those bits of paper from my window? They block the light.'

She gave no sign of having heard.

'Oh, I almost forgot! Pressies! You first, Dr Frazer, as you've got to rush off.'

She crammed his weak arms with parcels.

'Just a little something for the children. You'll love little Katy's present! It's a doll that gets nappy rash when it wets itself! Isn't that a hoot? Whatever will they think of next?'

The minions duly hooted.

Catherine watched her ex-husband's feet tangle and tear wrapping paper. He sat down heavily beside her on the floor, pushing parcels out of his way, and pulled her to him. His shirt, an obvious Christmas present, perhaps from someone who wished he was with her now, burst open at the neck.

'I still fancy you, you know.'

The whisky smell was like a metal gate across his mouth. She wanted to howl and weep and, failing John's, any old shirt would do, even this one, smelling so new, with a frill down the front.

'Your shirt. I'm sorry.'

'It doesn't matter. I didn't like it anyway,' pressing a button into her eye.

The bookshop. Mr Hermitage. Pat. Christmas. I'll get through this one, she thought, then the next one and the next. But this will be the worst. The years ahead. Each day that she would not go to the surgery, would not pick up the phone. She saw a series of bleak victories, a lone soldier capturing pointless hills when there was no one to see.

* * *

'Do you want to watch the children opening their stockings?'

John realized that she had never had to ask this before; the Christmas tree wavered into a green glass triangle shot with lights; Mary's face, above her pink dressing-gown, was pale and wary; she had sensed his absence beside her in bed and come to find him, and now excited sounds were coming from the children's rooms.

'I love you,' he said.

For a moment, before he followed her upstairs, the doctor placed his hand over the pain in his heart. He knew it was incurable.

George Egerton

Virgin Soil

The bridegroom is waiting in the hall; with a trifle of impatience he is tracing the pattern of the linoleum with the point of his umbrella. He curbs it and laughs, showing his strong white teeth at a remark of his best man; then compares the time by his hunter with the clock on the stairs. He is florid, bright-eyed, loose-lipped, inclined to stoutness, but kept in good condition; his hair is crisp, curly, slightly grey; his ears peculiar, pointed at their tops like a faun's. He looks very big and well-dressed, and, when he smiles, affable enough.

Upstairs a young girl, with the suns of seventeen summers on her brown head, is lying with her face hidden on her mother's shoulder; she is sobbing with great childish sobs, regardless of reddened eyes and the tears that have splashed on the silk of her grey, going-away gown.

The mother seems scarcely less disturbed than the girl. She is a fragile-looking woman with delicate fair skin, smoothly parted thin chestnut hair, dove-like eyes, and a monotonous piping voice. She is flushing painfully, making a strenuous effort to say something to the girl, something that is opposed to the whole instincts of her life.

She tries to speak, parts her lips only to close them again, and clasp her arms tighter round the girl's shoulders; at length she manages to say with trembling, uncertain pauses:

'You are married now, darling, and you must obey' – she lays a stress upon the word – 'your husband in all things – there are – there are things you should know – but – marriage is a serious thing, a sacred thing' – with desperation – 'you must believe that what your husband tells you is right – let him guide you – tell you –'

There is such acute distress in her usually unemotional voice that the girl looks up and scans her face – her blushing, quivering, faded

174

face. Her eyes are startled, fawn-like eyes as her mother's, her skin too is delicately fair, but her mouth is firmer, her jaw squarer, and her piquant, irregular nose is full of character. She is slightly built, scarcely fully developed in her fresh youth.

'What is it that I do not know, Mother? What is it?' – with anxious impatience. 'There is something more – I have felt it all these last weeks in your and the others' looks – in his, in the very atmosphere – but why have you not told me before – I –' Her only answer is a gush of helpless tears from the mother, and a sharp rap at the door, and the bridegroom's voice, with an imperative note that it strikes the nervous girl is new to it, that makes her cling to her mother in a close, close embrace, drop her veil and go out to him.

She shakes hands with the best man, kisses the girl friend who has acted as bridesmaid – the wedding has been a very quiet one – and steps into the carriage. The Irish cook throws an old shoe after them from the side door, but it hits the trunk of an elder-tree, and falls back on to the path, making that worthy woman cross herself and mutter of ill-omens and bad luck to follow; for did not a magpie cross the path first thing this morning when she went to open the gate, and wasn't a red-haired woman the first creature she clapped eyes on as she looked down the road?

Half an hour later the carriage pulls up at the little station and the girl jumps out first; she is flushed, and her eyes stare helplessly as the eyes of a startled child, and she trembles with quick running shudders from head to foot. She clasps and unclasps her slender, grey-gloved hands so tightly that the stitching on the back of one bursts.

He has called to the station-master, and they go into the refreshment-room together; the latter appears at the door and, beckoning to a porter, gives him an order.

She takes a long look at the familiar little place. They have lived there three years, and yet she seems to see it now for the first time; the rain drips, drips monotonously off the zinc roof, the smell of the dust is fresh, and the white pinks in the borders are beaten into the gravel.

Then the train runs in; a first-class carriage, marked 'engaged', is attached, and he comes for her; his hot breath smells of champagne, and it strikes her that his eyes are fearfully big and bright, and he offers her his arm with such a curious amused proprietary air that the girl shivers as she lays her hand in it.

The bell rings, the guard locks the door, the train steams out, and as it passes the signal-box, a large well-kept hand, with a signet ring on the little finger, pulls down the blind on the window of an engaged carriage.

Five years later, one afternoon on an autumn day, when the rain is falling like splashing tears on the rails, and the smell of the dust after rain fills the mild air with freshness, and the white chrysanthemums struggle to raise their heads from the gravel path into which the sharp shower has beaten them, the same woman, for there is no trace of girlhood in her twenty-two years, slips out of a first-class carriage; she has a dressing-bag in her hand.

She walks with her head down and a droop in her shoulders; her quickness of step is due rather to nervous haste than elasticity of frame. When she reaches the turn of the road, she pauses and looks at the little villa with the white curtains and gay tiled window-boxes. She can see the window of her old room; distinguish every shade in the changing leaves of the creeper climbing up the south wall; hear the canary's shrill note from where she stands.

Never once has she set foot in the peaceful little house with its air of genteel propriety since that eventful morning when she left it with him; she has always framed an excuse.

Now as she sees it a feeling of remorse fills her heart, and she thinks of the mother living out her quiet years, each day a replica of the one gone before, and her resolve weakens; she feels inclined to go back, but the waning sun flickers over the panes in the window of the room she occupied as a girl. She can recall how she used to run to the open window on summer mornings and lean out and draw in the dewy freshness and welcome the day, how she has stood on moonlight nights and danced with her bare white feet in the strip of moonlight, and let her fancies fly out into the silver night, a young girl's dreams of the beautiful, wonderful world that lay outside.

A hard dry sob rises in her throat at the memory of it, and the fleeting expression of softness on her face changes to a bitter disillusion.

176

She hurries on, with her eyes down, up the neat gravelled path, through the open door into the familiar sitting-room.

The piano is open with a hymn-book on the stand; the grate is filled with fresh green ferns, a bowl of late roses perfume the room from the centre of the table. The mother is sitting in her easy chair, her hands folded across a big white Persian cat on her lap; she is fast asleep. Some futile lace work, her thimble, and bright scissors are placed on a table near her.

Her face is placid, not a day older than that day five years ago. Her glossy hair is no greyer, her skin is clear, she smiles in her sleep. The smile rouses a sort of sudden fury in the breast of the woman standing in her dusty travelling cloak at the door, noting every detail in the room. She throws back her veil and goes over and looks at herself in the mirror over the polished chiffonnier – scans herself pitilessly. Her skin is sallow with the dull sallowness of a fair skin in ill-health, and the fringe of her brown hair is so lacking in lustre that it affords no contrast. The look of fawn-like shyness has vanished from her eyes, they burn sombrefully and resentfully in their sunken orbits, there is a dragged look about the mouth; and the keynote of her face is a cynical disillusion. She looks from herself to the reflection of the mother, and then turning sharply with a suppressed exclamation goes over, and shaking the sleeping woman not too gently, says:

'Mother, wake up, I want to speak to you!'

The mother starts with frightened eyes, stares at the other woman as if doubting the evidence of her sight, smiles, then cowed by the unresponsive look in the other face, grows grave again, sits still and stares helplessly at her, finally bursting into tears with a

'Flo, my dear, Flo, is it really you?'

The girl jerks her head impatiently and says drily:

'Yes, that is self-evident. I am going on a long journey. I have something to say to you before I start! Why on earth are you crying?'

There is a note of surprised wonder in her voice mixed with impatience.

The older woman has had time to scan her face and the dormant motherhood in her is roused by its weary anguish. She is ill, she thinks, in trouble. She rises to her feet; it is characteristic of the

177

habits of her life, with its studied regard for the observance of small proprieties, and distrust of servants as a class, that she goes over and closes the room door carefully.

This hollow-eyed, sullen woman is so unlike the fresh girl who left her five years ago that she feels afraid. With the quiet selfishness that has characterized her life she has accepted the excuses her daughter has made to avoid coming home, as she has accepted the presents her son-in-law has sent her from time to time. She has found her a husband well-off in the world's goods, and there her responsibility ended. She approaches her hesitatingly; she feels she ought to kiss her, there is something unusual in such a meeting after so long an absence; it shocks her, it is so unlike the one she has pictured; she has often looked forward to it, often; to seeing Flo's new frocks, to hearing of her town life.

'Won't you take off your things? You will like to go to your room?'

She can hear how her own voice shakes; it is really inconsiderate of Flo to treat her in this strange way.

'We will have some tea,' she adds.

Her colour is coming and going, the lace at her wrist is fluttering. The daughter observes it with a kind of dull satisfaction, she is taking out her hat-pins carefully. She notices a portrait in a velvet case upon the mantelpiece; she walks over and looks at it intently. It is her father, the father who was killed in India in a hill skirmish when she was a little lint-locked maid barely up to his knee. She studies it with new eyes, trying to read what man he was, what soul he had, what part of him is in her, tries to find herself by reading him. Something in his face touches her, strikes some underlying chord in her, and she grinds her teeth at a thought it rouses.

'She must be ill, she must be very ill,' says the mother, watching her, 'to think I daren't offer to kiss my own child!' She checks the tears that keep welling up, feeling that they may offend this woman who is so strangely unlike the girl who left her. The latter has turned from her scrutiny of the likeness and sweeps her with a cold criticizing look as she turns towards the door, saying: 'I *should* like some tea. I will go upstairs and wash off the dust.'

* * *

178

Half an hour later the two women sit opposite one another in the pretty room. The younger one is leaning back in her chair watching the mother pour out the tea, following the graceful movements of the white, blue-veined hands amongst the tea things – she lets her wait on her; they have not spoken beyond a commonplace remark about the heat, the dust, the journey.

'How is Philip, is he well?' The mother ventures to ask with a feeling of trepidation, but it seems to her that she ought to ask about him.

'He is quite well, men of his type usually are; I may say he is particularly well just now, he has gone to Paris with a girl from the Alhambra!'

The older woman flushes painfully, and pauses with her cup halfway to her lips and lets the tea run over unheeded on to her dainty silk apron.

'You are spilling your tea,' the girl adds with malicious enjoyment.

The woman gasps: 'Flo, but Flo, my dear, it is dreadful! What would your poor father have said! *No wonder* you look ill, dear, how shocking! Shall I – ask the vicar to – to remonstrate with him? –'

'My dear Mother, what an extraordinary idea! These little trips have been my one solace. I assure you, I have always hailed them as lovely oases in the desert of matrimony, resting-places on the journey. My sole regret was their infrequency. That is very good tea, I suppose it is the cream.'

The older woman puts her cup on the tray and stares at her with frightened eyes and paled cheeks.

'I am afraid I don't understand you, Florence. I am old-fashioned' – with a little air of frigid propriety – 'I have always looked upon matrimony as a sacred thing. It is dreadful to hear you speak this way; you should have tried to save Philip – from – from such a shocking sin.'

The girl laughs, and the woman shivers as she hears her. She cries –

'I would never have thought it of Philip. My poor dear, I am afraid you must be very unhappy.'

'Very,' with a grim smile, 'but it is over now, I have done with it. I am not going back.'

If a bomb had exploded in the quiet, pretty room the effect could hardly have been more startling than her almost cheerful statement. A big bee buzzes in and bangs against the lace of the older woman's cap and she never heeds it, then she almost screams:

'Florence, Florence, my dear, you can't mean to desert your husband! Oh, think of the disgrace, the scandal, what people will say, the' – with an uncertain quaver – 'the sin. You took a solemn vow, you know, and you are going to break it –'

'My dear Mother, the ceremony had no meaning for me, I simply did not know what I was signing my name to, or what I was vowing to do. I might as well have signed my name to a document drawn up in Choctaw. I have no remorse, no prick of conscience at the step I am taking; my life must be my own. They say sorrow chastens, I don't believe it; it hardens, embitters; joy is like the sun, it coaxes all that is loveliest and sweetest in human nature. No, I am not going back.'

The older woman cries, wringing her hands helplessly:

'I can't understand it. You must be very miserable to dream of taking such a serious step.'

'As I told you, I am. It is a defect of my temperament. How many women really take the man nearest to them as seriously as I did! I think few. They finesse and flatter and wheedle and coax, but truth there is none. I couldn't do that, you see, and so I went to the wall. I don't blame them; it must be so, as long as marriage is based on such unequal terms, as long as man demands from a wife as a right, what he must sue from a mistress as a favour; until marriage becomes for many women a legal prostitution, a nightly degradation, a hateful yoke under which they age, mere bearers of children conceived in a sense of duty, not love. They bear them, birth them, nurse them, and begin again without choice in the matter, growing old, unlovely, with all joy of living swallowed in a senseless burden of reckless maternity, until their love, granted they started with that, the mystery, the crowning glory of their lives, is turned into a duty they submit to with distaste instead of a favour granted to a husband who must become a new lover to obtain it.'

'But men are different, Florence; you can't refuse a husband, you might cause him to commit sin.'

'Bosh, Mother, he is responsible for his own sins, we are not bound to dry-nurse his morality. Man is what we have made him, his very faults are of our making. No wife is bound to set aside the demands of her individual soul for the sake of imbecile obedience. I am going to have some more tea.'

The mother can only whimper:

'It is dreadful! I thought he made you such an excellent husband, his position too is so good, and he is so highly connected.'

'Yes, and it is as well to put the blame in the right quarter. Philip is as God made him, he is an animal with strong passions, and he avails himself of the latitude permitted him by the laws of society. Whatever of blame, whatever of sin, whatever of misery is in the whole matter rests *solely* and *entirely* with you, Mother' – the woman sits bolt upright – 'and with no one else – that is why I came here – to tell you that – I have promised myself over and over again that I would tell you. It is with you, and you alone, the fault lies.'

There is so much of cold dislike in her voice that the other woman recoils and whimpers piteously:

'You must be ill, Florence, to say such wicked things. What have I done? I am sure I devoted myself to you from the time you were little; I refused' – dabbing her eyes with her cambric handkerchief – 'ever so many good offers. There was young Fortescue in the artillery, such a good-looking man, and such an elegant horseman, he was quite infatuated about me; and Jones, to be sure he was in business, but he was most attentive. Everyone said I was a devoted mother; I can't think what you mean, I –'

A smile of cynical amusement checks her.

'Perhaps not. Sit down, and I'll tell you.'

She shakes off the trembling hand, for the mother has risen and is standing next to her, and pushes her into a chair, and paces up and down the room. She is painfully thin, and drags her limbs as she walks.

'I say it is your fault, because you reared me a fool, an idiot, ignorant of everything I ought to have known, everything that concerned me and the life I was bound to lead as a wife; my physical needs, my coming passion, the very meaning of my sex, my wifehood and motherhood to follow. You gave me not one weapon in my hand to defend myself against the possible attacks of man at his worst. You sent me out to fight the biggest battle of a woman's life, the one in which she ought to know every turn of the game, with a white gauze' – she laughs derisively – 'of maiden purity as a shield.'

181

Her eyes blaze, and the woman in the chair watches her as one sees a frog watch a snake when it is put into its case.

'I was fourteen when I gave up the gooseberry-bush theory as the origin of humanity; and I cried myself ill with shame when I learnt what maternity meant, instead of waking with a sense of delicious wonder at the great mystery of it. You gave me to a man, nay more, you told me to obey him, to believe that whatever he said would be right, would be my duty; knowing that the meaning of marriage was a sealed book to me, that I had no real idea of what union with a man meant. You delivered me body and soul into his hands without preparing me in any way for the ordeal I was to go through. You sold me for a home, for clothes, for food; you played upon my ignorance, I won't say innocence, that is different. You told me, you and your sister, and your friend the vicar's wife, that it would be an anxiety off your mind if I were comfortably settled –'

'It is wicked of you to say such dreadful things!' the mother cries, 'and besides' – with a touch of asperity – 'you married him willingly, you seemed to like his attentions –'

'How like a woman! What a thorough woman you are, Mother! The good old-fashioned kitten with a claw in her paw! Yes, I married him willingly; I was not eighteen, I had known no men; was pleased that you were pleased – and, as you say, I liked his attentions. He had tact enough not to frighten me, and I had not the faintest conception of what marriage with him meant. I had an idea' – with a laugh – 'that the words of the minister settled the matter. Do you think that if I had realized how fearfully close the intimacy with him would have been that my whole soul would not have stood up in revolt, the whole woman in me cried out against such a degradation of myself?' Her words tremble with passion, and the woman who bore her feels as if she is being lashed by a whip. 'Would I not have shuddered at the thought of *him* in such a relationship? – and waited, waited until I found the man who would satisfy me, body and soul – to whom I would have gone without any false shame, of whom I would think with gladness as the father of a little child to come, for whom the white fire of love or passion, call it what you will, in my heart would have burned clearly and saved me from the feeling of loathing horror that has made my married life a nightmare to me – ay, made me a murderess in heart over and over again. This is not exaggeration. It

182

has killed the sweetness in me, the pure thoughts of womanhood – has made me hate myself and *hate you*. Cry, Mother, if you will; you don't know how much you have to cry for – I have cried myself barren of tears. Cry over the girl you killed' – with a gust of passion – 'why didn't you strangle me as a baby? It would have been kinder; my life has been a hell, Mother – I felt it vaguely as I stood on the platform waiting, I remember the mad impulse I had to jump down under the engine as it came in, to escape from the dread that was chilling my soul. What have these years been? One long crucifixion, one long submittal to the desires of a man I bound myself to in ignorance of what it meant; every caress' – with a cry – 'has only been the first note of that. Look at me' – stretching out her arms – 'look at this wreck of my physical self; I wouldn't dare to show you the heart or the soul underneath. He has stood on his rights; but do you think, if I had known, that I would have given such insane obedience, from a mistaken sense of duty, as would lead to this? I have my rights too, and my duty to myself; if I had only recognized them in time.

'Sob away, Mother; I don't even feel for you – I have been burnt too badly to feel sorry for what will only be a tiny scar to you; I have all the long future to face with all the world against me. Nothing will induce me to go back. Better anything than that; food and clothes are poor equivalents for what I have had to suffer – I can get them at a cheaper rate. When he comes to look for me, give him that letter. He will tell you he has only been an uxorious husband, and that you reared me a fool. You can tell him too, if you like, that I loathe him, shiver at the touch of his lips, his breath, his hands; that my whole body revolts at his touch; that when he has turned and gone to sleep, I have watched him with such growing hatred that at times the temptation to kill him has been so strong that I have crept out of bed and walked the cold passage in my bare feet until I was too benumbed to feel anything; that I have counted the hours to his going away, and cried out with delight at the sight of the retreating carriage!'

'You are very hard, Flo; the Lord soften your heart! Perhaps' – with trepidation – 'if you had had a child –'

'Of his – that indeed would have been the last straw – no, Mother.'

There is such a peculiar expression of satisfaction over something

– of some inner understanding, as a man has when he dwells on the successful accomplishment of a secret purpose – that the mother sobs quietly, wringing her hands.

'I did not know, Flo, I acted for the best; you are very hard on me!'

Later, when the bats are flitting across the moon, and the girl is asleep – she has thrown herself half-dressed on the narrow white bed of her girlhood, with her arms folded across her breast and her hands clenched – the mother steals into the room. She has been turning over the contents of an old desk; her marriage certificate, faded letters on foreign paper, and a bit of Flo's hair cut off each birthday, and a sprig of orange blossom she wore in her hair. She looks faded and grey in the silver light, and she stands and gazes at the haggard face in its weary sleep. The placid current of her life is disturbed, her heart is roused, something of her child's soul-agony has touched the sleeping depths of her nature. She feels as if scales have dropped from her eyes, as if the instincts and conventions of her life are toppling over, as if all the needs of protesting women of whom she has read with a vague displeasure have come home to her. She covers the girl tenderly, kisses her hair, and slips a little roll of notes into the dressing-bag on the table and steals out, with the tears running down her cheeks.

When the girl looks into her room as she steals by, when the morning light is slanting in, she sees her kneeling, her head, with its straggling grey hair, bowed in tired sleep. It touches her. Life is too short, she thinks, to make anyone's hours bitter; she goes down and writes a few kind words in pencil and leaves them near her hand, and goes quickly out into the road.

The morning is grey and misty, with faint yellow stains in the east, and the west wind blows with a melancholy sough in it – the first whisper of the fall, the fall that turns the world of nature into a patient suffering from phthisis – delicate season of decadence, when the loveliest scenes have a note of decay in their beauty; when a poisoned arrow pierces the marrow of insect and plant, and the leaves have a hectic flush and fall, fall and shrivel and curl in the night's cool; and the chrysanthemums, the 'goodbye summers' of the Irish peasants, have a sickly tinge in their white. It affects her, and she finds herself saying: 'Wither and die, wither and die, make compost for the loves of the spring, as the old drop out and make place for the new, who forget them, to be in their turn forgotten.' She hurries on, feeling that her autumn has come to her in her spring, and a little later she stands once more on the platform where she stood in the flush of her girlhood, and takes the train in the opposite direction.

Ailsa Cox

Just Like Robert de Niro

This is flesh-and-blood me, moving inside the machine. Music's coming up the gutters along Butter Street, Jerusalem Place, Artillery Street, and beyond these shadows the city lights are showing. The streets untangle into junctions, squares and tidal flows; then the orange lamps lead you into Hulme, where there's no sleep, where Michael is, which is Michael.

You get so you don't hear the music any more. Your limbs move of their own accord. I'm stretched thin, strung across the stacked balconies and boarded-up windows and dead lights of Hulme. I'm tired. I like being tired. At night, I like to feel the pressure of strangers all around me. I'm nowhere. Somewhere they're kicking down doors, the sirens are calling out for someone, everyone's looking out there, among the batteries of people, none of whom is ever Michael.

By day, the concrete's like every rainstorm that ever fell on Manchester, frozen in a grey ice age. They're rocks, the crescents. Look at them – Charles Barry, John Nash, Robert Adam, William Kent, they'll last for ever. They'll outlast any hope of mine, winging its way round the rows of washing, doorways, walkways. I remember two flats boarded up completely, then brown curtains – past another boarded up, I think. But I could be wrong. And they all look like that. The council must be giving out those shit-brown curtains. If I picked the right crescent, if I picked the right storey, the doorways would still be as numerous as the dead.

He said, 'I can't take you in there. It's a fucking shithole,' and slammed the door and walked too fast for me. He stopped, leaned over the edge and said, 'Where do you live then?'

There has to be such a thing as luck. I'll give up on justice, but there has to be such a thing as luck in life. So I come back here every time to look for him at random. Beneath me there's the warm brick of the Zion Hall where they filmed the Chicago scenes in *Reds*, and it does look like a film set, too good to be true, glowing vermilion by the pneumonic sixties grey. Diane Keaton trudged through all of Russia looking for Warren Beatty and she found him, she had to. He was hers; he was dying. Michael leaned over the edge, and all we saw was the repetition of the crescents in the rain.

I know this won't be Michael. There's a door-bell. But I'll try. I hear movement, rest, then movement again.

'Who is it?' a woman's voice calls, keeping behind those shut brown curtains.

'Excuse me. I'm sorry to disturb you . . .' When you say the words often enough, you don't hear them any more.

The face is greasy pale, spotty, lovebites on her neck. You can feel the neatness of the flat behind her. You can hear the telly.

'Is he a white guy?'

'Yes, he's about my age, tall, fair hair.' I don't go on adding all the other things he is. It sounds like I'm making him up. 'You can't miss him – very tall, very fair.'

'There's some students on the third floor,' she says doubtfully.

I still can't believe the Aaben's really shut. I thought it was me being insecure when I saw the lager running low, the spirits drained. I always waited for the movies to come to Hulme. I was there every Wednesday, no matter what was showing in the city centre. There was a time when the Aaben advertised in posh papers. There was a time when people brought their cars here, but soon there were only people like me, the holes in their coat linings full of old bus tickets.

I was there, making a fifth or sixth in the seats. Once I thought I was going to be the whole audience. Cameras rolling, action, just for me. I picked the dead-centre seat. I felt like Citizen Kane, until I realized when the lights were down I'd be in just the right spot for a Hitchcock murder. And if I dropped my cigarette packet, they'd know it was me.

I loved that place. I sat through a piece on *Monaco – Fairyland by the Sea*, then I waited while they tried to sell me the ultimate jean, Bacardi on the rocks, the bank that likes to say, for the ninety-ninth time – and then there was movement behind me. I could hear fidgeting, coughing, laughter.

The old Polish man in a trilby says, 'There's no one like that here. There's some students over the other side.'

'Real students? Or they look like students?'

He gets his keys out, sighs. 'Next time, make sure you get his address.'

Because you can't see through the windows, there aren't any clues. People are always kind, but if they aren't Michael, they're nothing.

Michael said, 'This place is finished. It's had it. Do you want a stereo? I'll get you one for ten quid. They'll steal anything and sell it for nothing, just to get fucking smack. I'll get you a stereo.'

The more I search, the less I believe in Michael. The young black men laugh and toss their dreadlocks, or they stand suspicious, tight-muscled, trim in the doorway. 'Go home. You won't find him.' The young white men are skinned rats, no relation to Michael. They don't answer me at all.

When darkness drops, I go home. There's a hole in my lining, but I've got a real coat with money in the pocket, and I'm scared. I've got a job, a crap job, but Michael's never had a job. I come from that part of Manchester where they still open little cafés and knick-knack shops. I don't need a new stereo. I've got one.

It wasn't a bad film. It was one of those heart-on-your-sleeve social issue movies. There was this grim-faced black detective who'd get to the truth, no matter what. I didn't mind, but it wasn't the kind of film that'd reach out and pull me inside. I could hear every rustle from the person behind me. It was worse than when you bring someone with you and they want to know who's who, and they sit with their arms folded while the tears are starting in your eyes. I could hear the wind racing round the crescents long before the credits were up. I could already feel the rain on my face. I wanted to go.

The other person held the door for me. 'What you think of that, then?'

'It was OK. I'll watch anything.'

'Yeah, it was rubbish.'

'Thank God for the Coppola on the telly.'

'Coppola,' he said, like a swear word, and he strode off.

They don't even make film stars like Michael any more, so why should he be here in Hulme? They don't even stand the short ones on boxes any more. So what makes me think I'm going to find Michael, with his superhero looks, leaning over a balcony ready to fly, no tricks, no strings, no coke, no heroin. I carry chalk with me to write in the pissy stairwells: I'M LOOKING FOR YOU MICHAEL. That way I can tell where I've already been.

When the phone rings, there's no chance of Michael, so I finish brushing my teeth, I mop my face and replace the towel carefully before I raise the receiver's weight.

I know who it is. It's that other guy Colin, saying do I want to go out for a meal? I don't want to sit still in a restaurant. I want to go out, because I can't stand being locked in. I've got to live. So we'll go dancing.

Michael and me, we like Klaus Kinski, Robert de Niro, Brando. 'You know,' he says, 'Robert de Niro goes swimming. He trains his body. That's what I'm doing. I go down Moss Side every morning, twenty lengths at a time, then straight in the gym.'

'He wasn't in very good shape in *Raging Bull*. He was twenty stone.'

He could do that. He could do what he wanted with his body. He's in control, just like I am.'

There's no phones working in Hulme.

It didn't seem strange the next week, to see Michael sitting on the Aaben steps. He said, 'I've got no money. I thought you might buy me a ticket.'

Michael says, 'I don't take drugs. I don't drink. I don't have sugar. Have you got anything to eat at your flat? What is it? I need a high-protein diet.' He says, 'I'm getting out of Hulme. I know a girl in the housing department, know what I mean?'

I smoke and I drink. I ride through Hulme in Colin's car. The indicator ticks at the crossroads. I turn the music louder – Baby be good to me – You don't have to cry no more – I'm sweet to you – till I can hear the songs no more.

Moss Side baths are nearly empty. I can see from the television screens there's nothing there, just young mums with their kids and some black lads cutting back and forth. When I'm moving through the blue water, I'm shot through light, the pure lights on camera, and I think: this is it, there's no one there. I'm going on for ever and I'll never sleep, night after day, day and night. I can't remember what he looks like any more. All I can see is the clean light of eyes and hair, but they can't be blue. The movie stars wear tinted contact lenses.

189

The phone's ringing. 'Listen, you're going to have to come to work. You aren't sick. You've been seen out. You're clubbing it.'

When there's a long pause at the end of the line, I know Colin's forgotten to turn the Ansaphone off. The mechanical voice begins: 'Hello. Colin speaking.' I needed him to buy me meals so I had enough money to pay for Michael at the pictures. I can't believe the Aaben's shut. And Michael gone. And it's only half-past nine, it's only eleven, it's two o'clock and I'm not asleep, five o'clock already, August already with no summer to speak of, one week, two weeks already off work. I need Colin's car to take me somewhere.

Television's not the same. Videos only remind you what you felt on the big screen. Bogart says, 'Sober up baby, I'm taking you home.' Trevor Howard leans over the table. He says, 'Shall I see you again?' Brando pours a couple of beers. The phone says, 'If you're not back on Monday, don't bother getting in touch.' The Ansaphone says, 'Hello. Colin speaking.' It'll be morning soon. I can go back to look for him.

I don't even know where I'm going. My legs move of their own accord. I know it's too late now, but I have to keep moving, just to know I'm alive. I'm getting rid of the phone. They've taken the telly and the video.

There's never anyone playing on the climbing frames and slides. The only kids are travellers' children, barefoot in rags. They brought their caravans right here, where there are endless boarded-up flats that nobody wants to live in.

The job was crap, but I need money. I can't pay my rent, but I can soon get a council place if I don't mind moving into Hulme.

Down the dole, everyone looks sick. No wonder he looks rough, standing in his line. I'm tired. My eyes are bad. But I know him. I'd know him anywhere, for the pride in his swimmer's body, bent as it is, the way tall people will hunch when they feel out of place. He knows me too. He looks over to me from out of his dark, demolished face.

In a movie, this is where we'd walk over to each other. There'd be close-ups of our smiling faces and the music would play louder. But you can't shoot a movie in a dole office. The lights turn everyone jaundiced. No wonder his face sags. No wonder the superman blue has gone from his eyes.

One day they'll knock the crescents down. Day by day they board more windows up, until entire rows are left vacant. One day Hulme won't be there any more. That'll be the shot, the big one – the crane swinging in the empty sky, then pan down to the rubble below, all of Manchester level at the camera's feet. But there's people in there – numb, nameless people, Michael. There has to be more than silence at the end, in the empty picture house. There has to be more than the sickness in his face.

In the movies, we walked out of line. In the movies, our hands met. We drove out of the city, we flew out of the sky. That's what always happens, in the movies.

Charlotte Mew

Spine

He saw now that they had always thought it, but it was only a year or two ago when his own crowd (he didn't count the family) had started chucking him, that that half-shaved amoeba Giles, who by the way, still owed him £15, had said to Billing that he had no spine.

It was not a fact. He had had it then. Wasn't he hawking his pen-and-inks round and getting some off at sweating prices and infernally insulted into the bargain? Hadn't he done the RA picture with Anna Baumann in it and those portraits for the Hotel Manager at Eastbourne – Self, wife and dogs? – he wanted to keep the dogs himself. And when he got the bounder's cheque hadn't he paid old Samuels three months off the year's rent owing; and £1 off the milk?

He must have been a pretty good tenant for old Samuels to have let it run on a year, and a pretty good customer to the milk people to have a bill of £6 odd. But they were neither of them pleased.

And if he had blued the rest on that little b– of a model Anna Baumann, that wasn't spending it on himself. Everyone knew she had gone straight for him (which of 'em hadn't) and he had come out of that dirty business very well. It had cost money. That was the worst of behaving decently; it always did. And nobody was pleased.

But if his work had gone to pieces he blamed old Samuels for kicking him out of the John Street rooms where he *was* working: six years and kicked out for nine months which he meant to pay. All Jews were dirt!

Then the tradespeople took old Sam's cue and behaved abominably; but the rooms had done it. No sitter would face the Studio stairs and the housekeeper was much too sweet on him. This open drain in the Caversham Road had given it the final knock. It would turn a Sargent into an Embankment screever – the wallpaper alone without the stove; the vile black tube with the vile square of red glass at the bottom.

A fire stood by you when you got home, dead sick of everything, to sit over, you and your pipe; but there was an enmity about the stove with its one red beastly eye that sucked the blood out of you, though the blighting enmity of the stove was the jocund dance to the filthy friendliness of that fungus, Mrs George; sizzling about the place like a cistern; saying everything over twice; pinching your bloaters with her poisonous thumb and coughing over everything.

She was not a liar, so from her point of view, he supposed the sheets were clean. They may have been before she started washing them – she liked them personally, as she did him; and refused to send them to the laundress because they had 'never left the house'.

That was *his* mistake. He ought to have bolted right off into another shanty and would, if it hadn't been for the job of getting one – at the price.

When he was going round for this, at one place they had offered him half a bed and said they could recommend the gentleman. He would have liked to see the gentleman – out of bed!

All said and done *he* was a gentleman: weren't half his people high up in the Services; two in the Treasury? Every starched one of them except himself battening on it, potting money out of it, having litters of jolly little kids (there was nothing like a jolly little kid for bucking you when you were down) he used to see the kids before the whole gang cut him, the whole swanky, dreary gang absolutely stiff with spine.

If it was worth while thinking of the Almighty – no one took Him seriously nowadays – he supposed He worked that way – a few good strokes and then He biffed it: and you were the result. But you were there: you were You, no one else exactly like you – the same nose: they always said he had the Aston nose that shoved through things and came out smiling. What had he done with it? His mother had had it too. What had she done with it? Simply kept her head above water; that was something; with a man like the Governor any other woman would have cheerfully gone down.

He was always fond of his mother. The others had rather laughed at it, but it wasn't funny. He had always liked women with sloping shoulders and behaved well to them for that reason. Anyhow, it was

193

a fact; there was the portrait, a genuine Lawrence to prove it, which he hadn't sold and didn't mean to sell.

His Aunt Emma had it too, the nose, and dug it gaily into all of them; but whoever drew the winning ticket no one had done more for her than he had, towing her round Galleries where he was known, telling her what to look at; driving about with her to drapers' shops and back to Hill Street to talk wash about the family – what his mother's was and the Governor's wasn't; giving her presents at Christmas that he couldn't afford, until he saw the utter folly of it all and waste of time.

It was *her* spine that was keeping her out of Kensal Green so long that they would all be past enjoying it when she got there.

Well, damn it! His had gone and he was fairly chirpy. At forty-two he wasn't looking for a new one or making any offers. He never had seen what there was in it; it merely took it out of you and didn't alter anything.

Take London, for instance; it was the same big gorgeous show whether you tossed up rotten sketches of it or not. A beautiful woman too – rather more so if you didn't. You enjoyed 'em for themselves.

It had never even mildly worried him till he met Mrs Eden. And then this insane, infernal craving had got hold of him – as bad as – well, certainly as bad as drink, which for nearly a year – God only knew why or how – he'd practically chucked for it.

It was in March, at Hill Street. He remembered the dinner because he hadn't had a bad imitation of one for days and it seemed his luck to have to put it away all at one go when it would have done him comfortably for a week. He hadn't sat by her, hardly noticed her; he had rather a going bit next to him and was taken up with her. Mrs Eden only dawned on him afterwards in the drawing-room when she got up and spotted that sketch of his skyed behind the piano, which the old lady had given him ten quid for the first time Samuels threatened to sell him up.

She liked it enormously; but it wasn't that! She wasn't young or particularly good-looking; distinguished, all that: they mostly were, the old blighter's crowd; but what struck him was the way she spoke, very quietly, as if she was interested and liked you and as if you really mattered.

They went down together and she said it was much too nice a

194

night to drive, so he walked with her from Hill Street to Wilton Street, up Piccadilly, the Park side, where the Westminster lights looked uncommonly clear and jolly.

At the door she said: 'I wonder if you would come and see me Thursdays? But then I shouldn't see you. What about Tuesday when I should?'

He couldn't place it – some silly impulse made him hesitate, but somehow she insisted without insisting.

And he had gone. They talked Art and the country; she told him they were taking a house near St Peter's, Bucks, for the summer. She thought he'd like it; there ought to be quite good sketching there.

At the end she said: 'You know, I'm coming to see your work,' and then broke off, and finished with a smile that was pure sunlight when it did come out, but wasn't in a hurry to – 'that is, if you'll let me?'

He went straight back and had a burst-up with Mrs George about the anointed piggishness of everything, and then knocked her clean out by telling her to take the whisky down; and next day he started to work like hell.

Out and out he'd never done anything better, half as good – with a few more square meals and a week, say, at Boulogne or Etaples where you could get the models, he saw himself pulling off something top-hole.

Later, he didn't see Etaples or France at all; there was something else at the back of his head, and it came out one evening as he was buying violets outside the Britannia.

It was Bucks. He would go down; St Giles or St Peter's; the Worcester crockery ought to do him a week at least and a new suit. This time he would go to Hartley's tailor and strike him dead by offering to pay up and probably wouldn't have to.

It occurred to him it wasn't only the grub, the poisonous air was half the trouble; he hadn't seen or sniffed the country for over a year, or more like two. That line of the Downs in spring, the smell of the wet leaves, the damp earth, there was nothing like it; and that peculiar crispness in the air, the snap of the morning, the touch of the wind; the blue-grey haze over the hills – purple later – they go that colour – behind the black hedges blown like a flame. The bare branches of the elms, the springy turf; the sort of country he used to hunt over; half the stiff-backed dreary gang were hunting over it now.

It wasn't bad sport if you hadn't a gun, to get a dog and make him fetch the rabbits out of the brushwood; and see 'em scamper up over the dips. But it wouldn't be spring: summer: everything shimmering and humming; the sound of summer – rather blurred, nothing quite clear, no time, no beat. Chopin had done it somewhere: Vi used to play it; very badly. It made you feel you weren't in the room, a rum sort of notion – Not here – Not here!

He wondered if Mrs Eden played. Perhaps she would ask him up. It didn't matter, she would be there, somewhere about. He'd never felt anything like it before. Yes! once. The day his mother died; they were sitting round the dining-room table after dinner, the Governor looking like a seedy goldfish, gulping down champagne and telling them all to bear up because he couldn't.

He flattered himself he had sat through the Governor in every other act, but he walked out in the middle of that one, up to his mother's room, and turned the sheet down and looked at her and said to himself: 'Dead – by God! dead!' And – odd, that! though she was lying there so out of it, she seemed more there than usual listening to him, saying in the old way: 'I know, Stuke, I have had worries too' – as he stood there looking down at her, wondering what the Governor was alive for, and swearing he would stiffen up.

On the 24th of July he got a note from Mrs Eden asking might she come at 3.30 on the 28th? He gave Mrs George two stalls for the Bedford and washed the china over again himself. She stayed an hour. He showed her all the last things he had done and she liked them immensely and the Worcester tea-cups. She was as keen on china as he was, but didn't mind Mrs G's glass sugar basin, and thought he was rather hard on Mrs G. Next time he promised to introduce her. They kept to small things, she seemed to like it; the bother of getting a first-floor room for twopence-halfpenny, and what things cost up there and the way he'd shut his bed off; she hadn't spotted it. It didn't matter what you said or what she saw; at first as if she wasn't there and then as if you'd always known her. He asked about the house in Bucks and she said it had fallen through; they had had to take another. She didn't say where and he didn't ask; but she wanted to know where he was going and he told her possibly Boulogne. She thought it was rather sordid wasn't it? and he said: 'I don't know; it's what you see.'

They were going downstairs; there was some scent on her glove like hay-fields, and she touched his arm and said: 'I think you always see beautiful things?' He didn't answer.

As he put her into the cab she said: 'I hope we meet in the autumn. I believe we're going to have lovely weather. Rumpelmeyers.' He told the man. She and the cab had clean upset the kids in the street. She must have given the little beggars something. He stood there too – one of them piped up something at him – and saw the taxi take the corner.

It was a swinking hot summer; everyone cleared out; but there hadn't been such a circus of cockroaches in the basement within Man's memory.

He fancied he spoke to about three people besides Mrs George, whom he didn't speak to. He got some picture postcards. His brother Warrington sent him a parcel from Goldings of old shirts and a suit and a book on hygiene, which he returned to Warrington at Goldings.

He borrowed a studio and pulled the picture off. There was no mistake about it this time. Six months ago he would have envied any chap who could put his name to it; but now the only thing he felt about it was that he was rotten tired.

He didn't sleep; he missed the whisky; he hadn't been drunk since March or April; he hoped he wasn't getting fussy. It used to be enough for him if models and so on were young and larky. French women though – another story. *Il y a façon et façon* in women, in everything. God! what an age since he heard that patter: '*En voilà des phrases! Dis, donc, ça c'est des bêtises!*' Poor little Renée and the rue Tournon and behind it all the St Sulpice bell!

Almost as queer as anything to think that at this moment while they were bawling cauliflowers down the God-forsaken road, Paris and all the rest of it was romping on.

This was November – in another month turkeys and Herald Angels would be on the job again. Next to the one when Vi was trying to

197

smash up their engagement and finally did, he couldn't remember a stiffer year.

In the middle of December he ran up against Mrs Eden one afternoon in Dover Street, coming out of a hat shop, looking very fit. She would have passed him, hadn't recognized him, but he pulled up, or something inside him pulled up and said: 'You don't remember me?' There was a shade of a pause, and then she said with extraordinary sweetness: 'Of course I remember you,' and she was evidently trying to get at his name. He said he was going on to his aunt's in Hill Street; she looked relieved and said: 'Dear Miss Aston! How wonderful she is! How is she? Do look us up one day', and something about the narrowness of Dover Street and its being so badly lit. He took his hat off: there was the same scent on her gloves; and she went on up Dover Street.

He wasn't expected in Hill Street, and at first the poor old sheep-biter was rather frosty, thinking he'd come to borrow money, but thawed when he took her off the hook, and told him he was looking ill. She did hope –. He said to her 'My good Aunt, nothing is so irrational as hope –' But she went on quite a long time about hope and the costs of his stomach. He didn't stop her; once or twice in his life he had spoken the bald truth to people and they had simply taken him for a bounder or slightly touched. He saw their point of view. He mentioned that he had just knocked up against Mrs Eden and she said: 'Oh! yes, you met her here. *He* is one of the Lincolnshire Edens; she has just brought out a book called *Flotsam* or *Wreckage* – something depressing of that kind. What can Alice Eden know about it? She lives entirely in her own world. She has just come into a second fortune.'

There was a jolly fire in the library and they sat on over it talking of Hartley's liver and whether Ada would get her divorce. What did he think? He said, as she meant to stick to India, he supposed she would still have her punkah-men to nag at if she did.

Afterwards he walked about and turned into the Pav for an hour. He thought it rather a smutty show. Going home he wished he could be as wrapped up in anything as Hartley was in his own inside.

He tried not to think of Mrs Eden. He saw that he must shake

198

her off. She had got idiotically on his nerves. Time was when he knew scores of women – more charm, the same sort (in the early days), better-looking, much younger, much younger. What in hell had Mrs Eden got to do with it? He tried not to think of Spine; one day he had looked it up in the dictionary and found: Spine, spin. n., a thorn; the back bone of an animal; the heart-wood of trees.

He saw now that she hadn't got it, neither had he. Charm didn't count, or work – work least of all – or whisky. It was going up, much higher – much higher; blue, wavering, cut off; the embers were smoking down below. It was there, right enough, but he was losing hold of it. He would get it again – when he was not so fagged – in the morning. It might go up, but he meant to get it. By God! he would!

He let himself in. There was no gas lit, there hardly ever was; and in the musty darkness Mrs George put her head round the kitchen stairs and wheezed out at him: 'Don't you be frightened of the 'addick, sir, if you should go down for your kettle and see it 'anging up in the scullery. It didn't 'arf give me the jumps up there on the 'ook, looking so strange and mother-o'-pearly, with the moon shinin' on it!'

He groped upstairs and went in and lit a candle and shut the door. There was a remarkable stillness in the room; it was like a room in which someone is lying dead. He stood there a moment, listening, expecting something to happen. He remembered that she had just come into a second fortune, and slowly, in the intense quiet, it came to him that there was no Mrs Eden; there never had been; she wasn't there. He went across to the window – he didn't hear – but he had the idea of a cab driving up. He said out loud to himself: 'Why not? Why not?' He looked out; and turned round on the room again.

There was nothing there. Not the wallpaper, not the stove; not really there; not solid, only like things that aren't; like tree-shadows, the ghosts of leaves. The sheets too – he remembered some in Brittany, at Douarnenez; he had sat up all night, what did it matter? If you slept; if you could only sleep . . . There wasn't light enough. He lit another candle. The picture, too, not solid, quite thin, like muslin, like smoke, like vapour.

This was wrong. No one ought to feel like this, whatever they'd done or hadn't done. No beast, no animal. There was nothing there.

199

The world was stark empty; a sort of pit; it made you giddy to look down at it; sick all over, nothing there; pure vacancy, not a living soul.

Nonsense! If you went out into the streets – the main thoroughfares – there were thousands – thousands – His eyes felt very stiff and hot: that was it; thousands of them and not one – not one! He thought suddenly of tomorrow; there was tonight too. Quite impossible. What about a drink? Why drink? He was too tired, dog-tired; better sit down, eat something; nothing but cocoa and an egg since morning. The haddock? That was (half of it) for tomorrow – tomorrow –! No – no! Sometime or other you died; everyone did; his mother had; they all would, sooner or later; a tough lot, hard to kill. This was exactly like it: like death, like life too. He was rather frightened, not of the haddock, though; he couldn't laugh. It must be pretty rank to look like that; perhaps it was swinging too – with the moon shining on it; everything else was; that dip in the Downs with the rabbits scampering over it. Rabbits, people, Warrington, Ada, Mrs Eden.

But in the midst of it all there was something quite steady and white and shining – the moon, the moon!

Anna Kavan

A Summer Evening

T his interminable, intolerable summer evening seems as if it will never end. Those responsible for the elongation of summer-time certainly can't have given a thought to the people, like myself, for whom it's far too long already, already moves in slow motion. More of it is absolutely the last thing we want.

The air is dead still, as it always is on these evenings, with a density which still further impedes time's passage, making it even slower. In the garden the leaves hang motionless, dusty, with the hard outlines of artificial leaves, ominously pointing down to death and defeat. Their greens are slightly unnatural, crude theatrical shades of viridian, peacock and arsenic green, like leaves on the stage. The fig-tree, in particular, has assumed an air of sinister melodrama with its poison-coloured bunches of armless thalidomide hands.

Weeks ago, an elder of ill-repute shed its dead florets in an untidy rain, and they still cover the ground thickly, as with big brown grains of sand. No one has attempted to sweep them up. Neither rain nor wind has dispersed them: although on the tree the embryo berries already form pancake-flat purgative clusters tempting to guzzling pigeons, whose excrement fouls the branches below with a morbid slime.

The atmosphere is oppressive, almost too heavy to breathe. Restless and apprehensive, I feel half-stifled, trapped in this endless evening, and acutely aware of my isolation. The garden is a sea of the darkest shadow, in which relentless fragments of memory swing ... out of place ... out of time ...

'Don't die. Don't leave me. I love you ... need you so terribly. I can't live without you.' Wasn't that enough reason for staying alive? Well, no, of course not ... I should have done better than that. Once more I enter the unknown room where he lies, changed,

201

smaller than I remember, in that narrow box, with the terrible marble absence of life, the enormous inhuman indifference. To avoid seeing it, I look at the beautifully-shaped hands which had the power to perform miracles, but which I now see are, after all, only bunches of little bones. How could I expect bones to save me? Outside in the street, leaves are blowing along the pavement, chased by an electrically-charged cat, pouncing on its imaginary prey with playfully lethal grace. An ex-member of Karl's orchestra, it still twangs and vibrates to his memory, utters unearthly cries, dedicated to a ghost. All elastic and velvet, it twirls on delicate hind legs, executing the wildest gymnastic bounds, a moon-mad cat ballet girl.

What am I listening for now, what do I expect to hear? Not the traffic in the main road, no more insistent than the throb of a distant dynamo. Not the far-off mournful hoot of a tug on the river. Not the sudden ghostly whispering overhead, which draws my attention to a great net flung across the sky, its meshes, fine as hairs, disappearing almost before there's been time to recognize the black, twinkling microscopic wings of a huge flock of starlings flying home to their roost in the heart of the city.

Immediately after this fragile sky-sound comes the other, far more personal sound for which my ears have involuntarily been straining. As I catch the first suggestion of it, something happens to me ... an instantaneous change, demolition, takes place, like a reduction of my corporeal being – I'm no longer aware of the ground under my feet. It's as if I'm suddenly in another dimension, inestimably remote, yet intensely personal ... intimately associated with my innermost self, which somehow takes precedence over my body ... All at once I'm suspended in universal time ... in the weird stretches of the continuum ... where I wait, caught in an obscure web of past events ... a ghostly entanglement which inevitably leads straight to the present moment ... when I hear that faint wordless muttering or humming under the breath, the low unintelligible murmur announcing the visitor's disembodied approach.

At precisely the moment when my ears pick up the sound, I see that its author is present already ... a shadow in his dark clothes against the dark shadowy trees, bare-headed, his domed head glimmering in the dusk. Something like an irresistible magnet of need draws me

202

towards him. Still I don't feel my feet touching the ground; which makes me all the more aware of the touch, intangible as a draught, on my face, and of a strange sensation, almost like running water, flowing along both arms, as if somebody's pulling me that way. At the same time, my physical disintegration becomes more marked, a displacement of tissue and bone, leaving only some essential inner quality ... as if I too ... as if something impossible is happening in this secret, sombre, secluded place, enclosed by walls and trees and blackish thickets of tall overgrown flowerless plants. Then suddenly the fluid bond seems to dissolve. He is here. But I have nothing of him. Only this tantalizing elusive shade.

Terrifying, how vague the memory of his actual face is already becoming; with such appalling speed the image of the living man dissolves into ghostly vagueness. Only my inner eye painfully holds an indelible imprint, like a snapshot in which, beneath a heartlessly happy sky, against the heartless background beauty of a mountain spring with flowers thick in the grass, the living, breathing human being stands smiling beside me in his physical self, accessible, touchable, *real* ...

At this point two alternatives are open to me. I can accept the apparition which represents him, and be frustrated for the whole of this limitless evening by its remoteness, its terrible incorporeality. Or I can refuse to listen to that heartbreakingly familiar singsong murmur, and hear instead the loud crude voices that belong to the world outside my walls.

As a matter of fact, it's hardly possible *not* to hear the people who park their cars at the top of the hill and walk to and fro between the tennis club and the pub, disrupting the stagnant stillness with bursts of harsh laughter. Shutting the cares of the day inside their places of work, they have come out relaxed, the lines smoothed from their faces, their smiles indicating a generalized goodwill. The atmosphere soon becomes gay, each one talks to his neighbour, they gather in compact groups to discuss the evening's amusement, and having decided, closely linked by arms over each other's shoulders, they charge down the quiet street, like a cavalry regiment, the cannonades of their laughter sweeping all before them. Nothing can stop these conquering heroes stocking their cars with drink and driving at a hundred mph through hundreds of miles of the countryside ...

heading for new adventures, for a night of intoxication, love-making and dangerous speed. For them the seconds must fly at the speed of light as compared to the tedious crawl of my time in isolation, when the hands of clocks and watches practically cease to move.

These evenings are no-times, not day and not night. Just as I myself, the garden, the trees, are no-things, projections of nothingness, isolation ... no reality except nothingness. I don't quite know myself any longer. I forget how to smile ... how to squeeze words out of my mouth. Everything drains away. Nothing is left but an empty world, in which Karl's face will never again be seen.

While he was here I felt safe, secure in his support and affection, in the supreme togetherness generated by cosmic rays. But now, of all that, nothing. Of all he gave so generously he has left me nothing. Nothing of himself, of his prestige, of his kindness. I am nothing to him. He is nothing. There is nothing in life any more. I try to find the way out, but people prevent me. Utterly heartless, they want to force upon me an unendurable existence, not seeing that I have already left their world.

I can never go back to the living world unless I am changed completely, not only in essence, but in outer aspect, transformed throughout the entire complex of body, brain, intellect, memory, feeling, the sum total of which is the individual being.

If this whole structure could be transmuted into something hard, cold, untouchable, unaffected by any emotion ... if flesh became something like granite, burning with mineral fires, so that, if a limb was snapped off, there remained an icicle dazzle of sparkling beauty, not a disgusting mess, then and then only, indifferent to isolation and independent of time, I might endure the world.

Composed of some iridescent substance, smooth, hard, cold as ice, with a ruby from Mogok for a heart and a diamond brain, inexhaustible and impervious, I would stride all over the world, seeing everything, knowing everything, needing nothing and nobody ... finally leaving the earth and the last human being behind me and turning away to the most remote galaxies and the unimaginable reaches of infinite space.

Janette Turner Hospital

❧

The end-of-the-line end-of-the-world disco

F
lutie reckons it's an even chance the world will end before the shearing cuts out, and therefore they shouldn't wait, they should have the party tonight. Sure, a train is coming from Brisbane, volunteers are coming, sandbags and sandbaggers, a train's on the way, but will it arrive in time? Already vultures hover, a sure sign. When Mike leans out the pub window, their shadows blacken him and his hurricane hair whips across his face. 'Hey, vultures!' he calls. He hoists his beer and gives them the finger, gives it to the helicopter pilots, to the Sydney producers, to the cameramen dangling from slings, to the whole bang lot of them. 'Hey, vultures! Stuff that up your TVs and poke it!' Grinning, grinning. 'Gonna be on *The 7.30 Report* tonight, mates,' he laughs, as he winds himself back inside.

'River's reached Warrabunga already.' Flutie pushes the phone back across the bar. 'She's coming down like a seven-foot wall, Paddy Shay says. How about another one, love?'

'Cooper's, is it?' Gladys asks, as though she hasn't been serving him beer in the Millennium Hotel every day and night for six months, as though in the last ten minutes she's forgotten every relevant detail about him.

'Drive a man to drink, Gladdie.' Flutie is baffled, exasperated, because she really is waiting for an answer. She really is not certain, in spite of the small regiment of empty Cooper's stubbies at his elbow. Or maybe she can't quite believe that a man in these parts would ask for anything but Four-X, and maybe she needs confirmation each time. Or maybe, as Mike maintains, she's just *slow*; but Flutie doesn't think that's the reason. She's still standing there with her watery blue eyes looking at him but not quite seeing him, blinking and waiting.

Waiting.

'Yeah,' he says, awkward. 'Cooper's.'

Mike rolls up his eyes, taps his forehead, grins at Flutie, but Flutie frowns. It drives him crazy, the way he feels protective of Gladys, and he's damned if he knows why, because she's no spring chicken, she's not a looker, she's skinny as a bloody fencepost, almost no tits at all. He thinks – for a reason he can't fathom out – that it's got something to do with the tired way she rubs the back of her hand across her eyes, and with that strand of faded hair which is always falling out of the loose bun she twists it into, always falling down behind her ear into a hollow of her shoulder-blade, and he always wants to brush it off her neck, tuck it into the elastic band, and let the pad of his thumb rest very lightly in the hollow below the bone. Jesus. He must be going soft in the head. It's almost frightening, that hollow, it's deep as a bloody egg cup. He wants to put his tongue in it.

She's staring at the spigot in her right hand, the spigot on the Four-X keg, having run him off a pot of draught without thinking. 'Oh fuck,' she says mildly. 'Sorry.' She reaches for a clean glass. 'Cooper's, wasn't it?'

'Wake up, Australia,' Mike says. 'You'll miss the end of the world if you don't watch out.'

'Why don't you bloody leave her alone?'

'What?'

'You heard me.'

'Jesus, mate. Keep yer shirt on.' There's a gleam in Mike's eye though. Flutie with the hots, well well.

Flutie scowls, embarrassed. He knocks back the Cooper's to clear a space, start fresh. 'Anyway,' he says, 'Paddy Shay climbed up to his roof last thing, saw the water coming. He's got the wife and kids in the ute, gonna run for it, should be here by dark. That's if he makes it. Another day, he reckons, and goodbye Charleville.'

Goodbye Charleville, good riddance, Gladys thinks. She leans against the glass doors of the refrigerator and closes her eyes and sees the swollen black snake of the river nosing south. A little higher than her head, preserved as curio, is the last flood souvenir, a decade old but still a clear corroded rust-brown line, threading its way across the white enamel wall behind the stubbies: the high-water mark.

Last time, the high-water level stayed exactly there for six whole

206

weeks. Nothing moved. Not so much as a damn cockatoo moved upon the face of the waters, and all flesh died, both of fowl and of cattle that moved upon the Queensland earth anywhere west of the Warrego. And the flood was forty days and forty nights upon the earth – so Mike says, and so Flutie says, and they can prove it from the *Courier-Mail*, though the figures were disputed in the Sydney papers – and every living thing upon the ground was destroyed, both man and cattle and crops and creeping things (except for the bloody mosquitoes and flies, it goes without saying). And only Noah O'Rourke the publican remained alive, and they that were with him in the ark of the Millennium Hotel, a regular zoo. And for forty days and forty nights the waters prevailed. Those are the nine last words on the subject from Flutie and Mike, who tell only the gospel truth.

Then Queensland unplugged her drains, glug glug. Ssschlooop. There was a swift season of sucking back. The regulars haven't stopped talking about the 'afterwards' party yet – there will always, damn it, *always* be an afterwards, Gladys thinks wearily. Oh, the regulars can trot out befores and afters from 1880 on, but the last afterwards party is particularly vivid. It was more or less yesterday, that resurrection party, that wild fishing-for-stubbies-in-the-mud party, that jamboree, wangaree, rainbow time. Wheee! what a way to come home.

'This hotel,' Mike will tell every visitor who leans across the bar, 'the river took 'er clear down to Cunnamulla in 1990, and then she came floating home on the backwash.' Hallelujah, is the standard response, and don't let the pint pot stand there. 'What we got', Mike explains, 'is life everlasting. What we got is the Hotel Indestructible, we gonna outlive the millennium itself in this here pub.'

Gladys presses back against the slick flood-surviving glass of the Millennium Hotel's stock of beer, feels the blessed frigidaire-coolness through her cotton shift, feels it sweet as a lover against her sweaty buttocks and thighs, feels herself go heavy between the legs. The wet blunt snout of the river is past Warrabunga. Here, baby, she murmurs, moving her hips.

Wavelets slap against the mirrored wall of the disco and the dance floor is two inches awash but in any case the musicians are on an island dais. Confidence is high. Some tried to flee – in cars, on horseback – but there was nowhere to go, with all the rivers running in packs and the creeks gone brumby. Water water everywhere, it's a bloody stampede.

The mirror tiles are pocked with black holes. A glittering rind of alum peels from the damp edges and leaves streaks that might be read as a map of the watercourses that are rising in convocation. Revellers arrive and arrive. Under the watchful eye of the helicopter, trucks and utes and horses and drays are still fanning out and then fanning in again like ants, for the disco lures them and where else can they go? This is the place of refuge, the end of the line.

This is the day and the hour.

The great inland sea, vouchsafed in vision to the prophet-explorers, has come into its own, so everyone's giving up. One by one, they are turning back for the Millennium. For a while, the regulars could watch in the upstairs TV lounge. There's Paddy Shay's ute, they could say. See? With that box thing he built on the back? He's turning back, keep a Four-X good and cold for 'im, Gladdie.

But now the power has gone.

The power went hours ago.

Gladys has strung up the hurricane lanterns, and volunteers have been working in shifts to see the beer safely stowed in iceboxes on the wide upper verandas. It's party time. No worries, mate. As for the sandbags and sandbaggers, the train was last seen, glugging at the windows, going slowly under somewhere west of Muckadilla. No question, this is the safest place to be. The beer is safe, and high time too, with the years spilling over the Warrego embankment, the years welling up and over like the zeros in an old Holden odometer, the century shifting, the party in full swing.

Oh when the saints . . . plays the motley band (one trumpet, one bass, three guitars, four harmonicas tuned to four different pitches, one jew's-harp, real drums, saucepan drums, about twenty people play-ing the spoons) *. . . go marching in . . .* The cymbals, two rubbish-bin lids, are banged with gusto by Noah O'Rourke himself.

'Marching? We're gonna *float* across the New South Wales border,' sings Mike. 'We're gonna float to kingdom come. We're gonna float into the next century, mates.'

Oh when the saints, booms the bar-room chorus, *go floating in . . .*

'Amen,' says Flutie. He watches Gladys coming downstairs with more beer. 'Put that bloody tray down,' he calls. 'It's every man for himself now, let 'em nick up and get it for themselves.' He can feel a sort of bright madness in his voice, he can see it dancing above the heads of every last one of them, tongues of fire, disaster excitement. He takes the stairs two at a time, whisks the tray from Gladys, puts it on the landing, and grabs Gladys round the waist. 'Come a-waltzing with *me*, Gladdie darling.'

He knows there's no way in the world she can resist him. He can feel the revving like a dynamo, the cyclone of final possibilities gallumphing down from the Gulf of Carpentaria, an irresistible force that sweeps her down the last few steps, past the bar, into the swampy space around the musicians. For just a half-second he feels her body stiffen, then she moves against him and with him. They're both barefoot, everyone's barefoot, and they stomp and splash like children at a wading-pool party. Big Bill, the Maori shearer playing guitar, leans out from the dais and booms the words in their ears. *'Oh when the saints . . .'*

'Go bargeing in,' Gladys sings back, and Flutie hears again that edge of wild and dangerous pleasure.

In the mirror, he sees musicians turning into dancers, dancers leaping on stage to have a go on drums or at the spoons. If the water doesn't weaken the foundations, he thinks, the stomping and clapping will. Any minute, the hotel could slip its moorings.

'Oh when the saints . . .' Flutie sing-shouts into the hollow in Gladys's shoulder-blade.

'How come', she gasps, breathless, slapping up a fan of water with the balls of her feet, 'they call you Flutie?'

'It's my baritone, my incredible bloody beautiful voice.'

'Come off it.'

'Hey,' he says aggrieved. 'Listen. You're talking to a winner of a Bundaberg eisteddfod. The nuns made me perform as a boy soprano, a fate worse than death. When me voice was breaking, I swung a punch at every kid who called me Flutie, but I never managed to beat off the name.' He puts his tongue into the dip in her shoulder. 'You've been here five months. Six maybe? You run away from a husband, or what?'

In the mirror, he sees her throw back her head and laugh. Her bun has come loose and all her faded red hair flies free. She cannot stop laughing. Flutie thinks they might all drown in her laughter.

Now the ground floor has been surrendered, the revelry transposed up several notches. Although it's far too hot and humid for sleeping, couples are disappearing into the rooms off the veranda. Flutie's looking for Gladys. Pacing the old veranda boards, he can hear the fizz and spit of concentrated life, it's like walking the deck beside a row of pressure cookers just before they blow. It's sensible, he thinks: telling death to fuck off. Where's Gladys?

At the veranda railing, interest in the swooping flotsam is intense. Will the milk-can pass the bucking sheet of corrugated roof-iron? Will that green thing (is it the top of someone's ute?) beat the fencepost down to Corones? Will the black water kiss the veranda in one hour, two hours, three, tonight, tomorrow night, or never? Bets are formally laid.

'Vultures!' Mike shouts, and yes, the whirlybirds are back, but what are they dangling? Not cameramen. No. It's a fat sausage-string of rubber dinghies.

They know something we don't, Flutie thinks. The water's still rising. In slow astonishment, because he has always, deep down, believed himself immortal, he says to no one: 'You know, we just mightn't make it.'

'Hey, Flutie!' It's Big Bill, the Maori shearer, strumming his guitar at the railing. Flutie has traded punches with Big Bill on the issue of wide combs or narrow combs for shearing. He can't believe his own life. 'This is it, Flutie,' the Maori says.

'We gonna make it, d'you think?'

'Dunno, Flutie. This is it, the Big Water.' He plucks at the strings of his guitar. *Oh when the saints* ... 'Hey, Flutie,' he grins. 'You remember that fight at Reardon's shed?'

A funnel of laughter descends on Flutie like a willy-willy and sucks him inside. 'The combs ...' he tries to say. 'We bet you Kiwis would never ...' But his voice goes spiralling upwards, round and round, faster, faster, beyond the reach of his breath and into the high whooping grace-notes of absurdity. And Big Bill enters the funnel with him, they are dizzy with glee.

'Jesus,' Big Bill bleats, in pain with mirth. 'You silly fuckers bet us ... You fuckers claimed that New Zealand wool ... You dumb fuckers lost your fucking *pants.*'

Through the fog of vertigo and laughter, Flutie sees Gladys fishing for dinghies with a pole. He sets his compass and strikes out for her shore.

Gladys thinks that at last has come a day with real *juice* to it, a day she can sink her teeth into. God, how come the bloody water's so cold when they're all sweating like pigs from the heat? She's got it now, she's hooked one of the dinghies. She'll have to share, damn it.

What she'd really like to do is stand in the dinghy and spread her arms and descend on New South Wales like one of the Furies, singing at the top of her lungs. Dimly she senses there'd be a letdown somewhere. There always is.

'Gladys,' Flutie says, encircling her from behind with his arms. 'Tell me why you came here. Because there's no time left, you know. You confess and I'll confess. I wanna know the lot.'

'Jesus, Flutie.' She can't believe men, she really can't. Boss cocky to the very last second.

'Where'd you come from?' he persists. 'Brisbane? Sydney?' Because he can smell a city girl, yes, that's partly what's been grabbing him, that dazed state of the city slicker in the bush, that *Where am I? What am I doing here?* bemusement, he's a sucker for that.

'Brisbane,' she says. 'If you must know.'

What will she tell him? She ticks off items in her mind: married twenty-seven years, three kids all grown up and married, Mum dying of cancer in Toowoomba; and while she sits at Mum's bedside, her old man buggers off with the neighbour's daughter. End of story.

How boring, how *embarrassing* a life is, once it slides down inside the tacky skin of words. Cheap skin, sharkskin, vulgar. Who could bear to say them? They had to be shoved away somewhere, in a suitcase under a bed. Goodbye words, good riddance; because what you felt afterwards, after the disorientation, when your clumsy tongue got free of dead explanations, was an immense and intoxicating freedom. You felt like singing your new self without any words at all.

211

You felt like a snake discarding the skins of past lives, sleek, unimpeded.

'When Mum died,' she says absently, smiling, 'I hopped on a train and bought a ticket for the end of the line.'

'Amen,' says Flutie.

'I didn't bring any luggage,' she says. 'No luggage at all.'

'Amen,' he says again. It doesn't matter if she tells him anything or not, they're both end-of-the-liners. Compatible histories is something he can taste, and he moves his tongue into the warm currents of her mouth.

When there's a space, she says mildly: 'I don't mind fucking you, Flutie, but I'm never going back.'

To a man, she means. To routine. To luggage. To intolerable ordinary life.

Then he realizes, *of course*, it's her sheer indifference, her unreachability, that's been driving him crazy.

'Hey,' he says sharply. 'Hey, your dinghy!' – because floating rubble, like a tank on the move, is ramming the rubber boat up against the railing, ramming the lattice, ramming the ship-wrecked veranda, oh Jesus, are they in the water or swamped on the deck? Chaos. He swallows an ocean. Veranda posts approach, an anchor holds, he is wrapped around something vertical and he can see her scudding out of reach, body-riding the dinghy like a surf-board queen.

'Gladysssss . . . !' He dingo-howls across the water.

She waves, or so he wishes to believe. Yes, she waves.

Gladys waves. But what she is seeing is the swooping green of the mango tree in Brisbane. The leaf canopy parts for her and she keeps flying. She is on that wild delicious arc of the swing, soaring up, up, and out from the broken rope. A sound barrier breaks. There are shouts, but they reach her only faintly through the pure rush of bliss, they are a distant and wordy murmuring of bees in mangoes.

We *begged* you not to swing so high . . . We told you the rope was frayed, we warned, we warned, we promised we'd fix but you just can't wait, you can't ever wait, you foolish stubborn little girl . . . you wilful impetuous . . . Buzz buzz to reckless ears.

'I don't care! I don't care!' she shouts. She has flown beyond the farthest branch of the mango tree, she is higher than the clothes-line,

212

euphoria bears her upward, she is free as a bird. Any second now, the broken legs waiting on the lawn will come rushing to meet her, but she doesn't care. This is worth it.

She waves. But all that comes back to Flutie is her laughter, the wild clear rapturous sound of a child on the last Big Dipper.

Notes on the Authors

ELIZABETH BOWEN (1899–1973) was born and grew up in Dublin. After her father was certified insane she travelled with her mother. On her mother's death Bowen was sent to school in England. She studied drawing at the LCC School of Art and, when her artistic career failed to develop, began writing stories. In 1923 she married Alan Cameron and published her first book of short stories, *Encounters*. She inherited Bowen's Court, County Cork, in 1930, and thereafter spent her time between England and Ireland, writing novels and stories. During the Second World War Bowen was an air-raid warden in London, and her wartime experiences were encapsulated in her novel *The Heat of the Day* (1949). Bowen believed that the advantage the short story has over the novel is that 'it must be more concentrated, can be more visionary, and is not weighed down (as the novel is bound to be) by facts, explanation, or analysis', a *credo* amply borne out by her own short fiction. Her novels include *The Hotel* (1927), *The Death of the Heart* (1939), *The Little Girls* (1964) and *Eva Trout* (1968). Her *Collected Stories* appeared in 1980.

KAY BOYLE, poet, novelist, short-story writer, was born in 1902 in St Paul, Minnesota. She was educated at the Cincinnati Conservatory of Music and also studied architecture at the Ohio Mechanics Institute, where she met – and, in 1922, married – Richard Brault, a French engineering student with whom she travelled to Europe. Her experiences in Paris among the expatriates (Gertrude Stein, Djuna Barnes, Ezra Pound, etcetera) are described in *Being Geniuses Together, 1920–1930* (1968). Her *Short Stories* were published in 1929, and a novel, *Plagued by the Nightingale*, in 1931. Kay Boyle has been married three times, is the mother of six children, has published more than thirty books and taught at several American universities (she was Professor of English at San Francisco State University from 1963 to 1979). She now lives in Oakland, California. Her most recent work is *Words that Must Somehow be Said*, a collection of essays that brings together her political concerns, and a volume of poetry, *This is Not a Letter*, both published in 1985.

AILSA COX was born in 1954 in the West Midlands. Her stories were first published by *Commonword*, a writers' project based in Manchester, where she now lives. Other work has appeared in the *STAND 1* anthology *Writing Women*, *Sunk Island Review*, and *Northern Writers 2* (Littlewood/Arc). She has an MA in Creative Writing from Lancaster University, and supports herself by teaching writing locally and for the Open College of the Arts. Ailsa Cox is a single parent, with one teenage son. She has recently finished a film script about women learner drivers trying to survive in the city.

GEORGE EGERTON (Mary Chavelita, *née* Dunne, 1859–1945) was born in Melbourne. She spent her childhood mainly in New Zealand and Chile, then studied in Germany. She worked at various jobs in New York, Dublin and London, and in 1887 eloped with the bigamist Henry Higginson to Norway, where she was influenced by Ibsen, Strindberg and Knut Hamsen, whose novel *Hunger* she translated on her return to London in 1890. In 1891 she married George Egerton Clairemont, a Newfoundlander, and moved to Ireland. Her first volume of short stories, *Keynotes*, which dealt in an outspoken way with the New Woman, was a sensational success when it appeared in 1893. *Keynotes* was followed by more volumes of short stories – *Discords* (1894), *Symphonies* (1897) *Fantasias* (1898) – and novels – *The Wheel of God* (1898) and *Rosa Amorosa* (1901). From 1901, after her marriage to a young drama critic, she turned increasingly to writing for the stage, with, however, far less success. She died at her home in Ifield Park, Sussex.

RAHILA GUPTA was born in London, although most of her formative years were spent in Bombay, her parents having returned there because they did not wish to live as second-class citizens in Britain. An Honours graduate of the University of Bombay, she came to London in pursuit of 'that thing called "an English education"

215

revered by people unfamiliar with the system'. She spent many years completing an M Phil in English Drama. Rahila Gupta is a single parent with two young children. She produces and edits publications for a voluntary organization on a part-time basis, and is a member of the Asian Women Writers Collective and Southall Black Sisters.

JANETTE TURNER HOSPITAL was born in Australia in 1942. *The Ivory Swing* (1982) won the Canadian Seal First Novel Award, and was followed a year later by *The Tiger in the Tiger Pit. Borderline* (1985) and *Charades* (1988) were both shortlisted for the Australian National Book Award. *Charades* was also shortlisted for the Miles Franklin Award. Many of Janette Turner Hospital's short stories have been anthologized and have appeared in magazines. 'The-end-of-the-line end-of-the-world disco', chosen for this anthology, has also been selected by Giles Gordon for *Best Short Stories 1992. Dislocations* (1986), her first collection, was given the Fellowship of Australian Writers' Fiction Award. A further collection, *Isobars*, and her latest novel, *The Last Magician*, appeared in 1992. Janette Turner Hospital is married with two children and spends half of each year in Australia (where she is Adjunct Professor of English at La Trobe University, Melbourne) and the other half between Canada and the United States, where she reviews for *The Toronto Globe and Mail* and *The New York Times*.

RUTH PRAWER JHABVALA was born in 1927 in Cologne of Jewish parents and educated in Jewish schools in Germany until her family fled to England in 1939. Her education was continued in Coventry and Hendon and Queen Mary College, London University. She was naturalized British in 1948. In 1951 she married Cyrus S. Jhabvala, a Parsi architect, and they lived chiefly in India until 1975, with their three daughters. *Esmond in India* (1958) depicts India from an – often prejudiced – Western viewpoint. In 1975 Jhabvala won the Booker Prize with *Heat and Dust*, which she adapted for the screen in 1983 as part of her continuing col-laboration with James Ivory. Her short stories were collected in *A Stronger Climate* (1968) and *How I Became a Holy Mother* (1976), originally published in 1971 as *An Experience of India*. Among her other novels are *A New Dominion* (1973), *In Search of Love and Beauty* (1983), and – her most recent – *Three Continents* (1987). Jhabvala's elegant prose explores the often ambiguous relations between East and West with wit and affection. Since 1975 she has lived in New York.

ANNA KAVAN (Helen Woods Ferguson, 1901–68) was born in Cannes. As a child she travelled extensively with her mother. She married Donald Ferguson, a Scot, and settled in Burma, where she began to write. Her first novel, as Helen Ferguson, was published in 1929. In 1930 she published *Let Me Alone*, and later took the name of the heroine, Anna Kavan, by deed poll. She became progressively unstable, and addicted to heroin, but continued to write. Returning to London, she worked as an interior decorator and as assistant editor of *Horizon*, the literary magazine founded by Cyril Connolly. In later life she lived quietly in Campden Hill. Her writing, which included science fiction and the collection of short stories and a novella published after her suicide as *My Soul in China*, can be seen as an attempt to free herself from the torments of her own life.

DORIS LESSING, *née* Tayler, was born in 1919 in Kermanshah, Iran, and grew up in what was then Southern Rhodesia. Educated in a convent school in Salisbury, she left at fourteen, taught herself secretarial skills and wrote two unpublished novels. At nineteen she married Frank Charles Wisdom, by whom she had two children. In 1945 she married for the second time, Gottfried Anton Lessing, and worked for the Rhodesian government and for a Marxist Black Liberation group. In 1949 she moved to England, publishing a novel, *The Grass is Singing*, in the following year, and short stories – *This Was the Old Chief's Country*, in 1951 and *Five: Short Novels* in 1953. The Martha Quest novels, *Children of Violence*, were published in five volumes between 1952 and 1969. Since then she has continued to write prolifically, including a series of five futuristic novels, *Canopus in Argos*. In *The Golden Notebook* (1962) Lessing expressed 'what many women were thinking, feeling, experiencing', in a work that 'spoke for other people'. Of *The Habit of Loving*, from which the story in this anthology, 'Flight', is taken, the *New York Herald Tribune* said: 'Controversial, blazingly angry ... powerful and imaginative artistry.' Doris Lessing's most recent book is *London Observed* (1991). She lives in London.

SHENA MACKAY was born in Edinburgh in 1944 and educated at Tonbridge Girls' Grammar School and Kidbrook Comprehensive, which she left at sixteen to do a variety of jobs. Her first publication was of two short novels, written when she was only seventeen: *Dust Falls on Eugene Schlumburger/Toddler on The Run* (1964). She married Robin Brown in 1964 and had three daughters. The novels *Music Upstairs* (1964) and *Old Crow* (1967) soon followed, but after *An Advent Calendar* (1971) she published no more until *Babies in Rhinestones*, a dazzling collection of short stories, in 1983. The next year saw the appearance of a novel, *A Bowl of Cherries*, followed, in 1986, by *Redhill Rococo*, which won the Fawcett Society Prize. A second volume of stories, *Dreams of Dead Women's Handbags*, came out in 1987. Shena Mackay's stories, of which the *Sunday Times* critic said that reading them 'is like walking on broken glass', have been frequently broadcast and anthologized. She reviews regularly for *The Times Literary Supplement* and *The Independent on Sunday*, and her latest novel, *Dunedin*, was published in 1992. Shena Mackay lives in London.

KATHERINE MANSFIELD (Beauchamp, 1888–1923) was born in Wellington, New Zealand, the daughter of Annie Burrel and Harold Beauchamp, director and Chairman of the Bank of New Zealand. She was educated at Wellington Girls' High School, where she wrote her first stories, and Queen's College, London, where she met Ida Constance Baker, the lifelong friend and helpmeet to whom Mansfield gave the *nom de plume* Lesley Moore. An early marriage to George Bowden in 1909 lasted a day, and she subsequently had a stillborn child in Bavaria by another man, events which were to provide the background and mood for some of the stories in her first collection, *In a German Pension* (1911) – a book which shows the influence of Chekhov and which, although a critical and commercial success, Mansfield soon repudiated as a 'lie'. Her relationship with John Middleton Murry, whom she married in 1918, also dates from that time. *Bliss and Other Stories* was published in 1920. By now her bitter struggle against tuberculosis forced her to spend a part of every year in the South of France and in Switzerland. A perfectionist, she worked obsessively and to the point of exhaustion, but, in the words of Elizabeth Bowen, 'that burning gaze of hers, her vision, gained in intensity', and she was increasingly perceived as an original and innovative writer. *The Garden Party and Other Stories* (1922) was published in the year she entered the Gurdjieff Institute, Fontainebleau, where she died in January 1923, aged thirty-four. *The Dove's Nest* and *Something Childish* were published posthumously.

PAULINE MELVILLE is an actor and a poet. Her collection of short stories, *Shape Shifter* (1990), won the *Guardian* Fiction Prize, the Macmillan Silver Pen Award and the Commonwealth First Book Prize. She lives in North London and is working on a novel.

CHARLOTTE MEW (1869–1928) was born in Bloomsbury. She was educated at Lucy Harrison School for Girls, and attended lectures at University College, London. There was a history of mental illness in her family, and two of her siblings were institutionalized. Her first story, 'Passed', was published in *The Yellow Book* in 1894, and until the outbreak of the First World War she continued to earn money from poems and prose in magazines. Harold Monro of the Poetry Bookshop published two collections of her verse, *The Farmer's Bride* (1916) and *The Rambling Sailor* (1929). Among her many literary admirers and supporters were John Masefield, Walter de la Mare and Thomas Hardy, who obtained a Civil List pension for her in 1923. However, the subsequent deaths of her mother and sister led to acute depression, and she killed herself (by drinking disinfectant) in a London nursing home. Her story 'Spine', included in this anthology, was apparently unpublished in her lifetime.

ALICE MUNRO (Laidlaw) was born in Wingham, Ontario in 1931 and grew up on the farm where her father raised silver foxes and turkeys. Educated at the University of Western Ontario, she married James Munro in 1951, and they had three daughters. She had already begun writing during her teens, and sold her first story to the Canadian Broadcasting Corporation at eighteen. Her first collection of stories, *Dance of the Happy Shades* (1968), won the Governor General's Award, as did the next, *Lives of Girls and Women* (1971). *The Beggar Maid*, originally published in North America as *Who Do You Think You Are?*, a series of interlinked stories that work both as separate entities and as a whole narrative, was shortlisted for the 1980 Booker Prize. *The Progress of Love* (1987) is one of the finest collections by a writer who was described by the *Washington Post Book World* as 'a born teller of tales who can transform the anecdotal or apparently digressive into a rich parable of life in our fickle times'. The stories from her most recent book, *Friend of My Youth*, have been extensively broadcast on BBC radio. Alice Munro, who won the Canada-Australia Prize in 1974, now lives with her second husband, Gerald Fremlin, in Clinton, Ontario.

GRACE PALEY (Goodside) was born in the Bronx, New York City, in 1922 of poor Jewish immigrant parents. She began writing poetry early, and consequently neglected her formal education, leaving Hunter and New York University without a degree. At nineteen she married Jess Paley and had two children. In her mid thirties, dissatisfied with her poems, she turned to writing short stories. Her first collection, *The Little Disturbances of Man* (1959), was an immediate critical success and displayed the robust humour and compression that characterize all her work. In the 1960s she became involved with anti-war activism, and attempted to write a novel 'because people said I should', but threw it out on the grounds that 'Art is too long and life is too short'. In 1972 she married the writer Robert Nichols. Grace Paley's other story collections are *Enormous Changes at the Last Minute* (1974) and *Later the Same Day* (1985). She teaches at Sarah Lawrence College, New York City, and divides her time between New York and Vermont.

DOROTHY PARKER (Rothschild, 1893–1967) was born at West End, New Jersey, the daughter of Henry Rothschild, a rich clothing manufacturer, and Eliza Marston, who died when Dorothy Parker was an infant. Educated at a convent school in New York City, she was twenty-three when she sold her first poems to *Vogue* and began writing fashion picture captions. In 1917 she became drama critic of *Vanity Fair*, where her meeting with Benchley and Sherwood launched her career as the wittiest member of the Algonquin Round Table. It was at this time that she married Edwin Pond Parker II.

Her best-selling volume of poetry, *Enough Rope*, appeared in 1926 and, as the Constant Reader, she reviewed regularly for the *New Yorker*, to which she also contributed the stories that were eventually collected in *Here Lies* (1939). In 1933 she married the actor-writer Alan Campbell (whom she subsequently divorced and later remarried), and they moved to Hollywood, where her film work included an adaptation of *The Little Foxes* by Lillian Hellman. Parker was an ardent left-wing political activist. *The Portable Dorothy Parker*, containing stories and poems, was published by Viking Press, New York, in 1944. She continued to write for magazines until the 1960s, but after the death of her husband in 1963 she became increasingly alcoholic and died alone in a Manhattan hotel room. The epitaph which she wrote for her own tombstone encapsulates her mordant wit: 'This is on me'.

ELIZABETH TAYLOR (Coles, 1912–75) was born in Reading and educated there at the Abbey School. She worked first as a governess and then as a librarian, and in 1936 married John William Kendall Taylor, a businessman, with whom she had two children. For most of her married life she lived in the village of Penn, Buckinghamshire. She published her first novel, *At Mrs Lippincote's*, in 1945, while her husband was serving in the Royal Air Force, and this was followed by a series of critically acclaimed novels and collections of short stories: *Hester Lilly and Other Stories* (1954), *The Blush and Other Stories* (1958), *A Dedicated Man and Other Stories* (1965), and – her finest and most accomplished collection – *The Devastating Boys* (1972). Elizabeth Taylor's novel *Angel* (1957), based loosely on the life and character of the writer Marie Corelli, was chosen as one of the Book Marketing Council's 'Best Novels of Our Time' in 1984. The last novel published in her lifetime, *Mrs Palfrey at the Claremont*, a penetrating and drily humorous study of old age, shows Taylor at the height of her powers, and bears out Elizabeth Bowen's contention that 'there is an exciting distinction about every page she writes'. Her final novel, *Blaming*, a book about bereavement and guilt, written when she herself was dying, was published posthumously.

SYLVIA TOWNSEND WARNER (1893–1978) was born in Harrow, Middlesex. Her father was a master at Harrow School, and she was educated at home. Moving to London on his death in 1919, she worked in a munitions factory; then, from 1922 to 1929, she was employed by Oxford University Press as one of the editors of the ten-volume *Tudor Church Music*, and during this time she published her first book of poems, *Espalier*. Her first novel, *Lolly Willowes* (1926), the story of a spinster who becomes a witch, was nominated for the *Prix Femina*. In 1930, with the poet Valentine Ackland, she went to Spain as a Red Cross volunteer. On their return, Warner and Ackland set up home in Dorset, where they were to spend most of their life together. They joined the Communist Party in 1935, an allegiance Sylvia was to maintain for several decades. A prolific writer (seven novels, four volumes of poetry, eight collections of short stories, essays and a biography of T.H. White), she contributed to the *New Yorker* for over forty years, and has been described by Hermione Lee as 'one of our most idiosyncratic, courageous and versatile writers'.

EDITH WHARTON (Jones, 1862–1937) was born in New York City and educated by governesses and European travel. Her first book, *Verses*, was published in 1878. In 1885 her marriage to Edward Wharton, a Boston socialite, launched her into the life of the society hostess, with half of each year spent in Europe. However, the marriage was unhappy, and after a nervous breakdown in 1894 she embarked on a serious literary career which included fiction, non-fiction and poetry. Of her many novels, the most successful and enduring are *The House of Mirth* (1905), *Ethan Frome* (1911), *The Custom of the Country* (1913) and *The Age of Innocence*, which won the Pulitzer Prize in 1921. After her divorce in 1905 she settled permanently in France, where she fell in love with Morton Fullerton, a relationship which was reflected in several of her novels. During the First World War she largely abandoned her writing, and for services rendered was awarded the Cross of the Légion d'Honneur. After the war she bought two houses, one near Paris and one on the Riviera, and the creation of their gardens was to become an abiding passion. Wharton's collections of short stories include *Descent of Man* (1904), *The Hermit and the Wild Woman* (1908) and – arguably containing some of her best stories – the three late collections of the years 1930 to 1936: *Certain People*, *Human Nature* and *The World Over*.

VIRGINIA WOOLF (Stephen, 1882–1941) was born in Kensington, the daughter of Leslie Stephen and Julia Duckworth. On her father's death in 1904 the Stephen family moved to Bloomsbury. Virginia Woolf was educated at home by her parents and took classes at King's College, London University. She began to write for periodicals and taught at Morley College, Lambeth. In 1912 she married Leonard Woolf. Despite early signs of mental illness, her first novel, *The Voyage Out*, was published in 1915. Leonard and Virginia Woolf founded the Hogarth Press in 1917, doing much of the work themselves. From 1919 – the year her second book, *Night and Day*, was published – the Woolfs divided their time between London and Rodmell, Sussex. *Jacob's Room* followed in 1922, and was acknowledged by friends such as T. S. Eliot to be a new development in the art of fiction. *Mrs Dalloway* appeared in 1925, *To the Lighthouse* in 1927, and the following year *Orlando*, her fantastical homage to Vita Sackville-West. *The Waves* (1931) confirmed her reputation as one of the foremost novelists of her generation. *A Room of One's Own* (1929) and *Three Guineas* (1938) were essays which have had a profound influence on feminist thinking. Virginia Woolf's short fiction was collected as *A Haunted House* in 1943, two years after she committed suicide by drowning.